WYOMING CALLS: JACK'S RISKY QUEST

WYOMING CALLS: JACK'S RISKY QUEST

THE FRONTIER CHRONICLES
BOOK 2

MARK GREATHOUSE

WISE WOLF
BOOKS

WISE WOLF BOOKS
An Imprint of Wolfpack Publishing
wisewolfbooks.com
1707 E. Diana Street
Tampa, FL 33610

WYOMING CALLS: JACK'S RISKY QUEST. Text copyright © 2024
Mark Greathouse

This book is a work of fiction. Any references to historical events, real
people or real places are used fictitiously. Other names, characters,
places and events are products of the author's imagination, and any
resemblance to actual events, places or persons, living or dead, is
entirely coincidental.

Paperback ISBN 978-1-957548-61-6
eBook ISBN 978-1-957548-60-9
LCCN 2024943262

Dedicated with love to my wife Carolyn, our two sons Mike and Matt, and the memory of my father John F. "Jack" Greathouse

Christ is my firm foundation (testify)
    The Rock on which I stand.

CODY CARNES, "FIRM FOUNDATION"

THE CAST

Jack O'Toole – *Sixteen-year-old son of Joseph and Kate O'Toole. He strives to carve a life from the Texas frontier on the easternmost reaches of the Comancheria.*

Kobe (a.k.a. Wild Horse) – *Sixteen-year-old son of a Penateka Comanche chief camped within the heart of the Comancheria.*

Mukwooru (a.k.a. Spirit Talker) – *The warrior name bestowed upon Wild Horse in recognition*
of his apparent connection with Taa Narumi (the Comanche Great Father) whom they confused with God. Mukwooru was the name of Spirit Talker's father's uncle.

Blue Flower – *Sister to Wild Horse. She's a year younger than her brother and is her father's treasure.*

George Freeman – *A Black cowboy driving cattle north; later an Army scout. He establishes a ranch on the North Platte River in Wyoming.*

Running Waters – *George Freeman's Pawnee wife.*

Kate – *Jack's eleven-year-old sister.*

Buck – *Jack's six-year-old brother.*

Mato (a.k.a. Bear) – *An Oglala Lakota warrior.*

Otaktay (a.k.a. Kills Many) – *An Oglala Lakota war chief.*

Isaac Fisher – *An Amish farmer from Pennsylvania seeking new opportunity on the frontier.*

Sarah Fisher – *Isaac Fisher's wife.*

Bear Grandy – *Elderly mountain man who advises Jack and Spirit Talker.*

Topsannah (a.k.a. Prairie Flower) – *Young Comanche girl captured and enslaved by Arapaho tribe.*

Hakan (a.k.a. Fire) – *Comanche shaman or medicine man that visits Penateka Comanche village as a prophet.*

Sam Collins – *Owner of the Circle C Ranch located near Jack's spread.*

Lieutenant Cort Johnson – *Army officer stationed at Fort Laramie.*

HISTORICAL CHARACTERS

Buffalo Hump – *War chief of the Penateka Comanche, the southernmost band of the Comanche people in the Comancheria. In the famous Council House Fight of 1840, he led roughly a thousand Comanche across Texas to the Gulf Coast where they ransacked Victoria and burned Linnville.*

Captain Nathan Benton – *Texas Ranger captain assigned to protect settlers* from Indians in the Leona River region northwest of Fort Inge. *(Benton eventually would serve as a lieutenant colonel in the Confederate Army, 36th Texas Cavalry.)*

Makhpia-Luta (a.k.a. Red Cloud) – *Chief of Oglala Lakota of the Sioux Nation.*

Tasunke Witko (a.k.a. Crazy Horse) – *Future chief of Oglala Lakota of the Sioux Nation. He is about nineteen years old at the time of this story but already gaining attention of tribal leaders. He will go on to lead the massacre of General Custer's troops at Little Bighorn (a.k.a. Greasy Grass).*

Tatanka Iyotake (a.k.a. Sitting Bull) – *Chief and medicine man of the Hunkpapa band of Lakota Sioux.*

August Klappenbach – *Early settler of Bandera, TX and owner of first general store and post office.*

Thomas Triss – *Indian agent assigned to administer to the tribes around Fort Laramie.*

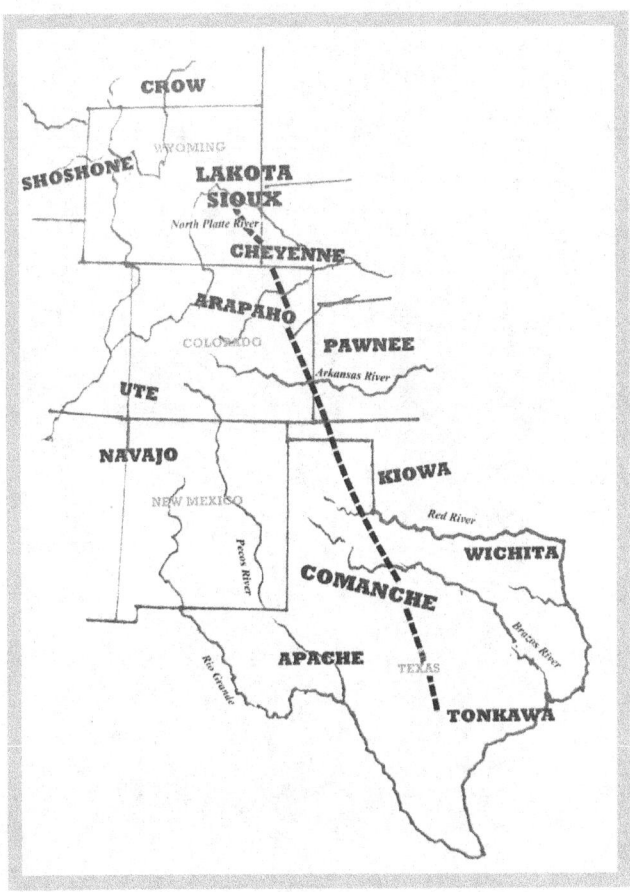

The trail Jack O'Toole and Wild Horse follow from Texas to Wyoming featured challenging landscapes and many tribes known to be hostile. (Map by Mark Greathouse)

YOU ARE INVITED

Dear Reader,

If you've read *Perilous Trails*, it's likely my story has grabbed you. This part of my tale occurs in 1856. You recall that I had been thrown alone and vulnerable by events beyond my control into the Comanchería, the most dangerous part of the frontier by a factor of 10x. I was now only sixteen years old. The Comanchería with its savage Comanche warriors was a virtual no-man's-land for White settlers.

Wyoming Calls: Jack's Risky Quest is the second of The Frontier Chronicles, continuing my adventures that call upon courage, faith, endurance, and pure grit. In this chronicle, my Comanche friend Spirit Talker and I set out on a daring journey from Texas to Wyoming. It was by meeting such tests of courage that we teenagers on the frontier grew up right quickly. From what older folks have told me, my story incorporates history not found in most school history books. Keep in mind that this book relates my tale as driven by fate and guided by God.

I met up plenty with Indians. My first encounters

were with Comanche and later with Lakota Sioux, so you'll find me using some of their language throughout *Wyoming Calls*. I have provided a handy glossary of Comanche and Lakota words toward the back of this book.

I'm a devout Christian, but I tried to understand the Comanche religion to better understand them. Their religion is based upon what is referred to as animism, in which every common natural item from fish and animals to plants, trees, waterways, and mountains were believed to have souls or spirits. The spirits and traditions connected with them guided the Comanche. Their passion for their spirits no doubt gave them their fearlessness as fed by the belief that they were protected in everything they did. Would they kill to defend their beliefs? Let's say that theirs was not a religion of love and forgiveness.

Could Indians like the Comanche become Christians? I have intended for my story in *Wyoming Calls* to unfold at the intersection of faith and culture. Historically, it was not unlike Saint Patrick's conversion of the Irish to Christianity by folding many of their less-offensive heathen rites into the Catholic faith. The British derisively referred to the Irish as "Black Catholics." Would this work with the Comanche? Well, it's part of the story I'm sharing with y'all.

As you follow my adventures, ask yourself whether you might be up to meeting the challenges I take on. Dangers? Privations? Hmmm. How might you have fared? Through it all, I first relied on the teachings from my family, then went on to learn from the raw and risky experiences I faced. I learned to trust in instincts forged from my biblical lessons.

To be straight here, I had no idea that my story was

going to fill multiple volumes until I began to write it all down. I invite you to follow my often perilous adventures on America's western frontier.

Kindest regards,

John "Jack" O'Toole

WYOMING CALLS: JACK'S RISKY QUEST

PROLOGUE

A COMANCHE WAR party presented a fearsome sight. Sitting astride decorated ponies, faces painted in broad black stripes, scalps adorning lances and shields, war clubs at the ready, and arrows nocked in bowstrings, they were a mobile fighting machine of which few could match. The Comanche could outride just about any cavalry on the plains. It was said that a Comanche warrior and his pony rode as one. It was little wonder that, with physical appearance, crazed war whoops, pounding pony hooves, swirling dust, and flying arrows, fear gripped the very inner souls of all those whom they chose to attack.

As frightening as appearances were upon seeing the savages, it was the talk and rumors of their brutality and sheer cruelty that hung foremost in most folks' minds. Homesteaders were advised that in the event they were overcome in an attack, save a last bullet for themselves. The stories of the horrors and indignities of torture and captivity were that terrifying.

All of this raced through young Jack O'Toole's mind as he prepared to defend Rising Cross Ranch.

ONE
INJUNS!

THE ARROWS SHOT into the cabin door got me fully roused. Isaac, Sarah, and Kate rallied to my shouts of alarm. In just moments, the gun ports we'd had the presence of mind to build into the walls of our cabin were filled with the muzzles of our rifles. Our cabin looked like a porcupine at first glance. But our quills were loaded! Isaac, Sarah, and even Kate joined me in the defense.

Did I say porcupine? Arrows filled the air, and many burrowed their way into wooden window shutters or stuck between the seams in our limestone walls. Blessedly, not a single arrow found its way inside.

I was confounded by what I could see beyond the sights of my trusty Springfield rifle. Under the light of the stars and half-moon, targets were tough to make out. Far as I could tell, the attackers wore the dress and war paint of Comanche. However, these warriors were none that I'd ever seen before. I reckoned they must have been of a Comanche tribe other than the Penatekas–perhaps Nokoni or Tenawa. No matter, we fired away. From somewhere deep within me the long-suppressed emotions of anger and vengeance from the murderous Comanche attack on my family less than a year ago welled up. It was all I could do to keep my cool under fire. I kept asking God for strength and unerring accuracy.

We had replaced the wooden roof with clay tiles just weeks before, an action driven by fear of being smoked out by attackers setting the wood and thatching afire. Our only vulnerability was access to water. Blessedly, the Comanche did not possess a siege mentality.

I feared for the barn and our livestock. Far as I could tell, the war party was comprised of at least twenty warriors. There was no way we could leave the shelter of our cabin to launch a counter-attack. I prayed. Oh yes, I prayed.

Flashes of light blazed from the muzzles of our rifles. Silhouetted against the moon, I made out the form of a Comanche warrior waving a torch and about to set the barn on fire. I aimed carefully and shot him from his pony. He was sorely wounded and scooped up by a fellow warrior. Thankfully, he failed to set the fire.

The Comanche were determined to steal our horses, and we were an inconvenience that stood in their way. Despite our mostly-accurate gunfire and the savages losing a couple of their band, either killed or wounded, they set about opening the gate to the corral. The half dozen horses in our corral were prime stock being readied for delivery to the Texas Rangers.

I stepped back from the gunport and looked around me. No words were spoken. Isaac and the womenfolk were shooting and reloading at a steady pace. Even six-year-old little Buck was busying himself replenishing supplies of ammunition. I took a step toward the door.

"What are you doing, Jack?" asked Isaac, pausing from his shooting. He'd answered one of my fears as to his ultimate survival in this hostile land, as he, by necessity, put aside his Amish teachings against shooting humans. However, the task at hand was nevertheless distasteful.

I heard Isaac and caught his imploring gaze. I was not to be dissuaded. "I must save the horses! Cover me!" I declared and headed for the door. I grabbed two Colt revolvers. Hopefully, all my target practice would pay off. I'd grown physically over the past few months, standing at a couple of inches over six feet tall and sporting plenty of lean muscle from all the labor building Rising Cross Ranch. I offered up a quick prayer under my breath, threw what I hoped was a reassuring glance at Isaac, and stepped through the door.

I instantly found myself face-to-face with one of the fiercest-looking savages I'd ever laid eyes on. The wild look in his eyes framed by black warpaint spoke of death–mine. Only the pony he sat astride kept him from lowering his warclub on my head. I'd faced Kiowa, Apache, and Comanche mostly at a distance; this was up close and personal. Instinctively, I swung one of my Colt revolvers up and fired. The bullet grazed the pony's neck and plowed dead center into the warrior's chest. He fell from his rearing pony and died in the Texas dust. I leaped past the fallen Comanche and, hooting, hollering, and shooting like a madman, headed for the corral.

One of the savages slid from his pony, charged toward me, and was about to strike me but fell, the victim of a shot from the cabin. I fired my Colts in all directions, as the Comanche seemed to be coming out of the darkness from everywhere at once. Dust, war whoops, yelling, and screaming ponies conspired to create a chaotic scene of blood, sweat, and death. I half remember snarling out, *"Isa peeka!"* I felt some sort of primal growl from my gut, as I shouted the words again and again. My words translated in Comanche to "wolf kills."

All of a sudden, one of the attackers, whom I judged to be their leader given the many feathers in his hair, raised his lance, let out a whoop, and waved the warriors to break off the attack. He laid a penetrating stare on me. *"Isa!"* he hissed, wheeled his horse, and led off with what remained of his war party. I could only guess that my crazed behavior coupled with shouting *isa peeka* must have gotten his attention.

I stood legs akimbo alongside the corral with a smoking revolver in each hand. Sweat poured from my brow. My breathing came in deep heaves. I scanned the yard. Five Comanche bodies littered the ground. Other dead and wounded savages had been carried off by their brothers. I heard whinnying and neighing behind me. The horses pranced around the corral. They could have cared less.

Isaac carrying a candle along with Sarah and Kate cautiously emerged from our cabin, while Buck merely peeked his face out from beside the doorjamb.

"Amazing...that was amazing, Jack," said Isaac, his eyes wide and jaw slack.

"You did mighty fair yourself, Isaac," I said. I looked off to the horizon at a vanishing silhouette of the retreating Comanche against the moonlight. The war party leader's invoking of the wolf spirit clung to me like buffalo glue. *Isa* was the Comanche word for wolf, and my Penateka Comanche friends respected me for it as part of my strong medicine. I was more inclined to think God had taken control of me and helped me aim true.

But if *isa* dissuaded Comanche warriors, I wasn't going to argue.

Kate began to cry. No, it was more sobbing welling up from deep within. I expect the attack had brought back memories of her having been taken captive, as our folks and siblings were being killed by Comanche at this very place. Sarah comforted her as best she could, and my sister's tears began to subside. I could hardly begrudge her such emotion.

I looked for little Buck. I feared that the attack might throw him back into the muteness experienced when he'd been kidnapped by the savages. "Jack!" he called and ran to me. I could nearly have cried with relief.

For me, this attack brought up the old guilty feelings I had felt at not having been present during that terrible attack, as though I might have performed as well nearly a year ago as I had this day. The many weeks on the trail with Wild Horse fighting Indians and bandits, engaging with wild animals, and fending off well-meaning soldiers had matured me very quickly. Perhaps too quickly.

————

I GUESS the noise from the ruckus at Rising Cross Ranch had carried quite a ways, as my old friend Captain Benton soon came galloping out of the darkness with about a dozen Texas Rangers. Benton pulled up in front of me and swung down from the saddle. As the dust settled and he looked about, an incredulous expression filled his face. He found himself speechless.

"Welcome to Rising Cross Ranch, Captain. You're late for the party," I offered drolly. I hoped a touch of humor would loosen the captain's tongue.

Benton shook his head ever-so-slightly and then

looked at our ragtag band of defenders one by one. "How many?"

I smiled. "It was dark, Captain. I didn't keep count."

In the candlelight, the five Comanche bodies could be seen still sprawled out in the dust between cabin and barn. "Dang, but them savages stirred the wrong nest of rattlesnakes," said Benton. He signaled to his Rangers to dismount. "We'll help y'all clean up this mess, Mr. O'Toole. We'll chase down that war party at daylight." I didn't miss the respect he was giving me by using my surname.

"It's late, Captain Benton. Why don't you have your men bed down, and we'll deal with all this in the morning after breakfast. Heathen or not, we'll give the Comanche a fitting burial. Beat up as they are, the war party won't get all that far tonight."

Benton thought on that for a moment. "Makes sense. They sure won't be heading back this way anytime soon." He went off to tell his men to make camp.

I turned to Isaac and our womenfolk. "Let's catch what sleep we can. We're safe. The Comanche won't be back." I had already begun to think of connecting with my Penateka Comanche brother Wild Horse. Clearly, other Comanche tribes were unaware of the peace made between Jack O'Toole and the *numunuu*, the people.

CAPTAIN BENTON and his Texas Rangers deeply appreciated the humble breakfast, especially the hot coffee, Sarah and Kate prepared for the chilly morning. Most of them joined us in blessing our meal, though we were being thankful for far more than a simple breakfast.

We wound up burying seven Comanche, as two more

were found lying beyond the barn. Little wonder they'd abruptly broken off the attack. To lose a third or more of their number in a single attack told them they were dealing with very strong medicine.

The burial was performed as respectfully as possible. Digging graves in the hard-packed soil was not easy, but we managed to dig the graves deep enough that varmints wouldn't be disturbing the remains. We buried them with their personal effects, as I'd learned about that part of their ritual from my chats with Wild Horse.

With burial complete, Captain Benton was anxious to pursue the Comanche war party. Before mounting up, he took me aside. "So, what happened to that darkie fella?" The phrasing of his question hit me hard, as it revealed more of the captain's inner man than I really cared to know.

"If you're referring to my friend George Freeman, Captain, he headed to the North Platte River country in Wyoming a couple of weeks back to raise cattle."

Benton gave me an appraising look.

I didn't especially care to be judged. Here was a man who held strong prejudices against anyone of color. Despite Benton's bravery in protecting settlers from predatory Indians, it nevertheless diminished his standing to my way of thinking.

"Escaped slave, wasn't he?" he persisted.

I pulled myself up to my full height. I realized that I was nearly a head taller than the captain, though he'd appeared larger and more intimidating on horseback. "So he said, Captain. He also spent time with the Pawnee, drove cattle for a rancher, and scouted for the Army. He earned our trust and respect as a God-fearing human being."

Benton snorted. "What about the Redskin boy?" he asked in a derisive tone.

I shook my head. The captain's prejudices were testing the graciousness with which we'd welcomed him. While I appreciated the protections offered by the Texas Rangers, Benton's very soul was off-putting. "He is of the Penateka Comanche people. He is my brother."

Benton's eyes grew wide. My response hadn't been expected given the recent raid and the devastating attack last year. To Benton, all Indians were the same. Tribal affiliations mattered not. "Hrumph!" he muttered. "Your call, Mr. O'Toole." With that, he ordered his Texas Rangers to mount up. They formed up a column of twos and headed out in pursuit of what remained of our attackers.

I must say that I had mixed feelings about their departure. Safety was a concern, but it was the future in a world of folks holding such prejudices that worried me. My ma and pa used to remind me to not be judgmental yet to be discerning. I guess they feared me getting mixed in the wrong company.

Isaac had watched out of earshot but observed the body language between me and the captain. "He seems to be a troubled soul, Jack," he observed.

"Sadly, there's more where he came from," I said, as the Rangers faded from view.

TWO
A QUEST BEGINS

UPON AWAKENING the morning following the departure of the Texas Rangers, I found myself struggling to recall a dream that had captured my heart as I slept.

"What's on your mind?" asked Kate during breakfast. She had become ever more adept at discerning any changes in my disposition.

I had developed a habit of occasionally kicking back and letting my thoughts wander off. I had honed this skill back in my days fishing for bass on the nearby Guadalupe River. These days, it seemed that I'd perfected this to where I might stop in the midst of mucking a stall, lean on the pitchfork handle, and let my mind wander off. It took a while for me to realize that there was a consistency to these episodes. I looked up absentmindedly at Kate, as she filled my coffee cup. "Just thinking, sis."

Kate looked around the table. "Thinking about what?" she asked.

Everyone had paused from eating their breakfast and seemed to have frozen in place awaiting my response.

"Going to be a few mares foaling," I blurted in a vain attempt to deflect Kate's question.

Kate gave me one of those looks that demanded an answer.

I had no choice but to be a straight shooter. "I've been thinking about visiting George up in Wyoming." There, I'd said it. Wyoming was calling.

Silence.

"I thought I might go visit Wild Horse and invite him to join me."

"What of Rising Cross Ranch?" asked Isaac.

"Y'all have a handle on operations now. It's safe. The Indians won't be bothering to come near." I felt a twinge upon saying it was safe.

With the initial shock of my revelation beginning to wear off, breakfast chatter resumed.

Kate shook her head resignedly. "When do you plan to go, Jack?" she asked.

I hadn't given that much thought. "Maybe in a week or so," I mumbled. "Yes, about a week from now." That would give me ample time to figure out what I needed to take on the long journey and ensure that much of the snow up north would have melted. The distance was more than a thousand miles. At twenty-five or thirty miles or so per day, it would take better than a month to reach George's ranch.

Kate's apprehension was writ large across her face, even as she forced a smile.

"We'll pray on it, sis."

That seemed to bring a bit of peace to her.

"You're gonna need help taking fifteen ponies to the Comanche, Jack," teased Isaac.

"I'm going to see Wild Horse," I said definitively. Much as I had begun to have longings for Blue Flower, I was not ready to pay the Comanche chief's dowry for his daughter. Yes, I had thought of her. She was likely a good match for me. It would take a bold, determined, self-sufficient woman to put up with Jack O'Toole. I still could not shake the memory of her saving my life by shooting White Knife, the Comanche shaman. And I surely could not lose the memory of her smile. Didn't hurt that she was downright pretty.

"Guess you'll ride Big Red," interjected Isaac.

Big Red had been the head stallion in the wild horse herd we'd brought in last year. He was a big chestnut-colored steed, and we'd developed a special bond. I'd swear that Big Red could read my mind. "Yep, Big Red will be under me heading north. I figure to only take one packhorse. More than that might attract unwanted company. If Wild Horse comes with me, he'll surely bring an extra pony or two. We should be quite a sight— a White and an Indian traveling together. Might get some folks to thinking." Of course, I was thinking how the two races could get along in peace. I was avoiding thoughts of how some prejudiced folks might take offense. "We'd better be well-armed, Isaac." I knew that he'd mostly overcome his Amish heritage and their views toward guns not being used against humans. The graves of dead Comanche out past the barn attested to that.

———

THE WEEK FOLLOWING the announcement of my quest seemed to blaze by. In addition to the normal chores around Rising Cross Ranch, I immersed myself in preparation. I'd be gone for at least three months. I'd be missing the prime growing season but was confident that Isaac, Sarah, and Kate were up to it. Even little six-year-old Buck was becoming a hard-working tyke. He even had his very own pony that he cared for. Dang, but children grew up fast on the frontier. Completing chores and owning responsibilities were a given. There was fun, too, as when Buck tossed a dead rattlesnake at Kate's feet and sent her screaming off to the cabin. My little brother was developing a near-diabolical sense of humor.

So, the day finally arrived for me to embark. Big Red nickered and pawed the ground with nervous anticipation. The packhorse was loaded with essentials, including food, utensils, a tarpaulin, extra ammunition, and the all-important coffee pot. I tied down a set of saddlebags, bedroll, and rain slicker behind the saddle cantle. I hung my rifle scabbard from the saddle horn. Within the scabbard's welcoming buckskin insides, I slipped a newly-acquired Sharps Model 1852 Saddle Ring breech-loading carbine. Its .52 caliber slug packed a wallop. I purchased a holster on another trip to Bandera, so eventually had a much-improved place to park my Colt 1851 Navy revolver. A second Colt lurked at the ready in my saddlebags.

A gift for Wild Horse was a must. I'd carefully culled a handsome pinto stallion from my growing herd. It was a steed fit for a future chief of the mighty Comanche, but even more befitting a friend and brother.

I was physically ready and equipped. I stood beside Big Red. Was I mentally ready? Here I was, a sixteen-year-old boy-man, about to undertake a journey that could never even be imagined by most children my age back east.

Everyone had gathered around to see me off. Forced smiles held back tears. The ranch was in great shape and would be fairly easy–relatively speaking–to care for. Our neighbors to the east promised to look in occasionally.

The growing town of Bandera was only a day's ride to the south. The horses would be well cared for, as I shared as much as I knew about the beasts with Isaac. I gave hugs to each. I was about to place my foot in the stirrup, when I stopped and turned back to my family. "Let's pray," I said.

There was a palpable sense of relief. We'd almost taken for granted our blessings at meals and even a ritual we'd worked out on Sunday mornings. We all bowed our heads.

"Lord, watch over Kate and Buck, and give Your protections to Isaac, Sarah, and baby Jack while I'm gone. Please make living here at Rising Cross Ranch easy for them and keep them safe. Bring good weather as is Your wish, Lord."

I was about to say amen, when Isaac interjected, "And keep Jack safe on his journey, dear God of love and peace. We pray that he joins with his friend Wild Horse in realizing the dreams You have set before them. We pray, too, for George Freeman, that he is in your watchful care. May we all ever be blessed, amen."

"Thank you, Isaac," I said from the depths of my heart and soul. Our prayers were never lengthy, but they overflowed with the spirit of the Lord, our God.

I mounted Big Red. This was the moment,; the beginning of my quest. Wyoming called. It seemed embedded in the depths of my very soul. How did it get there? Only God knew.

As I gave Big Red his head westward, I didn't look back. I waved–half-heartedly. I didn't want anyone to see me cry. Even Big Red looked out toward the pasture and gave a look of longing to his mares. The pinto pranced along behind on a long string.

———

I HEADED up to the Guadalupe River to where I reckoned I'd eventually reach the Pinta Trail northwest to the Pedernales River and find the Penateka Comanche encampment. It didn't take long to pass my favorite fishing spot. It was only a couple of miles from the cabin. I recalled taking seemingly endless quantities of bass from the Guadalupe. They made for good eating. By my thinking, if there was a stream nearby, a man would never go hungry so long as he knew how to fish.

Plenty of clouds danced across the sky. They were the billowy variety and portended wet weather. If that were so, it could very well be a summer of plenty. Big Red quickly got into my spirit of adventure and plodded along right easily. Assuming no interruptions, I figured to reach the Pinta Trail by sunset. I stayed ever alert, as mountain lions, wolves, and bears were known to prowl the region and rattlers were ever a lurking danger.

I wondered how I would be received in the Comanche village. It had been nearly six months since Wild Horse and I had parted company. Might he have forgotten what I taught him of Christ and reverted to *Taa Narumi*, the Comanche deity? I had sown the seeds and could only hope and pray the seeds of faith had taken root.

I made great time and made camp at the intersection of the Pinta Trail and the Guadalupe. The cedars lining the riverbank cast their long shadows compliments of the setting sun. Those big puffy clouds had long since dumped their cargo of life-giving rain well to the east of me, so I gazed upward into a clear sky decked out with millions of stars. It was so quiet, I could almost hear them twinkling. My, but it was glorious to behold. I took it as an early sign that I was on a path God had chosen for me. The mournful howl of a coyote brought me back to the here and now.

I gathered some mesquite branches and built a small cooking fire. I chose the mesquite, because it smoked the least of the alternatives. There was no point in drawing unnecessary attention to myself. The meal Isaac's wife Sarah had prepared was delicious, and I fully appreciated the apple pie she'd hidden in the food sack.

I looked forward to building my friendship with Wild Horse, assuming he was ready to join my call to Wyoming. My mission with George, aside from pure friendship, would be to establish a ranching relationship. We might trade horses and cattle for profit. I also looked forward to seeing Blue Flower. Would she still smile at me? How patient might she be? Was Buffalo Hump still asking fifteen ponies? I figured to have plenty of time to think about that.

THREE
PINTA TRAIL

THE MORNING BROKE in all its glory, as shards of sunlight burst from the east. I took stock of where I was. It seemed that we were so busy at the Rising Cross Ranch that I rarely had time to truly appreciate the beauty of my surroundings. I'm not counting those dreamy episodes Kate called me out on. I simply sat and took in the wonder of God's creation. In addition to the cedars, my morning was graced with mountain laurel, live oak, and prickly pear cactus mixed in among buffalograss, windmill grass, and curly mesquite. A herd of deer ambled down to the river and sated their thirst. I reckoned there was plenty of animal life around that simply preferred not to be seen.

My peaceful interlude was broken for an instant, as a mountain lion found his breakfast among the deer. The helpless squeals of the doe and splashing of water ended quickly, and the herd bolted for safety. The cat's yellow eyes glanced my way for a split second, but he apparently could have cared less about a human dessert. I chuckled. Perhaps word had gotten out that this human had killed one of the lion's brothers. Paying no further attention to me, he turned defiantly and proudly dragged off his prize.

Hunger and a desperate need for coffee finally inspired me to rise from my bedroll. As I stood, a chill coursed up my spine. What could have caused that? I stood tall and began to look about. About halfway through my visual sweep, my eyes locked onto a pair of pale-blue eyes framed in gray fur. *Isa*, the wolf, had found me, and he had company.

Big Red began acting up, but the wolf simply ignored the cayuse. The wolf's eyes, beautifully framed by his great head, focused upon me. What was going through his mind, I could not imagine. Wild Horse told me that wolves were known for their intelligence. *Isa* cautiously walked close and sniffed at my bedroll. A female stood behind him. About the time I was calculating how quickly I could reach one of my Colt revolvers, *isa* cocked his head, blinked, and nuzzled my boots. I reached out, and he actually allowed me to touch him. I went to give him a scratch behind his ear, when he backed away silently and began to trot away with his pack dutifully following. The female paused and looked over her shoulder knowingly at me before turning back to follow her mate. Could she have been the wolf whose life I'd saved? Judging by the behavior, well, why else would they up and leave with virtually no aggression? Did wolves owe life debts like the Comanche? I chuckled at my own musings. Nevertheless, I was fully amazed. I'd have to tell Wild Horse.

———

I WASTED NO FURTHER TIME, as I devoured breakfast, gulped my coffee, and packed for the trail. Once again, Big Red was excited. He easily disposed of one of the sugar cubes Kate had squirreled away in my bag. I stroked the pinto. The look in his eyes said he coveted a piece of whatever Big Red had enjoyed. I obliged.

While I anticipated no trouble on the trail, I was ever wary. Originally carved out by Indians, it had seen mountain men, miners, travelers like myself, and bandits. It was the last of those that concerned me the most. With my rudimentary ability to speak the Comanche language and palaver with them, I figured the local tribes would be no problem. In any case, being the well-armed traveler that I was, most folks would be reluctant to challenge me. There was also the simple neighborly respect of the trail. Most folks had legitimate business purposes to tend to and weren't up to causing trouble. The Pinta Trail had become overgrown a bit from disuse, so its very roughness discouraged all but the most experienced travelers...or the ones seeking to avoid being seen. It was the latter bunch that I figured to avoid.

———

MY MORNING RIDE went about as smoothly as could be expected. I was glad that I'd worn chaps, though we mostly avoided thorny overgrowth. Roughly every hour, I dismounted to walk and give Big Red a break. There were plenty of small creeks brimming with snowmelt, so we didn't go thirsty.

Ever since riding with Wild Horse, I had developed the woodsman's sense of lurking dangers. That sense struck me shortly after mounting up from a watering hole. A tingle crept from my boots to my hat. The Sharps rifle found its way into my hands. With keen eyes, I scanned the surrounding forest. Something or someone was watching. If it was a human and simply blinked, I'd likely see the movement.

A dove cooed and lifted itself aloft. It had been disturbed. The faintest of movements alongside a live oak trunk caught my eye. Human? I raised the Sharps and pointed its muzzle toward the spot. An eye blinked.

At the click of my pulling back the hammer, a warrior stepped into full view...then another...and another. There were five in all. No warpaint decorated their faces, so I reckoned this was a hunting party. But, what tribe? They weren't Comanche, so were likely ranging far beyond their territory. I lowered the muzzle of the Sharps and raised my hand as a sign of peace. I was at a loss for words, so asked the first Indian his name. *"Unha haksi nahniaka,"* I asked in the Comanche tongue.

The warrior's eyes widened at my words. Most Whites hadn't a clue as to the languages of the Indians. He raised his hand. *"Tasiwoo Tenahpu,"* he responded in Comanche. His name was Buffalo Man.

I pointed to myself. "Jack *Isa,*" I said, invoking the powerful spirit of the wolf. All Redmen recognized the strong medicine associated with the wolf, and Buffalo Man was no exception.

Buffalo Man nodded his recognition as did his companions. Apparently, they were impressed.

We began to sign mixed with halting Comanche. It turned out that they had ranged farther than expected in search of buffalo. They had seen Comanche, likely my Penateka friends, but had avoided engaging them. They were Cheyenne. Buffalo Man managed to work in battles he'd been in with the Crow tribe. As I'd move north toward Wyoming, I would learn more of the predations of the Crow and likely encounter some Cheyenne. It was a stark reminder of what lay ahead.

I decided not to share too much, as they might not cotton to my friendship with the Comanche or relationship with the Kiowa. I did tell of my recent encounter with the pack of wolves, and it seemed to deepen any respect they had for me.

Normally, we might sit around and get better acquainted, but it was clear that we were all on a mission. I told them that there were plenty of buffalo to the north of the Pedernales, and they seemed to appreciate that. While not certain as to the warlike inclinations of the Cheyenne, I reckoned that sending them up through Comanche and Pawnee territory might cure their inclination to range so far south. For all I knew, they could be a scouting party. I was relieved to move on with no trouble.

———

THE PINTA TRAIL might have been more aptly named the Danger Trail, as I encountered an abundance of rattlesnakes, a black bear, numerous foxes and coyotes, a couple of herds of javelina, and plenty of Indian signs. I saw a few tracks from shod horses, but nothing to be concerned about. I was especially leery of the javelina, as they stink to high heaven as well as being nasty critters.

I maintained as steady a pace as possible. The pinto pony I intended to gift to Wild Horse was spirited but behaved himself. Despite the signs of fellow travelers, I had no further encounters. Before I knew it, I had reached the Pedernales River. My hope was that the Penateka Comanche hadn't moved their encampment during the winter. That was unlikely, but one could never be sure. In any case, the sun was creeping toward the western horizon, and I figured to rest up and head to Wild Horse's village in the morning. I chuckled to myself with the realization that I was probably being watched, and Wild Horse already knew that I was headed his way.

I took stock of my situation, as I curried Big Red and then removed the bundle of supplies from my packhorse. The pinto seemed content to simply watch. The cayuses were none the worse for wear, save for a scratch or two from thorny branches reaching out into the trail. My chaps had their share of digs and cuts. The roughness of the Pinta Trail never let us forget the challenges it presented to those venturing along its meanderings.

I felt at peace, ate my fill of grub, and fell asleep beside my small cooking fire. So far, my journey was living up to expectations.

———

I AWAKENED TO VOICES.

"Jack? *Isa?*"

I shook away the cobwebs of sleep. There was something familiar in the speaker's tone. Then it struck me. I sat up. "Wild Horse! *Kobe!*" My travels had indeed been observed. The Penateka Comanche scouts had alerted Wild Horse, as I'd traveled nearer their village.

I stood in my underwear. "*Ana o'a hi'it?*" I said, stirring the campfire coals and inviting him to breakfast.

Wild Horse laughed. He pointed to my pants and shirt. "We go. *Ana o'a hi'it,*" he said pointing to the northwest along the banks of the river. His companions had already begun gathering my belongings.

I dressed as quickly as possible, ensured that the bundle on the packhorse was secure, and mounted up. I did sorely miss enjoying a cup of coffee, but that paled given the elation of my reunion with Wild Horse. I gave Wild Horse a once over, as he'd very clearly matured quite a bit over the winter. The scars from the mountain lion lent an aura of strong medicine to his appearance. I sensed that he had much he was anxious to share.

"Jack bigger," he observed, making a muscle and holding a hand high overhead. "*Isa* strong."

I was tempted to share my recent encounter with the wolf pack, but decided to wait until we were gathered in his teepee smoking a pipe. "*Puuta* strong," I responded. I noted that he wore the necklace of claws from the mountain lion I had killed to save his life. From the necklace's center hung a carved cross.

Wild Horse glanced at the pinto stallion and flashed me a quizzical look. "No fifteen ponies?"

I laughed. "Not yet." With that I walked over to the pinto, grasped its halter, and led him over to my Comanche friend. I took Wild Horse's hand and replaced my grip on the halter with his. "He is yours, my brother."

Wild Horse's eyes went wide in amazement and gratitude. "Jack generous," he said. "I grateful." He began to stroke and examine the pony. He looked questioningly at me.

"Yes, he's ready to ride," I said with assurance.

Wild Horse's companions were already chattering about my generous gift.

I finished packing and mounted up.

"How George?" Wild Horse asked.

I didn't reckon on dealing with my quest to Wyoming just yet. "George go north to Wyoming," I answered.

Wild Horse nodded. "No lose scalp," he laughed at his own humor, as he found George's shaved head a bit of a conundrum. The former slave had no desire to have his hair dangling from an Indian lance.

I shared in the joke. We made small talk about what we'd been up to over the winter. It was clear that we both had much to share, as we picked up our pace. I can say that I've rarely felt so secure as when accompanied by a dozen of the fiercest-looking warriors on the planet. I did notice that several sported rifles in addition to traditional weapons. Hopefully, Captain Benton wasn't near.

———

IT WAS clear that I was quite a celebrity as we rode into the encampment. Dozens turned out to see the return of Jack O'Toole, the *isa*. Wild Horse rode beside me rather than lead the way, a sign that he still saw us as brothers. A hundred yards ahead stood Buffalo Hump's teepee. The chief stood erect with a full headdress and arms folded. Blue Flower stood to one side and the chief's new wife on the other. Even at this distance, I could see in her eyes that she held disdain for Blue Flower. She was likely frustrated at having no control over Buffalo Hump's beautiful, feisty, spirited daughter.

Of course, the eyes I was most interested in were riveted on me. In my haste to dress, I did have the presence to grab a clean buckskin shirt from my bag. I sat my saddle tall and locked in on Blue Flower's gaze.

Wild Horse was smiling. He couldn't miss the heavenly dynamic decorating the atmosphere between me and his younger sister. He laughed. Wild Horse grew serious as we approached his father. "I have new name," he said with a certain pride. "No *Kobe*, now Mukwooru," he shared. It translated to Spirit Talker and implied strong medicine. "You will see."

I was impressed. "Strong medicine," I observed. "Mukwooru," I repeated respectfully.

"Was name of Buffalo Hump uncle," Spirit Talker added. It added all the more significance to the deep respect with which the name had been bestowed.

Spirit Talker and I pulled up before Buffalo Hump and dismounted.

Blue Flower's quizzical smile simply couldn't be avoided, yet I dared not dishonor her father. I walked up to Buffalo Hump and took his hand that had been extended as welcome. I did steal a wink at Blue Flower and was certain the chief missed it.

Buffalo Hump looked past me at my packhorse. "Where ponies?" he asked a bit more seriously than Spirit Talker.

I saw Lion Hunter suppress a grin. He raised his hand toward the pinto. "Jack give to Spirit Talker."

Blue Flower gave me a penetrating look.

Buffalo Hump's eyes shifted from the pinto to me. He cocked his head.

"Ponies soon, great Chief. Soon. My herd grows."

The chief smiled and whispered, "Blue Flower wait."

I was considerably relieved.

"*Ana o'a hi'it,*" invited Buffalo Hump, as he motioned us to enter his teepee. It was time to eat.

As I entered, I was overwhelmed with the aromas given off by a veritable cornucopia of delicacies. Deer, buffalo, corn, berries, and more captured my visual and olfactory senses. Buffalo Hump, Spirit Talker, and I were joined around the fire by two subchiefs, Man Who is Unafraid and Ironside. A pipe was lit and dutifully passed around. It was clear that we were all hungry.

Just as Blue Flower and the chief's wife were about to serve us, Spirit Talker paused. He caught me fully off guard as he looked at me and pointed skyward. "We thank God and *Taa Narumi* for our food," he said before motioning the women to serve the meal.

Spirit Talker's attempt at a blessing was humble but much appreciated. That he'd incorporated the Comanche Big Father was an interesting, if not respectful, twist. It left me wondering what sort of spiritual talk might have filled Comanche conversations during the winter. From the body language within the circle, it was clear that Buffalo Hump and the subchiefs held the spirituality of the chief's son in great respect. White Knife, the rogue medicine man, was no longer around to challenge new ways of thinking.

We enjoyed a fine meal. Upon finishing, Buffalo Hump lit a pipe, took the first draw, and began to pass it around the circle.

"Spirit Talker learning White man way. Must learn more," said Buffalo Hump. He realized the importance of understanding the invasive force settling upon what had long been Comanche lands, and it opened the door to my proposal to travel to Wyoming.

There was no time like the present to make my proposal. "I invite my brother Spirit Talker to go north with me to Wyoming."

Spirit Talker's broad smile revealed that the invitation had instantly resonated with him. He noted Buffalo Hump's approving nod and turned toward me. He waved aside the smoke from the pipe and smiled. "Spirit Talker go," he responded. I could tell that he was unfamiliar with the North Platte River country and was anxious to explore.

In anticipation of his next question, I said, "Three moons. Wyoming far away."

Spirit Talker nodded enthusiastically.

I caught a pout from Blue Flower. Her dreams of being the bride to Isa would be put on hold.

"It shall be," said Buffalo Hump. The decision was final.

With that, we put the pipe aside and began to once again fill ourselves with the bounty of the Texas frontier. Laughter filled the teepee, as tales of hunts and battles were shared. I told of my encounter with the wolfpack that served to confirm the strong spirit of isa with which the Comanche regarded me.

Each of us left the teepee at one time or another to answer nature's call. I also wanted to be sure that Big Red was comfortable. It was during such an interlude that Blue Flower followed me.

FOUR
NORTH PLATTE COUNTRY

THE EASY MOUNTAIN breeze wafting its way through the forest was deceptive, like the White man's treaties. The wind's invisible journey brought the scent of evil to Otaktay, as he sat on the edge of a cliff and gazed through the aspen boughs off to the snow-capped peaks of the distant mountains. *Wanbli*, the bald eagle, soared majestically on outspread wings. His eyes focused below, he tucked and dove to rob an unsuspecting osprey of its meal. A sign? Perhaps.

Otaktay's gaze shifted further off, as he watched the progress of the distant billows of dust kicked up by wagons moving along what the White men called the Oregon Trail. His eyes dropped to the beautiful meandering waters of the Shell River below him. The Whites called the river the North Platte. The river spat sprays of white as it tumbled over rocks passing willow, boxelder, and ash trees in its journey. Patience was not Otaktay's strongest virtue. He had earned his name through bravery in battle, as his Lakota name translated to Kills Many. If it were up to him, all the White interlopers would be killed. Many scalps would grace his lance. The Treaty of Fort Laramie was a mere five years old and already being violated by the hated Whites. And they kept coming.

There were rumors of a yellow metal that the invaders coveted. The Lakota had endured many years of the mountain men trapping beaver, but now men came to hunt buffalo merely for their hides or to simply engage in the perverse pleasure of the kill. Kills Many shook his head in disgust and resignation. What might the yellow metal bring?

Worse still were the Long Knives, the mounted Blue-coats with their flashing swords. He'd seen and heard of their treachery. His people had believed the White man's words. To Otaktay, the Horse Creek Treaty, agreed to back in 1851, had been a joke. Thirteen tribes had attended, but not his Lakota brethren. Not a single Oglala Lakota attended. Even the Comanche, Kiowa, and Apache stayed away. Otaktay heard that famous Whites like mountain man Jim Bridger, surveyor John Fremont, and Jesuit Father Peter De Smet, the famed "black robe" missionary, had been there. The treaty terms were one-sided and could never be lived up to. Besides, figured Otaktay, the tribes had no ownership of the lands and thus no standing to agree to the terms of the Whites.

Not far off had been the place but two years earlier where the Sicangu Lakota were falsely accused of stealing a cow from a Mormon traveler. The misunderstanding resulted in the massacre of more than thirty soldiers under the command of 2nd Lieutenant John Gratton but more importantly marked the emergence of Lakota teenager Crazy Horse who would become a fearsome leader of his people. Regrettably to Otaktay's thinking, the Sioux did not follow-up their advantage and overrun a weakened Fort Laramie. Soon after, the Army had sent General William Harney to punish Otaktay's people, earning the general the epithets "Woman Killer" and "Mad Bear."

Otaktay sighed. His eyes tracked off to the east of his clifftop roost. A man that acted like the Whites but had black skin had built a cabin on the banks of the North Platte. He was big, but the physical characteristic that confounded Otaktay was that the man had no hair. He lived with a woman of some other nation. Lakota scouts had told him that the man spoke the Pawnee tongue and the woman was of that tribe. He shook his head with curiosity at the inconvenience of the man having constructed a cabin and fences. Otaktay's teepee was far more convenient, especially as it facilitated moving with the buffalo. The Lakota warrior watched intently. The man looked to be working hard. Cattle with exceptionally long horns grazed the prairie lands around his cabin and watered at the river.

At last, Otaktay stood, rolled his blanket, and slowly made his way back to his pony. Before mounting, he looked over his shoulder and took a final long, almost-mournful, look at the majestic landscape around him. What might the Whites do to his treasured hunting grounds? Would there be more cabins and fences? He knew the answers before the questions came to mind.

———

THE STRANGEST FEELING swept over George Freeman, as he leaned against the cabin doorjamb. He knew that he was being watched from afar. His two years with the Pawnee following his escape from slavery had taught him the essence of tapping into the senses of good and evil, including being aware of the prying eyes of friend or foe. His deep and abiding faith in Christ had seen him through all of his challenges.

Running Waters slipped in beside him and followed his eyes to the distant bluff overlooking the river. Something had caught her man's eye. "What do you see?"

George looked down and smiled. Running Waters was already with child, and they'd been together barely six weeks in their Wyoming abode. He pointed to the faraway spot. "Someone watched us. He is gone now."

"Danger?" asked Running Waters.

"Don't know. I think that the Treaty of Fort Laramie isn't worth the paper it was written on. The tribes are getting stirred up," he responded. "We must always be watchful." He gave her the broad reassuring smile that was his trademark.

Running Waters responded with the demure smile that ever captivated the big Black cowboy, as she acknowledged her husband's caution. "Do you think your friends will visit?"

At that, George laughed. He turned and wrapped his big arms around her in a hug. "Perhaps. Young Jack has a ranch to build, and his Comanche friend surely has obligations."

"Are you hungry?"

"Ah, my sweet wife, you needn't ever ask that." he said laughingly. "Especially for your cooking," he added. He took another gander at the distant bluff before joining Running Waters at the rough-hewn table inside the cabin.

———

THE SENTRY on duty at Fort Laramie opened the gate. He breathed into his cupped hands to take away the morning chill. The bedraggled column of a cavalry patrol rode on through. Heads hung just a tad low. Even the unit's colors hung limply. The bandages on two of the Bluecoats bore evidence of a skirmish with Indians, possibly Lakota but likely Cheyenne.

The sentry counted the soldiers, as they passed. All were accounted for. No scalps graced some savage's lance this day.

Originally a fur-trading post, the fort had been acquired by the Army in 1849 to protect settlers heading west along the Oregon Trail. Walls of adobe and lime concrete were constructed to replace deteriorating log palisades. Stables, two-story officer quarters, soldier quarters, a bakery, a guardhouse, and a powder magazine to house and support the fort garrison were quickly constructed. Up to three hundred fifty men would be stationed at the fort at any given time. Prime daytime chores were chopping wood or breaking river ice.

The sentry closed the gate and watched as the lieutenant dismissed the men and turned his mount to the commandant's office. At the officer quarters, he dismounted and strode past the guard with nary an acknowledgment or permission to report to the fort commandant. It would be a brief and essentially meaningless account of the skirmish and noting the increased incidence of such encounters.

———

THE BUCKSKIN MARE was feeling a tad frisky as though anticipating the warmer weather the spring day would bring. "Easy...easy," soothed George. The cayuse nickered a bit.

The horse punctuated the quiet with a sudden sharp whinny. As George leaned forward slightly to offer a comforting pat atop her neck, he heard the whoosh of an arrow and felt its fletching graze the back of his neck. Had he not leaned forward when he did, his bald scalp would likely have decorated a Cheyenne lance.

He dug his heels reflexively into the mare's sides and bolted in a dead run for the homestead. For all it mattered, he pulled his Colt and fired off a couple of wild shots toward his rear. He hoped Running Waters would hear and be ready with loaded rifles.

The mare hadn't galloped more than a hundred yards, when George realized they were heading straight toward the attackers. Faced with better than a half dozen Cheyenne warriors coming at him in full war paint, he skidded to enough of a stop to cut a hard right. He might not run through them, but might be able to outflank them. The whooping and yelping savages fell in behind for the chase.

Timing was everything. The Cheyenne were slowly gaining on George's mare, and she was about ready to collapse under him. Only her big heart kept her obeying the desperate urgings of her rider. George calculated that he'd reach the cabin just about the time he'd be feeling the breath of the warriors' ponies on his back.

The buckskin was galloping fast enough that she was barely able to stop in front of the cabin door. George leaped from the mare and bolted through the door held open by Running Waters, but the poor cayuse took a couple of arrows intended for him and tumbled to the ground. She'd given her all.

Running Waters handed George a rifle, and he turned

to face the attackers. Raising the muzzle and barely aiming, he blew a Cheyenne warrior from his pony. Running Waters handed him another rifle. Now able to breathe and calmly aim, a second savage quickly fell to George's unerring marksmanship.

Now, the remaining warriors began having second thoughts. They pulled back to reassess their situation. It seemed quite clear that the black-skinned man was bad medicine.

The Cheyenne were totally taken off guard when George suddenly emerged from the shelter of the cabin, took careful aim, and wounded another warrior. The amazed Cheyenne pulled back further. The black-skinned one was definitely very bad medicine. They decided they'd had enough. After delivering some halfhearted whoops and yells from a safe distance, the remaining attackers rode away in full retreat.

Running Waters joined her husband, as he stood watching the raiders ride off. "They will tell their brothers to stay away," she observed.

"I reckon so," responded George. "I'm more worried about the Lakota. Our government isn't holding up its part of that danged treaty. The Lakota never agreed to the treaty anyway."

"We must be watchful," she sighed. "Come, let's eat." She tugged at George's sleeve to urge him back into the cabin.

He scanned the space around the cabin. There were two Cheyenne warrior bodies lying out in the grass. His loyal buckskin mare had succumbed to the Cheyenne arrows. George turned to Running Waters. "Guess I'll take care of old Sally after breakfast. She gave it her all to save me." He figured it was the least he could do to give the mare a proper burial. As for the dead Indians, he knew that the Cheyenne would sneak back at night and recover the bodies. They would be no further bother to him and Running Waters. George stretched his arms. As he folded them in to touch the back of his neck, he felt the welt from the fletch of the arrow that had whizzed by him at the outset of the attack. He looked up prayerfully to the skies. "God is good," he whispered.

———

OTAKTAY HAD PAUSED upon hearing gunfire from the direction of where he'd watched the Black man. It was enough to bring him back to the promontory from where he could observe the Black man's successful defense of the home he claimed. He lifted his head pridefully, even arrogantly, as the Cheyenne retreated. "Squaws!" he muttered. Otaktay was confident that his warriors would fare much better against the black-skinned man and his squaw. He was confident that his time would come. His patience was wearing thin. It would be soon.

He took another look at the people he considered squatters on Lakota lands. An evil smile creased his lips, as he considered a raid. Indeed, the time would be sooner than later.

FIVE

HEADING NORTH

I SENSED Blue Flower's presence as I stood beside a tree answering nature's call. The situation was as unsettling as embarrassing. I avoided the temptation to glance over my shoulder at her.

Blue Flower was not exactly pleased. Her disappointment had begun when I entered the village with no string of fifteen ponies strung along behind me. The announcement of the long and arduous trip to Wyoming clinched her distress.

My proposal to visit Wyoming had been irresistible to the men. It was impossible for Spirit Talker to even consider refusing, and Buffalo Hump's word on the matter was final. The men had no appreciation whatsoever for Blue Flower's hopes and dreams.

Blue Flower gazed off at the hills, patiently waiting to gain my undivided attention.

I stared into the bark of the tree for what likely seemed like an eternity. Finally, I sighed. It was high time to face up to the music. I slowly turned toward her. "Blue Flower...I...er...I've missed you."

"Blue Flower no believe."

I looked down at my trail-worn boots. I glanced over at Big Red. He seemed far more at peace than me. My boots and horse seemed to be the only comfort existing in the situation. How could I express how much I yearned to be with her without showering her with unbridled affection? I looked up and waited until her eyes met mine.

Tears had begun to gather in the corners of her eyes, yet she stood with a jutted jaw and folded arms.

I gulped hard. "My heart belongs to Blue Flower." She slowly unfolded her arms. "I will bring ponies."

Her gaze softened. She knew that my heart was true. "Five moons?"

Five moons would mark the end of summer. "Five moons," I said decisively.

She smiled and stepped toward me.

I so desperately wanted to embrace her. The temptation was very hard to resist. I gently grasped her in both hands at arms-length and gazed deeply into her eyes. My hand softly stroked her cheek. I sighed. "We must return," I said motioning toward the teepee.

———

THE TIME for departure arrived sooner than I had expected. I awakened to find that my weather-beaten boots had been replaced by moccasin boots. The cuff at the top of the shaft was decorated with a beadwork pattern. As I pulled them on, I caught Blue Flower's smile from the opposite side of the teepee. "I am grateful," I offered.

She blushed. "Gift from brother," she revealed in halting English. Then, she smiled again. "Moccasin soft.

Jack sneak up on enemy." She made a little walking motion along her forearm with two fingers. I think she was justly proud to have learned a bit of English.

I had to admit that the moccasins were practical in that sense, though they'd be a challenge so far as slipping my feet into stirrups.

As I stood to admire my new boots, another gift caught my eye. Lying beside my bedroll were a bow and quiver full of arrows. Spirit Talker was apparently intent on teaching me some Comanche ways. I picked them up and strode from the teepee.

Spirit Talker was waiting outside sitting astride the pinto pony I'd gifted to him, and it was easy to see that horse and rider were made for each other. He nodded to me in recognition of the quiver of arrows slung on my back. "Jack learn shoot," he said with a broad grin. I had the feeling that he relished the idea of teaching a tenderfoot the skill of the bow and arrow.

Buffalo Hump stood proudly in full regalia to see his son off.

Spirit Talker dismounted and strode over to his father. The chief spoke to him in the Comanche tongue so rapidly that I could only make out a word here or there. It's amazing what can be forgotten in just a handful of months. He embraced his son who nodded to his sister and promptly clambered back astride the pinto.

As I watched, I could feel Blue Flower's eyes on me. In my peripheral vision, I caught Spirit Talker smile and nod toward her. I wasn't exactly feeling comfortable. My gut told me that her demure smile would be very hard to part from. I nevertheless finally turned my gaze toward her. I wasn't disappointed. What could I do? I returned her smile. I dared not carry the emotion of the moment further, or we'd never get out of the village. I turned Big Red and urged him to an easy walk.

In short order, I found myself leading us northward with my Comanche brother riding alongside and two packhorses trailing on long tethers. We paused at the edge of the Comanche encampment. I glanced back. Blue Flower waved.

"Why stop, Jack?" asked Spirit Talker.

"Figure to bless our journey, Spirit Talker." With that, I bowed my head, and Spirit Talker followed suit. "Lord, watch over our journey, guide us, and keep us safe. And please keep our loved ones safe while we are on our journey."

"Amen," offered Spirit Talker.

We urged our mounts onward.

———

WE RODE about a dozen miles or so with nary a word spoken. I found myself trying to adjust to the reality of what lay ahead and assumed my brother was experiencing the same feelings. We rounded the bend in an arroyo, and I looked up to see a huge pink rock. With my curiosity fully aroused, I began to head us toward the monolith.

Spirit Talker pulled up. "No go," he said firmly.

I looked over at him questioningly.

"Strong spirits…bad medicine," he responded.

Sizing up the rock, I found myself drawn to it as though by some magnetic pull. The rock was easily more than four hundred feet high and was quite obviously a single piece of granite. I turned to Spirit Talker. "What spirits?"

He urged his mount eastward to skirt around the

rock. "Many die from bad spirits," he responded with obvious reluctance to go into detail. "We go around."

I glanced at the horizon to the west and noted the sun moving ever lower toward it. "Camp here?" I asked. I think I was taunting my brother in a perverse sort of way. He seemed genuinely unsettled by whatever magic surrounded the place.

"We ride," he said cryptically.

Looking up at the huge thing as we rode by at a distance, I strove to understand why some might think of the place as enchanted. I shrugged and sighed, "We make camp soon," I finally said. I truly would have loved the adventure of climbing to the summit.

———

I JUDGED that we traveled another eight or ten miles past that rock with all its supposed evil spirits.

Spirit Talker pulled up at a small stream and slid from the pinto. "We camp here," he offered definitively.

Off to the west, the sun was just about ready to sink below the horizon. The horizon? It was my first clue as to what lay ahead. The vista ahead was pretty doggone flat. "*Kohto*," I said as I began to pull together wood for a fire. "*Ana o'a hi'it?*" I asked whether my Comanche brother was hungry, as I set about bringing a fire to life.

Spirit Talker smiled and gave me a look as though I needn't have asked. He began preparing some of the victuals his sister had packed for us.

We ate well. Sitting in the glow of the firelight after dinner, we finally had a chance for just the two of us to talk. I opened by telling him of the attack by Comanche on Rising Cross Ranch. "I think they were likely Nokoni or Tenawa," I ventured.

Spirit Talker nodded. "Nokoni," he said assuredly. Angry at *tosa*. Fear White man."

I told him about my acting crazy and shouting *isa peeka* at them.

My brother laughed. "Jack know *isa* big medicine to Comanche. When *tosa* shout, Nokoni afraid."

"Jack meet *isa* pack on Pinta Trail. They were friendly."

All of a sudden, Spirit Talker grew serious. "Jack have big medicine."

I smiled. "If I have any medicine, it comes from God, not *isa*."

He chewed on that a moment. "Maybe God talk through *isa*?"

Now, there was a thought. But no, I'd never heard of such a thing. "God uses His power in many ways," I shared.

He looked over at me from the opposite side of the fire. "Penateka believe follow *Taa Narumi*," he said with his voice trailing off. Then he looked up at a distant star. "*Pia Wa'óo Hoikwa* follow Jack's God," he said with conviction.

I began to ask myself whether to be so bold as to baptize my brother. Call me less than confident, if you will, but I didn't feel the moment was right. I really hadn't shared Christ's story of dying for mankind's sins. Spirit Talker needed more of a perspective to truly understand baptism much less Christ dying on a cross and rising from death. There was a lot of trail laying ahead of us and plenty of time to talk about the Trinity and all that went with Christianity. I didn't want my Comanche brother to be under any illusions. God wasn't about any perceived strong medicine on my part, and Spirit Talker must understand that. I decided to change the subject for now. "I hope George is well," I said.

"Many enemy," Spirit Talker said as he pointed northward.

"How do you know?" I asked.

"Hear stories from Quahadi brothers. Numunuu fight many enemy." He looked at me with a very serious expression made more so by the deep scars from the mountain lion attack from which I'd saved him. "Pawnee, Arapaho, Cheyenne...bad medicine." He paused and stirred the coals thoughtfully with a stick. "Oglala Lakota strong where we go," he finally shared. "Ride like Comanche. Count many coup and take many scalps."

I felt an icy cold chill run down my spine. What was I taking us into?

"We shoot arrow in morning," he said with a grin. "Learn hunt quiet. No gun."

That made sense to me. I yawned. The day had caught up with me. The fire died out, as we both drifted off to sleep. I felt secure. It didn't occur to me that we'd soon be taking turns keeping a watch at night.

———

I AWAKENED BEFORE SUNRISE. As I opened my eyes, I found myself in a stare down with a rattlesnake. I thought about the Colt revolver under my bedroll at my shoulder. The snake's triangular-shaped head gave no hint yet as to whether it felt threatened enough to attack. As I thought about what to do, I heard a whoosh and saw an arrow drill right through its evil-looking head. It seemed that Lion Hunter was up before me.

He put a finger to his lips as though to keep me from

speaking and then placed his hand to his ear as a signal to listen.

Sure enough, I detected the faint sound of hoofbeats.

"Texas Rangers," Spirit Talker whispered.

"What of our horses?" I whispered back. There was virtually no cover where we had camped. The gurgling of the stream did little to mask any noise we made.

"Horses lie down," he assured me.

With the horses out of sight, we stood a fair chance of avoiding discovery. I crawled over to Big Red to keep the spirited stallion at ease. He seemed to sense the moment and stayed still.

We heard a lot of splashing and horses whinnying, but they passed on down the stream as though we didn't exist. I peeked over Big Red just long enough to recognize my old friendly nemesis Captain Benton. I suspected he was out hunting for Comanche. This was not going to be his day.

Once the Rangers passed on, we broke camp. There was no point in lingering in Texas Ranger hunting grounds.

SIX
THE PANHANDLE

WE LEFT the hills behind and were now carving our own trail northward across a vast prairie that was pretty much flat. My dear brother Spirit Talker decided that we would avoid the Quahadi Comanche for now. By that, he confirmed what I'd been told about the on-again-off-again love affair among the various Comanche tribes.

We saw nary a soul for the next few days. If we were seen, whomever saw us must have decided that we were not a worthy target. That rather surprised me given that our packhorses carried large loads. As best as we could figure the distance, we made a routine of riding two miles and walking one. This gave the horses plenty of rest. Water was plentiful enough, and there were plenty of grasses for the horses to feed upon.

Spirit Talker took it upon himself to share his skills with bow and arrow. It was almost scary how quickly I caught on.

On the fourth day of our journey, Lion Hunter set a few stick targets with pieces of buckskin attached at what I guessed to be forty or fifty yards. That's a pretty fair distance for bow and arrow. I think he was chuckling to himself at the challenge he was putting to me.

Upon completing the target placements, he leaped aboard the pinto, took careful aim with his bow and arrow, and put a shaft through one. He turned toward me and nodded for me to try. Three targets still stood unscathed.

Big Red stood steady. There was no wind. The sun was high and visibility was good. I nocked an arrow, drew back the string, aimed, and let fly. The arrow penetrated the target. Before Lion Hunter could nock another arrow, I shot a second. Another target bit the Texas prairie dust.

Spirit Talker's eyes widened. "Jack good. Strong medicine." It was his way of saying that I was a fast learner.

"Spirit Talker good teacher," I responded.

Just then, three pronghorn antelopes ventured unusually close. They are normally skittish beasts that will bound away at the slightest provocation. Spirit Talker already had an arrow nocked. He shot seemingly without aiming. We would be feasting on pronghorn this night.

He told me how the weapons were crafted. The bow itself was usually fashioned from a piece of juniper, hickory, or ash about a yard long. It would be shaped such that the middle was thicker to make a grip, while the ends were thinned to enhance flexibility. The shaping was done with rough stone, bone, or knives. The bowstring was made from gut, rawhide, sinew, or woven plant fibers such as from milkweed, nettle, or hemp. The weapon Spirit Talker had given me featured a string made from fibers. Such a string was more difficult to make but resisted stretching and was not so susceptible to humidity.

Arrows were made from straight shoots of trees such

as black locust, dogwood, ash, and birch. They were scraped, sanded or heated, and bent as needed to make them straight. Arrowheads were chipped from materials such as obsidian (volcanic glass), flint, or chert, a quartz-like rock, though steel and copper arrowheads crept into use with the onslaught of Europeans. They were attached with hide glue or pitch and sinew into a split at the head of the arrow. Buzzard or turkey feathers were attached to the rear of each shaft as fletching to better ensure accurate flight.

The crowning glory so to speak were any decorations the maker added. These might include feathers, strings of beads, or pieces of horsehair. The grip was usually wrapped with rawhide.

I was quite impressed with the process, though I imagine Spirit Talker would have been equally impressed with the manufacturing process that went into guns and ammunition. Whether the devices were used to hunt food or kill humans, they demanded the utmost care and respect.

———

WE HAD BEEN TRAVELING for several days. The sameness of the landscape was underwhelming. We plodded along, ever alert for lurking dangers. Riding the prairie left us exposed thanks to the scarcity of any growth taller than grass.

I had inched a horse length or so ahead as we rode downward within a narrow but shallow swale. Big Red drew up suddenly. A couple of feet ahead was a rather steep drop off. From our vantage point lay an incredibly awesome sight. So far as the eye could see was a gaping crevasse that had been carved from the prairie floor.

Spirit Talker pulled up alongside, curious as to why I had stopped. His jaw dropped. "Is place of hole in ground!" he exclaimed.

A few hundred yards ahead meandered a stream. Getting to it presented a monumental task. I scanned off to left and right. "We must find a path," I said aloud. The sound of my voice seemed in stark contrast to the awesome silence of the great canyon that lay ahead.

"Go this way," he announced confidently and pointed to our left.

My questioning look drew a smile.

"Old ones told me of this place," he assured me.

"How far?" I asked.

"Four days."

He was telling me that the canyon was more than a hundred miles long.

It didn't take long to discover a gentle trail to the floor of the canyon. In the couple of miles that we traveled, we stirred up a herd of mule deer, coyote, rattlesnakes, and a pair of lynx. We would not be going hungry, as game was obviously plentiful.

The canyon was teeming with wildflowers and grasses along with stands of mesquite, cottonwood, juniper, and willow. The sun was wending its way toward the horizon when we settled on a spot near a stream that was screened by willows. Years later, I'd learn that this stream was the Prairie Dog Fork of the Red River.

The rugged beauty of the surroundings was breathtaking. Despite lurking predatory wildlife, I found myself relaxing for the first time on our journey.

Spirit Talker wasted no time bagging a small mule deer. After feasting on the deer, we decided to take a day of rest from our travels. It would also give us the opportunity to make some venison jerky.

After feasting on the deer with pemmican as a side, we sat cross-legged around the fire. Spirit Talker stirred the coals with a stick. He seemed to be in a thoughtful spirit.

"Why you believe in God?" he finally blurted.

I might have asked him the same thing of his *Taa Narumi*, but that wouldn't have been productive. I picked up a nearby stick and thought to stir the coals, but put it aside rather than mimic my brother. "I guess my pa and ma taught me of God. They had His written word, called a Bible."

Spirit Talker nodded but persisted, "Why?"

"Peace of mind," I responded, pointing to my head. "Life offers many dangers, many challenges. God gives me the strength to overcome them." I could see from Lion Hunter's facial expression that he wasn't quite understanding. "Life hands us challenges like mountain lions, like enemy numunuu, and lurking death." I gazed into my Comanche brother's eyes. "We have choices. We can choose challenges to avoid or confront, or we can let challenges choose us. God gives me peace and comfort in making the best choices. The Bible tells me that God renews my strength and mounts me up with wings like eagles, like pia huutsuu." I sighed and looked into the flickering flames. "I trust God, and that is my why."

Silence emanated from the opposite side of the campfire. Spirit Talker stirred the coals a bit more. He was obviously in deep thought. He surely earned his name. "Much pulls us away from God," he said with a profoundness.

I was caught off guard. Despite having learned to appreciate my brother's raw intelligence, his powers of observation ran impressively deep. "There is much to tempt us from the path of good," I shared.

Spirit Talker nodded, then smiled. "Like Comanche *wa'ipu*."

Yes, the path of good. I swallowed hard and nearly choked. "Like Blue Flower," I said, finally conjuring up a knowing laugh.

The floor of the canyon was a tad warmer during the day but chilled at night. We decided to keep our fire going and take turns with sentry duties. My Comanche brother had raised thought-provoking questions, and they'd be fodder for more campfire conversations.

———

AS SHARDS of sunlight danced across my face, I awoke to the aromas of venison steak and coffee. I vaguely recalled Spirit Talker shaking me awake in the middle of the night, so I could take my turn at sentry. I stayed awake for at least a couple of hours before awakening him shortly before sunrise. Thankfully, the night was uneventful.

Lion Hunter smiled, as he watched me sit up. "We make jerky. Find berries. Make pemmican." He had a busy day lined up.

I stood and stretched. Upon taking a few strides toward one of the willows to answer nature's call, I nearly stepped on a rattlesnake head. It was just the head lying there with its empty eyes staring into space. I glanced over at Spirit Talker.

My Comanche brother smiled broadly. "Eat snake. Is good." With that, he popped a sizzling piece of snake meat from the frying pan to his mouth. He lifted the pan in my direction. "*Isa* try," he chided.

The morsel was delicious.

We spent the day making venison jerky and pemmican, taking time to explore. Spirit Talker told me that the Comanche settled in what they referred to as the secret place many years ago. They didn't frequent it so often these days, but Cheyenne, Arapahoe, and Kiowa explored its depths many times over the years. It was good hunting, but not necessarily a place to be during heavy rains. Flash floods were a very real danger in the canyon. I thanked the Lord for the crystal-clear blue sky, the big sky that stretched the boundaries of the horizon.

———

IT WAS with some reluctance that we broke that first campsite in the canyon. As we wended our way northward, we remained ever mindful of the dangerous varmints that lurked. Our vigilance was especially directed at those venomous rattlesnakes. If its bite didn't kill you, it could make you awfully sick.

We were into our third day of travel when Spirit Talker pulled up. He pointed to the east rim of the canyon. Sure enough, there was a party of perhaps a dozen Indians. They were likely a mile away. The coloration of our horses and outfits likely offered enough camouflage to make us difficult to spot in the canyon floor, but Spirit Talker ushered us over to a stand of cottonwood to ensure we wouldn't be spotted. We dismounted. It was time for a rest anyway.

"Quahadi Comanche," Spirit Talker said with an ironic smile.

"They friendly?" I asked.

"Not want to find out," he responded. It was obvious that he took no chances. Recalling that there were as many as thirteen Comanche tribes, I reminded myself that they could be enemies one day and friends another.

The Comanche band passed on with no further incident. We remained dismounted and continued to follow the stream northward. Twice, rattlers blocked our path. We could have had plenty of good snake eating had we chosen to kill the critters.

We soon remounted out of an abundance of caution.

Spirit Talker pulled up at a bend in the river. "*Puuka* thirsty," he observed. Indeed, the dry air in the depths of the canyon led to our horses becoming more thirsty than usual.

I slipped from Big Red's saddle and let him guzzle from the water's edge. Once he was satisfied, I fell to my knees and slurped my fill. As I pushed myself up, a chill swept over me. I looked up. A pair of yellow eyes were fixated on mine from the opposite stream bank. "*Pia wa'óo*," I whispered in Spirit Talker's general direction. I could see Big Red's ears prick up, yet he remained silent as did Spirit Talker's pinto. The packhorses whinnied nervously.

My Comanche brother stiffened a bit. He absentmindedly stroked the claws of the mountain lion necklace I'd given him, as if to draw some extra strong medicine. "*Pia wa'óo*," he echoed through tight lips.

The cat raised its head from the stream. His tail twitched. Fight or flight was likely running through its brain. How hungry was he? Did he know that he faced a man who'd killed one of his kin? A low guttural hiss spewed forth from its jaws.

I lay still at the edge of the stream perhaps twenty feet from the tawny mass of muscle and its deadly claws and teeth. Visions of the cuts Spirit Talker had endured back when I saved him from an even bigger lion raced through my mind. I hoped my friend was nocking an arrow at this incredibly tense moment.

I heard a whoosh cut the air.

An arrow struck deep into the lion's throat. Spirit Talker hadn't let me down.

The big cat rolled on his back, clawing desperately at the deadly shaft protruding from him.

As I stood, a second arrow found its way into the lion. He lay on his side, breaths becoming ever shallower. He took a final mournful look at me and breathed his last.

"Come, Jack," called Spirit Talker, as he waded into the stream.

Soon enough, we were dragging the big cat's remains across the stream. We went to work skinning it. Coyotes and buzzards would take care of the carcass. It hardly seemed a fitting end to such a magnificent beast, but an end it was. Spirit Talker collected the mountain lion's claws. He'd apparently already decided to fashion a necklace like the one I had gifted to him.

We would have to tan the hide later, as we both felt pressed to get on with our journey to George's ranch. We hadn't even left Texas yet. Transporting the hide posed a bit of a problem. My Comanche brother Spirit Talker scraped any fat and remaining flesh from the hide and rubbed it with salt that we'd had the foresight to bring with us. The salt served to draw moisture from the lion's pelt. However, the hide had to be transported flat. Soon enough, we would stretch it and begin the tanning process.

I was initially a tad disgusted by what he did next. "What are you doing?" I asked.

"Tan hide," he responded, as he gathered mountain lion brain and body fat in a buckskin bag.

I didn't exactly appreciate that some of the contents

oozed through the seams, but Spirit Talker didn't seem to mind.

I shook my head resignedly and held back the contents of my stomach.

Spirit Talker grinned. "You see."

———

WE ROUNDED a bend in what was now barely a creek, and I found myself staring at a rather majestic sight. Had I been back east, I might have been looking at a lighthouse. The rocky spire sure resembled such a structure, without the great flashing warning lights of course.

Spirit Talker simply nodded at my amazement. He had a habit of staying cool, calm, and collected, rather nonplussed.

I wondered whether there were any spirit stories surrounding the towering rock, but my brother offered no such tale. I reckoned it simply didn't hold the enchanting magic or bad medicine of that big rock now far to our south.

SEVEN
LEAVING TEXAS

WHETHER SPIRIT TALKER fully appreciated it or not, I remained quite conscious of the fact that we were in the heart of the Comanchería. Upon departing the canyon, we traveled over more flat prairies before the landscape turned to rolling hills. Three days after leaving the canyon, we arrived at the *Goo-al-pah* or Canadian River. From what I'd been told, we were drawing ever closer to the Texas border and would soon be entering what the folks in Washington called the Indian Territory.

The broad prairies gave us plenty of opportunity to travel side-by-side and talk about the cultures we'd grown up in, religion, the challenges we'd already faced, and hopes and dreams for the future. It fascinated me that Spirit Talker still clung to the life debt created when I'd saved him from the mountain lion and certain death. No matter that he had saved my life a time or two, the life debt was an obligation that endured. Shucks, I owed him my life. In a sense, we were mutually indebted.

Blessedly, the Canadian River was broader than deep. Crossing wasn't a special challenge, as the horses never lost their footing and seemed nonplussed at the current. We dried out rather quickly in the ever-warmer rays of the mid-spring sun.

We set up camp a few miles north of the river. It was a chance to truly dry out from the crossing, and Spirit Talker could go to work on the mountain lion skin. He gathered sticks of various lengths and lashed them together to form a stretching rack. He proceeded to dig some roots and mash them to a semi-fibrous pulp. I soon learned what the lion brain and fat was for, as Spirit Talker mixed them together with the mashed roots and began rubbing the concoction on the hide. Apparently, the roots served as a makeshift form of tannin. Ultimately, this process would ensure a soft pelt that could serve as decoration, cape, or fashioned into clothing. In any case, I observed and tried to learn. Oh, and it did get me to recalling the Mexican hiders back in Texas who rustled and then skinned cattle just for their hides, leaving the carcasses to rot or serve as meals for local buzzards and four-legged predators. I'd just as soon have forgotten that experience.

Next morning, I awakened to the aroma of damp fur. During his turn at sentry, Spirit Talker had placed the mountain lion pelt over my shoulders. It was a worthy gift for which I'd be ever grateful.

We now presented quite a sight to the world. The sun had served to tan my face and hands, and my hair had grown to my shoulders. I was fully outfitted in buckskins, though increasingly shed my shirt as the weather warmed. It was late April, and we had a long way yet to go. We both had our quivers of arrows slung over our shoulders with bow near at hand. My 1851 Colt Navy revolver was nestled in a homely but serviceable holster at my waist, while my Sharps rifle hung in a scabbard from the saddle horn. A Bowie knife was fastened to my belt at my back. Spirit Talker was no less impressively armed. In addition to the aforementioned bow and arrows, he carried a lance with no scalps dangling from it, war club, and knife all readily at hand. We'd have been an even more fearsome pair had we decked ourselves out in war paint!

The sun was moving mighty close to the western horizon when we came upon some fairly substantial adobe ruins. This was apparently a place called Adobe Walls that had served as a trading post in the past. As Spirit Talker explained to me, a trading outfit named Bent, St. Vrain, and Company had built the place to trade with Kiowa and Comanche. Nearby Bent's Creek was named for William Bent. When the trading operation failed, a fellow named Kit Carson reopened it back in 1848. Again, the enterprise failed. Bent himself wound up blowing the trading post to smithereens in 1849. Over the ensuing years of disrepair and piles of adobe rubble, the ruins became a familiar landmark to travelers who dared to venture into the heart of the Comanchería.

We hobbled the horses and enjoyed the ample water supply and the semi-shelter of what remained of the adobe walls. We managed to scrounge up enough wood to build an adequate fire for warmth. Dinner was jerky and pemmican, as we reminded ourselves that we would need to hunt if we were to enjoy fresh meat.

"Jack say God is three," Spirit Talker stated, referring to the Trinity.

I nodded. "That's what we were taught and what we Christians believe," I answered.

Spirit Talker stared into the fire. "Three strong medicine," he observed.

I thought it was an interesting way to describe the

Trinity. Strong medicine indeed. "God, Jesus, and the Spirit are three in One," I said.

"Jesus die on cross?" he asked for the umpteenth time as though trying to grasp that sort of torturous death.

From descriptions of Comanche torture, I was rather surprised that he would think of crucifixion as any more or less of a gruesome a method of killing. "Yes. And he buried in cave and came alive in three days."

"Can prove?" Spirit Talker asked.

"Many saw him alive."

"He alive today?"

"He stayed a short time to deliver His message, then went to live with God."

Spirit Talker pondered my latest revelation. He locked on to my eyes.

I strove with my gaze to reinforce what I'd just shared.

"Spirit Talker tired," he said. He nodded and gave a hint of a peaceful smile before covering himself with his blanket and nodding off to sleep.

I supposed I had satisfied his curiosity. I stood and sat on the remains of one of the adobe walls. The moon had risen high into the night sky. Along with the stars, it was a right peaceful scene with plenty of light to spot any threats. The quiet? It was almost deafening but for an occasional coyote howl. I draped the mountain lion skin over my shoulders to ward off a slight chill and cradled the Sharps rifle in the crook of my elbow. Tomorrow, we would likely push into western Kansas, and the risk of hostile Indians would grow. Cheyenne and Arapahoe would be lurking.

Long about what was likely a tad after midnight, I tapped Spirit Talker to take a turn at sentry. We swapped places, and I passed along the rifle. He'd learned over the winter how to use a rifle though chose not to carry one, as he thought the things were too heavy, and he much preferred the stealth and light weight of the bow and arrow.

Spirit Talker looked at me questioningly as though asking whether I had seen anything. I expect his silence was a reflection of the quietness that surrounded us.

We heard a coyote howl. Or was it?

A sense of eeriness crept over me.

"Jack stay," Spirit Talker whispered. He handed the Sharps back to me and picked up his lance.

I waited while Spirit Talker disappeared from view into the night. A few minutes passed, and I heard a grunt and groan from somewhere out among the darkness. That was followed by a whoop and another grunt. Silence.

Spirit Talker emerged from the darkness.

Much to my chagrin, two scalps now decorated his lance. The scalps were grisly, and blood still dripped from the point of his lance. My mind flashed back to the day my freshly-scalped pa had passed away in my arms.

"Cheyenne," he said, appearing to take no notice of the horror written across my face.

"I thought *Kutseena* the coyote howled," I said.

"Cheyenne sound different," he responded.

I reckoned that the Cheyenne must have mimicked the coyote's howl with some sort of accent. I was grateful that Spirit Talker recognized the Indian signals, or our hair might have been decorating Cheyenne lances. "Spirit Talker strong medicine," I said as a compliment to my Indian brother.

Spirit Talker shrugged. "Watch careful. Cheyenne bad

medicine. This Pawnee land...Arapaho land. They friends," he observed, then added, "Cheyenne hungry."

His wasn't the greatest English, but the message was clear. The Cheyenne had apparently moved far to the south of their regular hunting grounds. It might have been that they were searching for buffalo. They happened upon us and figured us to be easy targets, and we were easy targets. We were likely safe for the moment but would have to be evermore watchful for lurking threats. Before long, we would be moving into Lakota territory, and I could sense foreboding in Spirit Talker's voice. The Lakota were reputed to be as savage as the Comanche, though I wouldn't dare mention that to Spirit Talker.

We decided to abandon Adobe Walls at first light. The sooner we resumed our journey northward, the better. I was naturally presuming that George's ranch would be safe.

We actually hit the trail just as the first rays of the sun poked above the eastern horizon. The Sharps rifle now rested across my lap rather than being stuffed into its scabbard. Afore long, we crossed out of Texas. The Santa Fe Trail, our next landmark of significance, was yet a day ahead of us.

EIGHT
MOUNTAIN MAN GREETINGS

THE SANTA FE TRAIL was easy to spot. There were the ruts from passing wagons along with the hoofprints of the oxen that pulled them. Abandoned furniture, an occasional wagon wheel, skeletal remains of animals, and clusters of the graves of travelers who reached the end of their life journey littered the trail. I can't say as I saw any Indian sign, but Spirit Talker paused several times to point out evidence of their presence. I strove to be a fast learner, as our lives depended on it.

By now, I was accurate with bow and arrow, cultivated my long hair with the addition of a wispy beard, had tanned nearly dark enough to be mistaken for an Indian, and fully enjoyed my moccasin boots. To some eastern tenderfoot, this sixteen-year-old man likely would present a rather fearsome sight.

We traced the trail for a few miles westward before peeling off to resume our journey north. The prairies faded behind us, giving way to a forested and more rugged mountainous landscape.

It was now early May. By my reckoning, we were

roughly halfway to George's ranch. We reached a river the Indians called the *Napeste* and White folks referred to by the name given it by the Spanish explorers–the Arkansas River. We easily crossed the river at a wide and fairly shallow place and wended our way northwestward until the rugged terrain and a distant mountain range hinted that it was time to turn due north. By my calculations, we'd arrive in North Platte country in about two weeks.

The countryside was downright magnificent. To say it was beautiful would have been an understatement. Game was plentiful, and the streams teemed with fish. This was God's country by any measure. I was pleased to introduce Spirit Talker to trout.

We were still managing roughly thirty miles per day and took care to keep our horses watered, fed, and rested. Big Red was every bit the strong stallion that had led an impressive herd of wild horses when I had first found him. I occasionally thought about how the Fishers and my sister and brother were making out back at Rising Cross Ranch tending to livestock and continuing to develop our holdings. Hopefully, the Texas Rangers were protecting them from further Comanche predations.

———

THE COUNTRYSIDE GREW MORE rugged after we crossed the *Napeste*. We had now entered Arapaho and Cheyenne territory. While they were mostly quite hostile, Spirit Talker assured me that they were not so savage as the Comanche.

"Arapaho...Cheyenne...*tabu*," he announced with confidence.

I doubted that these tribes were cowards, despite Spirit Talker's assessment. I read his smile and decided he was purposefully exaggerating. I laughed. "We must be careful of *tabu*." Underestimating enemies had sent many to early graves.

The countryside, as we passed through the foothills with its magnificent peaks to our left, offered minimal cover from ambush, as mountain juniper and mahogany dotted the rolling hills. Game was plentiful.

Over the next five days, I sharpened my skills with bow and arrow. There was no point in announcing our presence to wandering parties of Arapaho and Cheyenne. I bagged two deer, so we enjoyed venison steaks over low cooking fires.

As our trail took us higher into ever more mountainous territory, we were blessed with forests of aspen, fir, pine, and spruce. It was somewhat of a relief, even a mixed blessing of sorts, to gradually leave the foothills with its sparse ground cover of mostly shrubs behind. While we had better cover in the forests, so did any potential enemies.

Little did we know that just a couple of years from now, the region would be swarming with miners seeking to tap the bountiful lodes of precious gold that lay within its rocks and streams.

On the fifth day after crossing the *Napeste*, we made camp beside a beautiful creek. We had just finished a meal of venison steak with a ration of pemmican and coffee, when a sound brought us to full alert.

"Wagh! Hail the camp," called out a gravelly voice in English. "May I join you?" Giving forewarning before entering a camp was a common courtesy of the west. Failure to do so could get a soul a meeting with his or her Maker. "Wagh" was a word of greeting commonly used by mountain men.

Spirit Talker and I hefted our weapons as a precaution. "Come in slow with hands empty," I called out.

What emerged from among the nearby stand of aspen seemed more apparition than human. The wrinkles across the man's face gave witness to advanced years. Crystal-blue eyes peered out from under long silver hair and were framed by a long scraggly beard, all of which was topped off by a gray fox cap. From the neck down, fringed tan-colored buckskins decorated with deteriorating beadwork led the eye to well-worn moccasins. A large knife hung from his belt and what appeared to be a large-caliber Hawken rifle was slung over his shoulder. He led a horse that seemed as old as he but appeared well cared for. An Indian-style saddle was strapped to the pony's back. Behind the horse was a mule, laden with the owner's stock of necessaries. As the man approached, he called out, "Bear Grandy, at your service!" He offered a nearly toothless grin.

I reckoned this Mr. Grandy was a throwback to the mountain men of years past. I'd been told that they were pretty much extinct, a vanishing breed. "Come enjoy some coffee, Mr. Grandy," I invited.

Grandy ambled on into our campsite. His eyes widened upon noting that my companion was an Indian, but he didn't break stride in grabbing the tin cup of coffee I offered to him. "Thanks kindly," he said with his eyes ever on my Comanche brother.

"I'm Jack O'Toole, and this is my friend Spirit Talker," I shared by way of introduction.

"Spirit Talker," he nodded in Spirit Talker's direction. Apparently, Bear Grandy spoke some Comanche language. "Nice to make yer acquaintance, Jack."

I motioned for him to sit. As I did, I noticed an arrow protruding from the back of his shoulder. He winced just a tad, as he sat.

"Appears you might need some help with that?" I asked, pointing to his shoulder.

"Dang! I plumb fergot. Fool Arapaho bushwhacked me yesterday." He smiled. "I'd be much obliged. I'd have yanked it myself, but it's tough to reach," he added. He nodded toward his mule. "Thought about lettin' Charlie over there chewin' it off, but then smelled yer fire."

I shuddered at the thought of the mule biting off the arrow. "I think we can help you out, Mr. Grandy."

"Y'all can call me Bear," he offered.

I nodded to my Comanche brother. "Let's take a look at your wound, Bear," I said and moved toward the throwback mountain man. "Spirit Talker has a poultice that will help heal."

Spirit Talker waved me off. "Me look," he said.

"Just hopin' the danged Arapaho savage didn't use no poison arrow," Grandy grumbled. He took a swig of coffee and permitted Spirit Talker to examine the wound. "An' be gentle with my shirt. Only one I gots."

Spirit Talker smiled, as he scrutinized Grandy's wound. "Humph!" he grunted. He slipped out his knife and cut Grandy's shirt just enough to better access the arrow. "Is deep but only muscle," he diagnosed. He handed Grandy a stick and motioned him to clamp it in his jaws.

Grandy shook his head. "Ain't hardly got no teeth to clamp it with," he responded.

Spirit Talker shrugged, took a firm grip on the shaft, braced himself, and slowly and excruciatingly worked the arrow from the mountain man's shoulder. The arrow finally came free of its fleshy home. "Wasápe take off shirt," requested Spirit Talker, translating the name Bear to Comanche.

Grandy looked over to me as he shed his shirt. "Yer friend talk good English, Jack."

I smiled and tilted my head toward Spirit Talker. "It's how he earned his name. Much respect among Penateka Comanche."

"An' a young'un, too," Grandy observed, as Spirit Talker applied a poultice and bandaged it in place with a couple of strips of rawhide.

The Comanche examined the arrowhead in the fading light. "Wasápe no poison," he assured Grandy.

The mountain man responded with an audible sigh, as much from relief as discomfort in slipping his shirt back on. "Mind if'n I set a spell?" he asked.

I smiled. "We expected you'd spend the night enjoying our hospitality, Bear."

"Wagh! Thanks, right kindly." And he stood, wobbled, and sat back down. "Guess the danged arrow got me more than I'd figured," he reluctantly observed.

I went over and saw to making his horse and mule comfortable for the night. Save for a nicker or two, Big Red and the pinto didn't seem to mind the company.

Upon returning to the campfire, I found Grandy smiling broadly and chewing on a strip of venison Spirit Talker had given him.

"You two be lucky you ain't lost yer hosses or scalps," he offered with a reassuring sort of grin. He watched our reaction. "Reckon y'all figure me to be some sort of throwback," he observed. "Well, I expect I am. Where you young'uns hail from?"

I figured I really didn't have to tell him that we'd learned how to travel with a low profile. "Comanchería," I responded, as though that said plenty. I figured to turn the conversation to Grandy. "You been around these parts a long time?" I inquired.

Grandy stirred the campfire embers with a stick. Stirring campfires with sticks seemed to be a common habit, as it apparently helped the thinking process. The mountain man looked from me to Spirit Talker and back as he cogitated for a few moments. He cleared his throat. "Come out here back in '21," he began. "Heard stories 'bout freedom of the mountains. Folks was makin' a livin' trappin' critters."

He stirred more coals, then leaned back against his saddle which I'd placed behind him. "Yep. Just me, clothes on my back, a sad excuse for a hoss, and my Kentucky long rifle. Well, I had just enough money to get a decent hoss, a mule, an' trade the Kentucky rifle for that there Hawken. Folks in St. Louis said I'd need a big slug to handle the critters out here." He leaned forward a bit, as he began to get into his story. He shrugged his wounded shoulder to ease the discomfort best he could. "Joined with a bunch of trappers, and by '23 found myself trappin' beaver."

I found myself joining in stirring coals. He had Spirit Talker's and my full attention.

"In '25, run into a fella name of Hugh Glass. Now, there was a man. Wagh! Stood with Jim Bridger, Jedidiah Smith, and them legends. Fella had serious scars from a grizzly maulin'. Spent time together, and he taught me a ton."

The mention of Hugh Glass grabbed my attention. "What do you know of Glass?" I asked.

"About as much as anyone...maybe a tad more," Grandy responded. "First, I learned that he was a Christian man. Yep. Strong in his faith in the Lord. Glass sailed the seas early on. His boat was captured by the pirate Jean Lafitte. Sailed under the skull and crossbones fer a couple of years afore escaping. He spent time with the Pawnee, then left to join trappers. He learned the mountain life right quick. One day, he was off with a trappin' party. He tailed off by hisself and came upon a big grizzly bear." Grandy glanced at our mountain lion claw necklaces and shook his head. "Bigger and meaner than any lion. Glass took on the griz' with his knife. He was tough but mostly a loser in the fight. Mauled pretty bad. The griz' died right on top of him."

I fondled the mountain lion claw necklace Spirit Talker had given me. "He wasn't killed?" I asked. His story had me fully in its grip.

"Well, the trappin' party fixed him up best possible, left him behind with young Jim Bridger and a ne'er-do-well name of John Fitzgerald and headed away. After a couple of days, Fitzgerald talked Bridger into leavin' Glass fer the varmints to dispose of, takin' his weapons, and rejoining the trappers. Even dug a grave beside him." Grandy took a swig of coffee. "Somehow, Glass crawled and staggered better than two hundred miles to Fort Kiowa. He recovered from his wounds and set out to get revenge on Fitzgerald and Bridger."

The mention of revenge brought a pang of remorse to me, as I had come to know the emptiness that came with vengeance. But for killing a mountain lion attacking Spirit Talker, I'd likely still be seeking revenge on the Comanche that had massacred my family and taken a brother and sister captive. "Did he get his revenge?" I asked.

"Sort of," responded Grandy. "He caught up with Bridger but forgave him. Wagh! He figured that the young mountain man had fallen under Fitzgerald's influence. Wasn't long after that he found John Fitzgerald.

The rascal had joined the Army and was out of Glass's reach so far as revenge. It wasn't comfortable, but Glass forgave him in exchange for getting his much-beloved weapons back."

"What come of Glass?" asked Spirit Talker.

"As I heard it, 'bout ten years later some Injuns killed him," answered Grandy. He stirred the embers a bit. "Where you unlikely friends headed?" he inquired, changing the subject with genuine curiosity.

"We have a friend up on the North Platte. Building a ranch," I said. It became clear from the curious look in Grandy's eyes that he was looking for more. "After my homestead was wiped out by Comanche, I was determined to avenge my family and save my brother and sister from the Comanche. I happened upon Spirit Talker being attacked by a mountain lion. I killed the lion, and Spirit Talker and I became friends. It taught me how shallow vengeance was." By now, I was growing weary. "We eventually freed my brother and sister. Now, I raise horses and beeves on my Rising Cross Ranch back in Texas. We're headed to meet our friend George to talk about selling horses and beeves in the North Platte country."

"You think yer friend George still has his scalp?" said Grandy, laughing.

Spirit Talker smiled, then laughed. "George black skin. No hair. No take scalp."

We all appreciated a bit of Comanche humor.

It was time to turn in. "I'll take first watch," I offered.

Spirit Talker and Grandy wasted no time burying themselves in their blankets.

———

I AWAKENED to the smell of coffee and the sizzling sound of meat being pan fried. It sent my salivary glands into high gear. The horizon had already released its grip on the sun.

Grandy clearly relished whipping up breakfast. Upon seeing me, he chuckled. "Mornin', sunshine. Yer Comanche friend is scoutin' aroun'. Wagh!" He poured coffee into a tin cup and passed it over to me. "Be leavin' yer company in a bit. Much obliged to Spirit Talker for fixin' my shoulder. I'd love to join y'all, but I travel alone. It's 'bout freedom and talkin' with God, my protector. Been saved more than once from savages by God's good graces."

I slipped on my moccasins. "Reckoned you were a God-fearing soul, Bear." I'd felt a strong hint of his faith, as he told Hugh Glass's story. I found myself reflecting again on the hollowness of revenge.

"Them moccasins will serve you well out here, Jack. Bow and arrow, too. Gotta be sneaky quiet. Soon 'nuf you'll be in Lakota territory. They be 'specially riled 'bout now." He sighed. "Oregon Trail cuttin' through their lands."

Spirit Talker padded back into camp. His facial expression hinted at his having found some serious sign.

Grandy glanced up at him and nodded knowingly. "Yep, they be out thar," he said. "Watchin' us as we set." He dumped the venison and quail eggs onto a couple of plates. "I won't be inflictin' myself on you much longer. Fewer of us travelin', the better."

Spirit Talker looked over at me and nodded agreement.

"You young'uns keep them hosses on a tight tether. Arapaho or Cheyenne would love to grab'em," observed Grandy. With that, he bowed his head briefly. "Bless this food, amen," he offered and then seemed to swallow the contents of the plate in one swift gulp.

Spirit Talker and I chuckled, as we silently chewed and thoroughly enjoyed every morsel of our meal. I figured that we might not see a square meal for a few days if Grandy was right about heading into Lakota territory.

"'Preciate y'all helpin' me," said Grandy, as he pulled his gear together, signaled us a goodbye, and led his horse and mule from camp. He swiftly and noiselessly disappeared among the aspens. The new growth of leaves fluttered in the wind as though to absorb Bear Grandy into their piece of heaven. Likely as not, he'd be communing with God and nature wherever he headed.

I cleaned up right quickly and doused the fire while Spirit Talker packed us up.

NINE
SOUTH PLATTE VALLEY

SPIRIT TALKER POINTED out Cheyenne signs several times as we headed into ever-higher country. I thought I was a pretty fair tracker, but he revealed more subtle signs that I never would have seen. I did get to see my first truly huge herds of buffalo. They were impressive beasts. Their numbers were such that the surrounding hills looked black.

"*Tasiwoo* danger," advised Spirit Talker, referring to the shaggy buffalo scattered before us.

Taking in the massive size of the beasts and observing their seemingly ornery nature, I wasn't about to doubt my Comanche brother. We skirted wide and clear of the herds when we came upon them. While plentiful, I never gave any thought to killing a buffalo. Given the need for us to move along, butchering a buffalo would take too much time and most of the beast would go to waste. As we journeyed, I did take note of the landscape. Herding horses or cattle would not be especially easy. There was plenty of water and forage, but the going was rough. It seemed more suited to the shaggy *tasiwoo* than longhorns, though horses would likely traverse the country more easily.

The buffalo were the least of our concerns. I held onto an ongoing conviction that we were being watched. More accurately, we were likely being sized up as worthy of being attacked.

About a day and a half after our encounter with Bear Grandy and as we plodded single file up a natural cleft in the hills, Spirit Talker stopped, put his finger to his lips, pointed to a rocky outcropping, and turned his pinto toward it. About the time we reached the shallow rock shelter, arrows had begun to whoosh past us. One of our packhorses took a couple of the deadly shafts and fell screaming onto the ground. I yanked out my Colt and mercifully put him out of his misery.

The rocky outcropping offered a modicum of shelter, but I doubted we could withstand any full-on attack for long. It would depend on how big the war party was. We hadn't yet had a chance to count our attackers.

I got our horses to lie under the natural ledge afforded by the rocks, and Spirit Talker and I took defensive positions as best we could. I had the presence of mind to grab my Sharps rifle. It had the advantage of being accurate at a far greater range than bows and arrows, but you still had to see your target.

"Cheyenne," declared Spirit Talker.

Well, the savages were definitely not going out of their way to expose themselves. They seemed perfectly happy to hide within a stand of aspen. This was especially so after I downed one at roughly a hundred yards. I suppose that was sort of an attention getter. They likely took it as bad medicine.

Spirit Talker nudged me. "Cheyenne want horses."

My first thought was that there was no way they were

getting Big Red. I thought on our predicament while Spirit Talker stared at me expectantly. We were still several days from where I figured George's place to be, and we would have no more bargaining chips were we to encounter more Indians. I wondered whether we might salvage supplies we would yet need from the packhorses before giving them over.

A Cheyenne warrior poked his head from behind a tree. Someone once told me that curiosity killed the cat. In this case, curiosity got this warrior killed. Dang, but the Sharps rifle was amazing.

I heard a thud followed by a shrill whinny.

Spirit Talker had cut the load from our remaining packhorse, slapped its haunches, and sent it trotting noisily toward the Cheyenne. Such was the answer to my unspoken question.

The Cheyenne must have figured that one horse captured from a couple of brave young travelers was face-saving enough. They had already paid a high price. I made out the fleeing backsides of perhaps a half dozen warriors heading for the ponies they'd likely hidden on the far side of the aspens. They dragged the lifeless bodies of two warriors with them, likely so they'd enjoy a fitting burial.

I looked over at Spirit Talker.

He nodded.

We breathed long sighs of relief.

The South Platte River valley beckoned. We'd soon be facing the mighty Lakota. I shuddered involuntarily at the thought. I prayed for our safety...no, our survival...as at least another ten days of travel lay before us.

———

ON THE SECOND day after the attack, we reached the South Platte. George's homestead lay somewhere south of Fort Laramie but well north of where we stood at the river's banks. As we drew ever closer to our destination, a feeling of accomplishment bred of overconfidence crept over us. We still kept a keen eye out for hostiles, but we were feeling quite upbeat despite the possible dangers ahead. With just Big Red and the pinto, we had become a less conspicuous target. We had loaded both cayuses with what was salvageable from our lost packhorses. Essentials like coffee and coffee pot, fry pan, fire making tools, flour, pemmican, venison jerky, and blankets were tied securely aboard our trusty steeds. The extra load did slow us a tad, as we gave both horses more frequent rests. We were grateful that there was still plenty of water and grass. Spirit Talker and I even enjoyed a cautious dip in the rushing and decidedly ice-cold waters of the river.

Once dried out after bathing, we mounted up and left the river behind us. I expect we hadn't gone more than a couple of miles, when we were faced with a natural trail through a thick stand of aspen and spruce. I felt a chill run up my spine and glanced over at Spirit Talker. We were still far enough from it to choose an alternate route, but time was now our enemy given our depleting supplies.

Spirit Talker had a deadly serious expression written across his face. Something lay ahead, and he was not liking whatever it was. He pulled his pinto to a halt.

I pulled up beside him.

"Cheyenne!" he spat out disgustedly. He knew this would not be solved with a packhorse.

We stood our ground and debated our next move. There was certainly not a chance that we'd make a mad dash through the ambush. We were in a good defensive position partially hidden by the surrounding firs, but we couldn't be certain that we hadn't been spotted by the savages.

Spirit Talker took his bow in hand and nocked an arrow.

I did likewise.

We dismounted as silently as possible. Big Red and the pinto must have sensed the danger, as they moved nary a muscle and made no sound. Only the pricking up of their ears and look in their eyes gave any hint of their being aware of the danger that lurked ahead.

Spirit Talker gestured to our right. He thought he saw an alternate path to the east of the Cheyenne.

Just as we were about to head for the place Spirit Talker had pointed to, whoops and shrill yells emanated from the forested slope that housed the waiting Cheyenne war party.

Spirit Talker froze in place and looked on in amazement. At least two dozen Lakota warriors had fallen upon the Cheyenne. A panorama of bloody hand-to-hand combat unfolded before our very eyes. The Cheyenne had been so confident in ambushing us, that they'd neglected to adequately guard their back trail. The battle, if it could be called a battle, was over in but a couple of minutes. Lakota warriors celebrated, waving fresh scalps and dancing wildly.

I gave Spirit Talker's arm a gentle tug. It was our opportunity to escape unscathed.

———

OVER THE NEXT THREE DAYS, we managed to steer clear of sighting a single human. That's not to say that we were not seen. There was this constant sense of prying eyes. Was there a Lakota war party out there that would decide to attack us?

Unbeknown to us, Otaktay had decided to track us. He may have been curious about the Indian from an unknown tribe traveling with a White man. Perhaps he wondered why two young boys were traveling alone. Would Kills Many live up to his name?

We had just completed packing up on the morning of the third day north of where we'd encountered the dust-up between the Cheyenne and Lakota. I finished snuffing out the last embers of our small cooking fire, upon which we'd fried some rattlesnake the night before. As I was about to mount up, I caught a startled look in Spirit Talker's eyes.

"Pray to God, Jack," he whispered and nodded behind me.

Standing alone on the path upon which we figured to be traveling was an apparition I would just have soon never seen. A single fierce-looking Lakota sat on his war pony. We were looking down the barrel of his 1857 Spanish Enfield rifle. I knew it was an Enfield, as I'd seen one back in Uvalde last year. His expression, his posture, gave not a hint of fear despite us outnumbering him. He raised the muzzle of the rifle. "*Táku un lel?*" he questioned in the Lakota tongue while signing with his free hand. Guess he wanted to know who we were.

Spirit Talker nodded. "*Unha haksi nahniaka?*" he asked our visitor what his name was in Comanche.

The Lakota warrior gave us a quizzical look, as he strove to figure out the strange yet familiar language. He'd heard the Utes speak in this manner.

Spirit Talker pointed to himself. "Spirit Talker," he said. He pointed to me. "Jack."

Otaktay nodded. He raised himself ramrod straight and pointed to his chest. "Otaktay!" he said proudly. He displayed the many scalps dangling from his shield.

Unfazed, Spirit Talker gestured toward me. "*Isa!*" he said emphatically, as though it was strong medicine. He touched his mountain lion claw necklace. "*Peeka pia wa'óo,*" he added, telling the warrior that I had killed a mountain lion.

I had a feeling that the Lakota's name symbolized something we'd as soon not fall victim to, but he seemed to understand enough of Spirit Talker's words to be impressed. "*Isa,*" the warrior repeated. "*Tanka.*" H=He nodded knowingly with a decidedly respectful shift in body language. The wolf was apparently highly regarded in the Lakota culture.

"*Ana o'a hi'it?*" Spirit Talker asked while moving his fingers to his mouth.

Why on earth was Spirit Talker offering food, when we'd just broken camp?

Otaktay blinked at Spirit Talker's offer. Whether it was the peace offering it implied or my Comanche brother's strange yet familiar language, the Lakota's gaze softened just a bit. To my eyes, he appeared to be someone of importance. Oh, he was a brave one, but there was a confidence and even touch of comfort born of living in the wilderness that seemed to ooze from every pore of his being. "Otaktay," he said, pointing to himself. "Oglala Lakota."

Spirit Talker nodded. "Penateka Comanche," he responded.

Otaktay's eyes widened at the mention of the Comanche.

I gathered that a mutual respect was forming.

Spirit Talker motioned again to the now extinguished

campfire and brought his fingers to his mouth as though eating.

The Lakota smiled and produced a pipe.

I figured this was a good sign.

Otaktay raised his hand, and two more Lakota appeared. He gestured to the youngest of the two. "Tasunke Witko," he said, pointing to the warrior who was likely around our age and signing a wild horse. He turned to the second warrior. "Mato," he said, making a bearlike gesture.

I looked at Spirit Talker quizzically.

Spirit Talker whispered an aside. "I think I understand. Young man name Tasunke Witko. Mean Crazy Horse, other is Mato. Mean bear. Strong names."

With a chill still lingering in the morning air, I built a small fire for us to gather around.

Otaktay dismounted and produced a pipe.

Soon, we were seated cross-legged around the campfire using a mix of languages and signs to get acquainted. Up to now, I had kept silent. I was clueless as to how to deal with this mix of tribal cultures. My pa told me that if you knew nothing about something, opening your mouth would serve to prove it.

Even Spirit Talker was subdued. It was obvious that he was impressed with the prowess of the three Lakota. By now, we had figured that Otaktay was a war chief. Mato hadn't said a word, but Tasunke Witko was making signs that he was ready to contribute to our conversation.

Tasunke Witko now turned to me after nodding deferentially to Otaktay and Mato. "*Wicasa unktehi?* He half asked and half stated.

Spirit Talker's eyes widened. This was a bold question. He turned to me. "Tasunke Witko ask whether you kill."

"*Eeetu paaka,*" I responded. "*Aruka...tenahpu,*" I added, telling him I used bow and arrow to kill deer and humans.

Tasunke Witko passed the pipe to me.

I took a long pull. "*Peeka pia wa'óo,*" I reminded him that I had killed a mountain lion. "*Sunipu natsuitu,*" I added that I had strong medicine. That seemed to resonate with the young warrior. Apparently, my halting use of Comanche was having a positive effect. It showed that I cared enough about the Indian cultures to respect their languages.

Tasunke Witko's dark eyes locked on mine with a penetrating earnestness. "*Takuwe?*" he asked in a measured, thoughtful tone. From his facial expression, I gathered the word translated to why.

"*Kahni,*" I answered in Comanche and gestured toward Spirit Talker. It was the closest I could think of to saving a life. I pointed to myself, "*Natsuitu* God." I spread my hands, flexed my arm muscles, and repeated, "*Natsuitu* God." I strove to communicate the greatness and strength of the God I worshipped, the God that I credited with my own supposedly strong medicine.

"*Ska kata wicasa,*" he said flat out with an implacable expression but using strong hand signs that gave evidence of strong underlying emotion. It was his rhetorical observation that the God I spoke of permitted the White man to kill. Whether he had ever heard of the White man's God or not, his facial expression remained outwardly nonplussed. He took a long pull on the pipe, as he was clearly moving on with his thinking.

I wondered whether this Crazy Horse youth was

trying to figure out whether I was a White man who killed Lakota.

Tasunke Witko suddenly seemed to think better of his judgment of me and my God. *"Wasake wakan tanka,"* he murmured thoughtfully, acknowledging the power of the wolf spirit.

Spirit Talker looked aside toward me and translated best he could. The Lakota tongue was a challenge. It was obvious that he didn't like the direction the young warrior's questions seemed to be headed toward. He was encouraged by Crazy Horse's change of tone with mention of a strong god and the wolf spirit. Those had apparently resonated with the young Lakota.

I was beginning to realize that this Tasunke Witko was a spiritual thinker and perhaps why someone so young rode with two experienced warriors. There was a humbleness about him and an introspection that revealed a depth of his mind.

Otaktay had heard enough. He looked questioningly at Tasunke Witko as though for approval then extinguished the pipe and stood.

I was getting the impression that Crazy Horse was the son of someone important among the Lakota.

Mato and Tasunke Witko stood as did we.

I followed Otaktay's eyes to Big Red and the pinto.

He seemed to be trying to decide whether it was worth a fight to take our horses.

Spirit Talker and I stood tall and forced our facial expressions to brim with strength. Set jaws, grim unsmiling lips, and a hardness in our eyes tended to get that point across. It was as though we dared them to try something.

"Iyaya," commanded Tasunke Witko. The young warrior was ordering them to leave, and they unhesitat-

ingly obeyed...without our horses. Crazy Horse looked from Spirit Talker to me as though one day we might meet again.

As they faded from sight, Spirit Talker turned to me. "*Sunipu natsuitu,*" he said, referring to the young warrior. Strong medicine indeed. "He be strong with *numunuu.*" He looked thoughtfully off into the distance. "Tasunke Witko is thunder dreamer," he said in a near whisper. "*Sunipu.*" He reiterated his observation of the big medicine this Crazy Horse represented.

I had to agree that the ability of the young warrior to hold the respect of his battle-experienced companions was evidence that he might rise to power within the Oglala Lakota people. Little did I know that his leadership wouldn't be fully realized for another twenty years at a place the Lakota called Greasy Grass and we referred to as Little Bighorn. As to our immediate situation, I could only hope and pray that Otaktay and Mato had no evil intentions so far as we were concerned. There was no telling what they might do without Tasunke Witko around to rein them in.

TEN

LAKOTA ATTACK!

AFTER BEING SO EASILY SNUCK up on by the three Lakota, we found ourselves being extra cautious. There was no room for carelessness. While Spirit Talker still spoke to his Comanche spirits, I found him praying to God as well. It was as though he was not taking any chances.

We made camp for the night by a small stream. The impromptu pow-wow with the Lakota weighed heavily in our thoughts.

"Jack *natsuitu*," Spirit Talker opined, as we sat around our small cooking fire under a rock outcropping alongside the stream.

"Trust," I responded. I did not know a Comanche word for trust. "I trust God...trust in His truth, his *natsuitu*."

"God *natsuitu*," he observed.

The roll of distant thunder reached our ears.

Spirit Talker gestured toward it. "*Ekakwitsʉbaitʉ natsuitu*," he said observing the power in the lightning. "Jack God like *ekakwitsʉbaitʉ*."

I shook my head. God was no flash of lightning, powerful as it was. "God protects from evil. He lives for all moons. More strong than *ekakwitsuḅbaitu*." I tried my best to communicate God's everlasting power.

Spirit Talker nodded his understanding. "Trust," he said in perfect English. "*Tumhyokenu*," he repeated in the Comanche tongue. He looked off at the storm. "Can trust evil?" he asked.

I joined his gaze at the distant storm. This was a powerful question. "God help fight anger, fear, and hate."

"Jack angry with Comanche?" he asked.

The attack on my family had been so long ago. It had apparently been weighing on Spirit Talker's mind. I recalled my own feelings of anger, guilt, and vengeance. It took a deep trust and faith in God to beat down those evil feelings. "*Aitu...hawokatu*," I said in Comanche, referring to anger as not good and vengeance as a hollow reward.

Spirit Talker nodded that he understood. "*Hawokatu*," he said, repeating my observation. He paused a long time and stared into the dying embers of our fire. "*Kooitu... where die?*" he asked. "*Tumah tuyai*," he added, referring to the Comanche afterlife.

I deeply appreciated how inquisitive Spirit Talker had become about Christianity. "Yes. Live with Trinity," I assured him and raised three fingers together for emphasis.

Spirit Talker smiled.

I had explained the Trinity before, so it seemed clear that he was beginning to grasp the concept of going to be with God when we die.

His smile broke into a broad grin that stretched the mountain lion scars on his face. "Blue Flower *tumhyokenu*." This revelation of her belief in God came out of the blue, totally unexpected. "Jack bring fifteen horses."

Now, I couldn't help but laugh. It was a dowry I fully expected to provide upon our return from visiting George. With that, I took first watch. Somehow, I simply found it difficult to trust the Lakota. Otaktay had seemed to ooze evil intentions. His frustration at the onslaught of White settlers was fast turning to anger. To my thinking, it wouldn't be long before it boiled over. In Texas, the Comanche and Apache were being held in check by the Texas Rangers. I didn't get the feeling that the Army had an especially effective protective presence here in Lakota territory. I reckoned we'd be doing a lot of praying.

———

AN EXPLOSION ROCKED MY EARS. Its echoes bounced off the landscape; every blade of grass and tree limb shook. It had to be from one powerful rifle. I looked over at Spirit Talker, and we instantly urged our mounts forward as if with unspoken command.

We dismounted barely a hundred yards up the trail, as there was no telling what lay ahead. I checked the load in my Colt and stuffed it back into my holster. We ground-hitched Big Red and the pinto and proceeded on foot. I gave a passing thought to grabbing the Sharps rifle but my senses told me to follow my Comanche brother's example and take my bow and arrows. Considering how silently we moved, I felt like some sort of ghost. We heard voices not far ahead followed by another deafening explosion.

Spirit Talker signaled us to stop just as we reached a small clearing.

The sight before us was horrifying to put it mildly.

"Oh dear Lord, protect us," I whispered.

An irritated Spirit Talker shushed me.

Bear Grandy lay with his back to a tree, blood streaming down his face and two arrows protruding from his left leg. His still-smoking Hawken rifle lay across his lap.

As we watched from the edge of the clearing, a third arrow found its way into Grandy's chest. He gasped and tried in vain to reload the Hawken.

A half dozen Lakota were approaching him cautiously on foot. They were decked out in full war regalia with painted faces, breastplates, shields, and bows and arrows. They launched a couple of more arrows into the mountain man. Poor Grandy never had a prayer of escaping his fate.

What were we to do? My natural inclination was to avenge Grandy's death. Hadn't I learned my lesson about vengeance?

Spirit Talker sighed and motioned for us to retreat. There was no point in engaging six Lakota warriors filled with the rush of just having killed a White man. As we pulled back, I did see at least two dead or badly wounded Lakota warriors. I recognized Otaktay and made a mental note of his savagery. It was small compensation that Grandy's Hawken had exacted a toll on the Lakota success.

Spirit Talker and I returned with all due swiftness to our horses. It was a blessing that the hostiles were so wrapped up in taking Grandy's scalp and any valuables that they were oblivious to us. We likely could have killed a warrior or two, but we would eventually face great risk. We made haste in skirting the area while the hostiles were otherwise involved.

"Lakota *aitu*," observed Spirit Talker, as we negotiated the trail ahead. Not good indeed. "*Tabu kutseena*," he added. In his overwrought state in which he fought back the in-bred desire to fight the warriors, he referred to the attackers as cowardly coyotes.

"*Tabu kutseena*," I agreed, then added, "*Kaahaniitu*." It seemed to me that the Lakota had been deceptive. Then again, had it not been for the presence of Crazy Horse, our scalps might have already been dangling from Otaktay's shield or lance. The Lakota war chief's name didn't translate to Kills Many without good reason. I turned to Spirit Talker, "We must hurry." I was intent on putting as much distance as possible between us and the savagery we had witnessed. And we had to remain on high alert, as Cheyenne and Arapaho also roamed the region.

———

I FIGURED we were perhaps two days from where I understood George's ranch to be. I prayed that I fully understood the Black cowboy's directions. I had yet to find any of the landmarks he had mentioned just before he left Rising Cross Ranch. Spirit Talker and I traveled on what could best be described as what folks called a wing and a prayer, or more realistically a horse and a prayer. While keeping eyes and ears alert for Indians, we continued doggedly blazing a trail northward ever on the lookout for Fort Laramie. George had described his ranch as located a few miles northwest of the fort along the southern banks of the North Platte River. We had already crossed a couple of rivers, but hadn't a clue as to what names they held. Neither Spirit Talker nor I would admit that we just could be lost up here in this hostile, yet majestically beautiful, wilderness. While we had chosen this journey, this challenge if you will, it increasingly seemed that the challenge was beginning to choose us.

The site of Bear Grandy's demise was now well behind us. I still couldn't help but lament his loss. I regretted that we were unable to give him a Christian burial. After more than thirty years in the wilderness, he'd fallen victim to a Lakota war party. There was an irony coupled with a sort of justice that so knowledgeable a frontiersman would ultimately fall victim to the very wildness of the frontier he embraced. It reminded me of the story he told of Hugh Glass, the mountain man who overcame great challenges only to meet his end on the shafts of Crow war party arrows. I thought back, too, on my brief backslide to vengeance upon witnessing the attack on Grandy. Thankfully, Spirit Talker had brought me to my senses. There was no escaping the reality of our present situation.

I got to thinking about folks back where I grew up in Pennsylvania who lived in denial of the violence of the frontier. They used to frustrate my pa. I sure would love to drag those deniers out here and open their ignorant minds. I was beginning to realize that people tended to avoid recognizing life's horrors by hiding from them, by avoiding reality. Maybe one day, I would have to share my experiences in a book or in a newspaper for the world to see. Then again, many folks likely still wouldn't believe me. They'd likely think my stories were simply more wild west shoot-'em-up fantasies.

Long journeys tend to offer plenty of opportunities for reflection. I was learning plenty of life lessons, likely far more than a typical sixteen-year-old. I prayed that Spirit Talker's faith would be strengthened such that he would have a strong Christian influence over his *numunuu*, his people.

ELEVEN
FORT LARAMIE BECKONS!

THE LANDSCAPE HAD BECOME NOTICEABLY ROUGHER. The hills in this part of the country made those back home near Rising Cross Ranch seem like mere bumps in the prairie. The terrain slowed us a bit. We remained extra vigilant for Indians, as there were plenty of places suitable for ambushing us.

Roughly a half morning journey due north of where we'd camped, we reached the rocky banks of a serious river. I figured it had to be the North Platte. It had been more than a month since we'd departed the Penateka Comanche village, so the timing was about right. Of course, there was no one around to confirm my assessment. I considered that it may have been wise to invite Bear Grandy to guide us, but then we likely would have been with him when Otaktay and his Lakota warriors attacked. Can't be crying over that. So, here we were sitting astride our travel-weary horses and staring at a river. We were sort of sheltered by a stand of aspens.

Spirit Talker gave me an inquisitive look and pointed to the rushing waters before us.

It was hardly reassuring to realize that my Comanche brother was as lost as I was. I rubbed my chin in thought. If this was the North Platte, my reckoning was that we needed to follow it in a northwesterly direction. I prayed that I understood George's directions that lingered evermore-vaguely in my mind. I nodded to Spirit Talker. "Go that way." I pointed off to our left. As I followed my own finger, I saw what was apparently a hunting party of Indians. As I pulled Big Red back among the trees, I didn't take the time to identify the tribe…not that I was especially adept at doing that just yet.

Spirit Talker joined me in hiding. "Cheyenne," he said. Seemed they were ranging into Lakota territory.

"We must reach Fort Laramie," I responded. "We wait." Of course, we would wait. There was no point in riding out in the open in front of the Cheyenne hunting party. The Lord's protections were surely based upon me having some common sense. I breathed as quietly as I could and hoped Big Red and Spirit Talker's pinto would stay silent. As tired as they were, quiet came easy for our mounts.

As a precaution, we both nocked arrows in our bows. Guess I was feeling confident in my marksmanship. Recognizing that confidence can be fleeting, I did check the loads in my Colt revolver and shoved it back in my waistband.

We waited what was likely an hour to be certain the Cheyenne were long past us.

———

THE SUN HAD BEGUN its dance on the western horizon, sending reddish-gold reflections over the rushing waters of the North Platte, when Fort Laramie beckoned. There it sat in all its rustic splendor just ahead of us. "There she is," I said with unabashed relief to Spirit Talker.

Spirit Talker nodded, as his facial expression mirrored my feelings.

The landscape around the fort was dotted with a few teepees and makeshift shelters, some of which resembled cabins. In the dimming light, I could just about make out the walls and buildings of the fort. The fort apparently attracted traders. Being that it was late in the day, there were very few people out and about so far as I could see. We were barely within sight of the fort, and it would be dark by the time we reached it. Big Red and the pinto were pretty bedraggled and could use some well-earned rest. Besides, I much preferred approaching the fort in broad daylight. I turned to Spirit Talker. "Let's camp here," I suggested.

With that, my Comanche brother slipped from the pinto's back and began to make camp.

Given our proximity to the fort and the many folks dwelling around its periphery, I figured we were safe from any attack.

We dined on the last of our pemmican and jerky. There seemed no reason to kill fresh game with the fort and the expectation of more normal dining so near at hand.

"*Eekasahpana paraiboo* know where George home?" asked Spirit Talker referring to the commanding Army officer. Would the long knives know where our Black friend's spread was located?

Whether he did or did not, I was confident that following the North Platte upstream would bring us to the Freeman ranch. God hadn't led us on this journey to miss our goal. "I expect he does. George should be about two days west," I responded reassuringly. Inside my head, I was praying that there would be good news about our friend. It simply wouldn't do to have come all this way to find our friend done in by Lakota or Cheyenne. I had to give my full faith and trust to the Lord.

The night was tolerably cool for the North Platte country in the waning days of May. I reckoned that snowmelt from the mountains was feeding the rushing river waters. I noticed plenty of campfires dotting the area around the fort, so figured adding one more wouldn't be troublesome. Taking the chill out of the night, our small campfire warmed us in body and soul. We actually hadn't built a campfire for the past four nights, given our fear of hostile Indians. There was no protection in my being accompanied by a Comanche. We were both potential prey.

"God keep promise," offered Spirit Talker. "Big medicine," he added, as he stirred the embers of our campfire.

I smiled sheepishly. "I was scared that we were lost," I confessed.

Spirit Talker looked up from the fire. He shrugged, then gave a grin that stretched the mountain lion claw scars on his cheeks. "Me too," he confided. "*Tumhyokenu* God." His admitting to his trust in God was huge. I foresaw great discussions about faith ahead, when we reached George's ranch.

With our humble admissions of fear out of the way, I began to think on what lay ahead. "We can resupply at the fort," I suggested.

"We bring gift," stated Spirit Talker.

I gave him a quizzical look.

"You see," he said knowingly. With that, he rolled out

his blanket, stared for a moment up at the starlit sky, and fell asleep.

———

I SHARD OF sunlight blasted its way into my nearly-closed eyes, forcing me to grudgingly sit up and recognize the new day. I rubbed my eyes and looked around. Spirit Talker was field-dressing a good-sized buck. I smiled. "Good morning," I said.

Spirit Talker turned toward me and smiled. "Gift," he said, pointing at the deer and then at the fort.

I nodded. "Spirit Talker generous *tenahpu*. Army like fresh *aruka*." I was still learning the Comanche tongue and occasionally worked it into my speech. I was proud of having recalled that *aruka* was Comanche for deer. I had begun to think that both of us might find it beneficial to learn Lakota.

We mounted up for our short ride to Fort Laramie. Spirit Talker had tied the deer carcass behind him on the pinto, so we made a right-tidy sight approaching the fortress. A sense of foreboding crept its ugly way into my mind, as I watched a pair of vultures floating along the thermals created as the day warmed.

The North Platte rushed along to our right. A bald eagle swept down and stole breakfast from an unsuspecting osprey. Somehow, that seemed appropriate.

As we drew nearer, we attracted a ragtag cluster of women and children from the teepees and shelters surrounding our path. They noisily pointed at us, laughing and shouting in a variety of languages. I made out some French and Spanish from a handful of White children, though it was difficult to distinguish the Indian tongues. God hadn't missed these folks with his Tower of Babel punishment. The common thread that seemed to run among these mostly women and children was desperation as evidenced by ragged clothing and under-nourished bodies. It was as though all had gone to seed after the Grattan Massacre of a couple of years before.

All of a sudden, Spirit Talker drew his reins. He looked about quizzically. "Comanche," he whispered to me. "Find later," he added. If there were any Comanche this far north, it was most likely they were enslaved captives. That possibility wouldn't escape Spirit Talker, as his own Penateka Comanche *numunuu* held enslaved captives as well.

I stole a glance over at Spirit Talker and nodded my understanding. It was a sensitive issue.

At last, we reached the entrance to Fort Laramie. I was singularly unimpressed. The envisioned construction of the fort had never been completed apparently owing to high cost and insufficient labor out here on the vastness of the frontier. Beyond the fort were the decaying walls of Fort William and Fort John, the trading post predecessors to Fort Laramie. It was effectively an open fort, and it was likely a blessing that it had never been over-whelmed by Cheyenne or Lakota. I was surprised that we were not challenged at the entrance to the grounds. In fact, there were people coming and going at will. I gathered that the fort was living up to one of its main functions of serving as a guidepost along a particularly lengthy stretch of the Oregon Trail.

"Pardon me, sergeant," I called out, hailing a soldier with three stripes on his sleeve.

The sergeant turned and looked intently at us as though sizing us up. Two wet-behind-the-ears young-sters. He finally decided we were worth responding to.

"The lieutenant is on patrol. Be back tomorrow." He turned his grizzled face toward Spirit Talker. "Yer friend is a long way from home."

Spirit Talker pointed to himself. "Me Spirit Talker… Penateka Comanche…son of Buffalo Hump."

"Well I'll be, the heathen knows English," spat out the sergeant.

"And he's no heathen, sergeant," I added.

The sergeant apparently decided that we just might be worth talking with. "Where you boys from?" he queried.

I was beginning to feel a tad comfortable here on what was apparently friendly ground. "Texas. Come to visit a friend near here."

The sergeant shook his head. "Many folks been burned out. Lakota and Cheyenne ain't too happy around these parts. Who's yer friend?"

"George Freem…," I didn't get to finish my response.

"The Black cowboy with no hair?" he laughed. "Injuns figure him and his Pawnee squaw be big medicine. Yep, he be about two days west of where you're standing. We been trading horses with him." He shuffled his feet. "Gotta watch yerselves, though. Lots of riled up Injuns between here and George's spread."

"Much obliged, sergeant. Anyplace we can get some supplies?" I asked.

Before the sergeant could respond, Spirit Talker nudged his pinto forward and slung the deer carcass from the pony's rump. "Spirit Talker bring gift."

The sergeant gave him a squirrely sort of look before nodding. "Much obliged, chief."

Spirit Talker took no visible offense at the sergeant referring to him as a chief, though grinned slightly upon catching me rolling my eyes.

"You can resupply up yonder," the sergeant said pointing to a building ahead of us.

"Thanks, sergeant," I said and nudged Big Red forward.

"This place bad medicine," offered Spirit Talker in a near whisper, as we headed for the fort commissary.

I glanced over my shoulder to see three soldiers hauling the deer to a barrack. I had a sense that the troops might not have been eating so well, as the three clearly relished my Comanche brother's gift.

Fort Laramie was not exactly a prime spit-and-polish example of what a military fortress should be. The walls were crumbling and only partially built in the first place. At least, there was decent shelter for the garrison. My Rising Cross Ranch was in far better condition.

"No stay here," urged Spirit Talker.

I nodded. Knowing that George was apparently alive and well, it seemed to make sense that we head upriver with all due haste.

Spirit Talker reached out and touched my arm. Intensity was writ large across his face. "We free Comanche boy," he said earnestly, as though there was no question that it was to happen.

That gave me cause to rein in Big Red. "Might be risky, my brother."

He nodded with a hint of a smile. "Jack strong medicine. We pray for God help."

What could I say to that? Now, I envisioned us searching for a young Comanche captive among the teepees surrounding the fort. We would resupply first, as we might have to make a quick getaway. A lot of praying was surely in order. If we were to put the fort behind us quickly, I figured we'd have limited time to inquire among the teepees dotting the countryside around Fort

Laramie. It would be sort of like looking for the prover-bial needle in a haystack.

———

THE FORT COMMISSARY WAS ACCOMMODATING, though woefully under-stocked. As we picked and chose among the supplies we considered essential for the next couple of days, I noted that Spirit Talker was pulling together more food than we would need. I decided that he must have some good reason, so I didn't question him.

As we finished packing, Spirit Talker looked over at me thoughtfully. "Wait," he said.

I stood patiently alongside Big Red, as Spirit Talker rode off.

Spirit Talker returned in what couldn't have been more than a half hour with a field-dressed doe draped over the pinto's rump.

I looked up at the sun. "We're wasting daylight, my brother."

He motioned me to follow and headed toward the path we'd followed approaching the fort.

What could I do but tag along.

"*Natsuitu numunuu, natsuitu sunipu,*" called Spirit Talker in even tones, as we rode among the teepees. Repeating "strong people, strong medicine" was designed to draw out the Comanche voice we had heard upon entering the area surrounding the fort. It sounded more as an offhand comment than any challenge. Spirit Talker hoped that the young Comanche was within hearing distance. Draped over top of the supply pack was the deer he'd managed to bag while I was negotiating for our supplies. We hoped it would serve as trade bait to food-starved tribesman

As we passed a rather forlorn-looking teepee, a small pair of eyes peered from behind the entrance flap. Whomever they belonged to was yanked back inside.

Spirit Talker pulled up and repeated his call just a tad louder, "*Natsuitu numunuu, natsuitu sunipu.*"

A youngster rolled from the teepee. I couldn't yet tell whether it was a boy or girl, as I sat Big Red beside Spirit Talker.

No sooner had the youngster nearly regained his or her footing than a stringy-haired hag wearing greasy buckskins chased after with a stick in hand.

In but a heartbeat, Spirit Talker nocked an arrow and fired the shaft into the dust in front of the woman and narrowly missed the youngster. As quickly, another arrow found his bowstring and was aimed at the haggard old woman. "Me Spirit Talker, Penateka Comanche, son of Buffalo Hump...*unha haksi nahniaka, wa'ipu?*" he demanded as much as asked the old hag's name. Then he delivered what I figured was the spirit crusher, a direct challenge to the woman's authority. "*Tenahpu?*" he asked where the man was.

She hung her head.

I found myself holding back a tear. This old hag who likely hadn't always been a haggard old crone, was struggling to merely survive. The captive youngster was all that stood between her and her certain demise.

"*Unha haksi nahniaka,*" persisted Spirit Talker, demanding her name.

"Flower Woman," she said in some language I didn't recognize.

"Arapaho," said Spirit Talker flatly, glancing over to me. By now, the old hag was literally quaking in her moccasins. Spirit Talker looked from her to the youngster. He guessed the child was a girl, but she was pretty much skin and bones. Suddenly, my Comanche brother seemed to soften a bit. *"Ana o'a hi'it?"* he asked whether she was hungry.

A desperate look swept across her face and that of the girl.

Spirit Talker un-nocked his arrow and slid from the pony's back. He unloaded a sack and motioned me to follow him into the teepee.

As I entered, I was almost overcome by the noxious odors that permeated the air. I threw back the entrance flap and raised the sides of the teepee as gently as possible so as not to further damage it. A cool prairie breeze began to quickly dissipate the stench. I found a certain irony in the contrast between the majestic beauty of the surrounding hills and the squalor within the teepee.

Spirit Talker stoked the fire and was soon roasting venison ribs with corn and potatoes.

The young girl ate ravenously, but the old hag was holding back. It was then that I realized that she had no teeth.

I proceeded to cut the meal up into bite-sized pieces.

Flower Woman smiled for the first time and then proceeded to stuff her mouth with food as though she had never eaten solid food before. I feared she would make herself sick by over-eating.

The next hour was well spent in service to an indigent woman and our God. By the time we were finished, Spirit Talker had negotiated for the release of the girl into our custody in exchange for much of our food supply. We learned that young Topsannah was Quahadi Comanche, captured in an Arapaho raid months earlier in which her family was killed. Flower Woman's husband had been mortally wounded in the battle and did not survive. She moved the teepee to be near Fort Laramie with the hope of living from the largesse of the Army.

With time having seemed to fly along, we bade our farewell to Flower Woman.

Topsannah sat behind Spirit Talker on the pinto.

It wasn't until Fort Laramie had faded into the distance behind us that I felt fully secure that the haggard Arapaho woman wouldn't change her mind. I knew intuitively that she wouldn't survive long without Topsannah to do her every bidding. It seemed a bit ironic to me. Here we were heading for the ranch of a former slave, and we had already dealt several times with the tribal habit of enslaving captives. Did a Black man enslaved by Whites have it any better than a White enslaved by Indians? Alas, slavery was slavery regardless of who was master. I surveyed the majestic scenery surrounding us and found myself more fully appreciating the freedom it symbolized. I looked to my God above.

"Amen," said Spirit Talker. It was as though he was reading my mind. He smiled and pointed skyward. "Is good," he added.

———

THE CLOUD-FILLED night sky lay its shroud of darkness across the countryside. I could barely see my hand a mere six inches from my face. The good news was that we couldn't be seen; the bad news that we couldn't see. We had chosen the campsite with a keen eye as to its defensibility, close to the river yet nestled among a stand of aspen with plenty of ground growth. It would have been difficult to spot us in broad daylight. Being in the heart of Lakota and Cheyenne territory, we couldn't be too careful. Dinner had been jerky and pemmican, since lighting a fire was inadvisable.

Not being able to see in the darkness did not eliminate the duty to keep a watch, so we took turns throughout the night.

I was sentry shortly after midnight when I heard Big Red nicker. Instinctively, my hand gripped the Colt in my lap. I couldn't see, but I sure could hear. Something out there was disturbing our horses. I figured whomever or whatever, it would have to be struggling to see. In fact, I got to thinking it was more likely animal than human.

As I sat helplessly trying to decide what to do, a cold wet nose nuzzled my hand. The nose moved up my arm, and a tongue swiped my cheek. An aroma of wet fur filled the air around me, as a large thickly-muscled dog-like body sat beside me. Yet, there was something familiar about it. "*Isa!*" I realized. How in the world?!

Just then, the clouds parted just enough to throw a hint of starlight on us. Sure enough, I found myself looking into the intense blue eyes of a wolf. He was big, and I began to rapidly convince myself that this was the same one I had encountered back in Texas. How could that be? I couldn't begin to guess. If so, how had he found me? We were a good thousand miles from the Texas hills. And where was his pack?

I could barely make him out as he backed a couple of feet away and lay staring at me. I strained to see beyond him and could barely make out a few shadowy figures well outside our camp. What to do? Isa wasn't giving me any sign. He simply lay there. Not a hint of aggression was evidenced. What could he possibly want? Should I attempt to awaken Spirit Talker? I still had the lingering feeling that he wasn't fully convinced of my interaction with the wolf months ago.

Isa continued to stare.

I tentatively reached my hand out toward him.

He cocked his great head and nudged forward just enough to smell my fingers.

Two hours must have passed. The cloud cover was dissipating, and the first light of the sun was creeping up the eastern horizon. In the gray dawn, I could see that the pack hadn't moved a muscle. I must have dozed. Any thought that the wolves were an apparition was rapidly disposed of.

Spirit Talker finally began to awaken. The first thing that greeted his half-opened eyes was the *isa* lying beside me. His eyes widened, and he cautiously moved to sit upright while simultaneously reaching for his bow and arrows.

"*Isa,*" I said softly and signaled him to put aside his weapons.

Isa regally turned his head as though to observe Spirit Talker.

I motioned with my hand for the great wolf to come to me. My, but he was big. He'd been eating quite well. His coat was a thick, luxurious pelt of shades of gray, and his crystal-blue eyes were fully alert. He arose, walked closer to me, and nuzzled my hand.

Spirit Talker's jaw dropped. "*Sunipu,*" was all he could say. Strong medicine indeed.

"It is him. It is my wolf from Texas," I fairly exclaimed in amazement. I leaned forward and stroked the wolf's head. He didn't flinch.

I reached into my bag and drew out a piece of jerky.

Isa sniffed it, grasped it with his fangs, and gently pulled it from my grasp. He about swallowed it without chewing. With that, he nuzzled my hand and rejoined his pack. He took one last look and led them off in single file.

"Jack *sunipu*," said Spirit Talker.

What could I say? I was as amazed as my dear Comanche brother. There simply seemed to be no accounting for the wolf's behavior save that it was God's work. Was this a sign? Isa had found me. Would he stay near? "God is great," I said. I stood. Paw prints were everywhere. This had not been a dream.

Spirit Talker shook his head and quietly began packing for the day's travel.

About this time, Topsannah awakened. She'd been totally oblivious to the visit from our furry friends. She smiled while munching on pemmican and venison jerky. She was soon mounted on the pinto behind Spirit Talker and cheerfully prattling on in the Comanche tongue, as we continued our ride westward along the North Platte.

———

LITTLE COULD we have known that Otaktay and Mato and perhaps four more warriors were watching us. They must have snuck away from the Lakota camp. Our horses were simply too tempting to resist. Despite the power of God and the spirits of the mountain lion and wolf that we had invoked, they had apparently decided that I was just another White man and that Spirit Talker was like a weak woman for associating with me.

That they hadn't attacked thus far likely evidenced that they respected us and wanted their ambush to be successful. Success would be measured in returning to their village with prizes and, most importantly, no loss of life.

We had alternately ridden and walked our horses for most of the morning. Spirit Talker pointed to his eyes and then made a sweeping motion with his hand. Like me, he sensed that we were being watched. I nodded and pointed to a stand of aspen up ahead. The so-called quaking movement of their leaves in the mountain breeze served as a bit of camouflage. "Let's rest here," I suggested.

I led us to the trees, dismounted, and loosened Big Red's cinch. I reckoned he could graze a bit on the lush grass. We were perhaps fifty yards from the south bank of the North Platte. But for the tension of that feeling that comes with being scrutinized by unseen eyes, the scene was relaxing. Another day and a half, and we should be riding up to George's home.

Upon dismounting, I had grabbed my Sharps rifle.

Spirit Talker had grabbed young Topsannah along with his bow and arrow. Her eyes widened, as she was held tightly against him with his hand over her mouth to ensure her silence. He sat with his back against a tree and surveyed the area around us. "Lakota!" he whispered.

How could he know? I saw absolutely nothing.

Spirit Talker dove to one side on top of the girl, as an arrow embedded in the place he'd sat just a second before.

We both dove for cover, dragging her with us.

Apparently, Otaktay had grown impatient. His anger at the encroaching Whites and lament for the future of his people had overtaken his good senses.

I thought back on a warning my pa had shared from the Book of Proverbs. It was something about a patient person having great understanding while impatience brought folly. While that made perfect sense at the moment, it had virtually no impact on the arrows being launched in our direction. Thankfully, they craved our horses enough that they aimed away from them. I gave a half thought to making a run for it, as Big Red was plenty close.

Spirit Talker must have sensed my thinking as he shook his head. He pointed to his belly. By the time I could tighten Big Red's cinch, I'd have taken enough arrows to resemble a porcupine. Besides, we were dug in pretty well behind the trees.

I raised the Sharps and aimed it in the general direction from whence the arrows were coming.

Spirit Talker pointed to grasses off to our left close to the river.

No question, there was a Lakota warrior moving among those grasses perhaps seventy yards away. It was near maximum range accuracy-wise for bow and arrow, but a right-easy distance for my rifle. If the warrior was trying to outflank us, he was about to be sorely mistaken.

I took careful aim, awaiting even the slightest sign of movement. An arrow stuck in the tree just above my head. Amazingly, I didn't even flinch. I finally saw the top of a bow and followed its curved shaft downward with the muzzle of my Sharps. I squeezed the trigger. In the next instant, a warrior was blown upward and backward with a hole in the center of his chest.

That must have given Otaktay pause as the arrows suddenly stopped.

I was surprised that the killing of a single warrior had caused a pause in the attack. It was even more of a surprise when the Lakota began moving away from us. In fact, they were wasting no time in silently, almost reverently, retreating. I heard guttural oaths that sounded like *ayústan* and *tanka* being repeated over and over by the attackers, as they moved away. I saw a wide-eyed Otaktay take a furtive look in our direction as he moved away, but I wasn't able to sight a clear shot with the Sharps.

Spirit Talker nudged me and motioned to our right. "*Isa*," he hissed.

The entire pack of wolves had appeared. Those crystal-blue eyes of the leader of the pack were riveted in on the retreating Lakota warriors.

"*Sunipu*," added Spirit Talker. It was strong medicine for sure.

Apparently, the Oglala Lakota held a deep spiritual respect for the wolf with its keen senses of sight, smell, and hearing and its place near the top of the frontier food chain. The wolf was seen as an intelligent spirit with the courage to protect its family at all cost. That my medicine was so strong to have apparently pulled in a pack of wolves had been too much for Otaktay. He figured to live to fight another day.

Spirit Talker held the now weeping Topsannah. She'd rightly been scared half to death by the attack. Perhaps, it had been reminiscent of the Arapaho attack on her people, her *numunuu*.

In my studied judgment, I reckoned that we'd seen the last of any Lakota war parties for now. I stood and scanned the aspens off to our right. Sure enough, there he was. Isa looked at me. He lifted his head and gave a yip before leading his pack away. "Dear God," I found myself saying, "thank you for your protection. Thank you for *isa*." I guess I had uttered the little prayer of thanks aloud.

Spirit Talker nodded. "Amen."

Topsannah stopped her weeping and looked at us in wonderment as though we held some sort of magical power. "*Sunipu*," she whispered to Spirit Talker. The poor girl had endured an attack by Arapaho, enslavement, rescue, and now an attack staved off by a pack of wolves. It had to be overwhelming to so young a girl.

A feeling of comforting safety swept over us. Sure there were other hostiles around, but it was quite apparent that we were being protected by a high power.

We were soon remounted and headed upriver. Hopefully, George's ranch would be reached by late the next day.

TWELVE
GEORGE'S RANCH

WE CONTINUED to journey northwest along the south bank of the North Platte, grateful to have Fort Laramie and the Lakota behind us. The sun had begun its inevitable descent to the horizon; not quite low enough to bathe the clouds in the glow of sunset. As the river took a sharp bend southward, we found ourselves looking out upon a vast meadow with perhaps two dozen horses grazing at leisure. The very lushness of the landscape was overwhelming in its beauty. Far off in the center of the meadow, a spiral of smoke arose from the chimney of a small cabin. I reckoned that this had to be George's place. It made sense that he'd built it with a view featuring a clear line of sight in the event of visitors, welcome or unwelcome.

I smiled broadly and turned to Spirit Talker. "That must be George's cabin," I announced, pointing animatedly at what amounted to a large log hut. I was about to dig my spurs into Big Red when Spirit Talker motioned off toward the river.

George was riding toward us on a huge black steed.

He was waving his hat about wildly and shouting, though he was yet too far off for us to hear.

We turned and headed his way. Big Red was tired, but he and the pinto still had just a bit of gallop left in them.

The reunion quickly became a chaotic near tragedy, as we nearly overran each other. Our cayuses bumped every which way before getting them under control.

"You made it!" shouted George. "Praise the Lord! You made it!"

Topsannah was totally confused as we all hugged while still mounted. She was as likely taken aback by the big strange black-skinned man with no hair being hugged in the middle of it all.

We all paused to breathe and take in the relief of having endured the challenges of our journey.

"Welcome, my brothers. Welcome to God's country." George's infectious grin couldn't have been any greater. "Let's head to yonder cabin. Running Waters will fix us some grub," he announced.

I glanced at Spirit Talker. We'd finally get to meet George's wife, and we were ravenously hungry.

———

RUNNING Waters stood smiling in the doorway with arms folded as we rode up.

We dismounted in a cloud of dust, ground-hitched the horses, and followed George toward the cabin. Topsannah followed fearfully behind, seeming to be nearly attached to Spirit Talker.

George halted a couple of yards from Running Waters. He bowed slightly from the waist and swept his well-muscled arm in a graceful arc from her to us. "My sweet wife, meet Jack O'Toole and Wild Horse."

He turned to us and added, "My wife, Running Waters."

Spirit Talker had blinked at the use of the name of his youth but didn't correct George.

I figured it was my turn to speak. "It is our pleasure, Running Waters. We have traveled many days. Much danger. My friend has been given a new name, Spirit Talker. It means Spirit Talker in my language."

Spirit Talker urged the young Comanche girl from behind him and gestured toward her. "Topsannah. She Quahadi Comanche captured by Arapaho."

A warm smile spread across Running Waters's lips. "Come little one. I need your help," she said gently, motioning with her hand. "We feed hungry men," she added with a laugh.

I watched awestruck, as Topsannah followed Running Waters into the cabin with not the slightest hesitation. It was as though the young girl was desperate for loving female company. Little wonder after two days horseback riding with a pair of teen males who couldn't begin to fathom her needs. Undoubtedly, her relief at escaping captivity had quickly turned to desperation for someone of her own gender who might understand her.

George chuckled at my expression. "Never try to figure them out, Jack." He turned to Spirit Talker. "I like your new name," he said thoughtfully.

Spirit Talker thought on George's observation for barely a moment. "Penateka Comanche hear my talk of God. See *sunipu*, strong medicine."

George nodded. I think he appreciated that my testimony to Spirit Talker had a lasting impact. "Let's take care of the horses and wash up. Then *ana o'a hi'it*." We would eat, indeed. He used the Comanche tongue in deference to Spirit Talker to invite us to eat.

Spirit Talker nodded in agreement. Then he patted the top of his own head while pointing at George. "Still no hair," he said laughingly.

Once cleaned up and with the horses enjoying the corral, I followed George and Spirit Talker into the cabin. Reflexively, I took a final scan around the area, but there was no sign of hostiles.

George led us to a great too-big-for-the-cabin table upon which lay a simmering bouquet of North Platte country bounty. Elk, corn, potatoes, gravy, cornbread, and berries competed for our culinary attention.

Salivating, I looked at Spirit Talker and he at me. In my peripheral vision, I saw young Topsannah smile. She danced happily around the table pouring coffee. She had clearly already become comfortable with Running Waters.

We sat. It was all I could do to not sweep the food onto my plate. But that was not yet to be. All heads turned expectantly to George.

"Let's bow our heads," he began.

His prayerful blessing wasn't all that long, but it seemed to take forever. I was convinced that everyone could hear my stomach grumble.

"And thank you, Lord, for keeping Jack and Spirit Talker safe on their travels and for saving Topsannah from captivity," George paused for what seemed like an eternity to my empty stomach. "Amen," he finally said.

The dining conversation was mostly about life here in the North Platte country. Every time we veered off to talk about our journey or Rising Cross Ranch, George diverted the talk back to the here and now.

"After chow, we'll gather 'round yonder fireplace, and you can tell me about your adventure," he finally said. It seemed clear that he wanted to be able to have a meaningful conversation uninterrupted by scraping plates, chewing elk steak, sipping coffee, and occasional belching.

Topsannah seemed to appear ever more appreciative of the contrast between her Arapaho captors and the world here at George's ranch. She eagerly helped Running Waters clear the table, as George, Spirit Talker, and I shuffled over to benches beside the fireplace.

Upon sitting, my eyes scanned the cabin interior. I saw a large bookcase. From what I could see at a distance, it teemed with literary treasures. My attention shifted to the windows which were mere slits more akin to gun ports. The roof was constructed of overlapping adobe tiles to retard fire. A half dozen carbines were placed at strategic locations. I assumed they were loaded.

George saw me assessing his cabin fortress. "Can't be taking any chances out here, Jack. The soldiers at Fort Laramie have been hunkered down since the Grattan mess a couple of years back. Those are .56 caliber breech-loading Burnsides. Danged hard to get hold of but right effective. Fended off a handful of Cheyenne the other day. We can be sure the Lakota are watching as we sit." He nodded at the bookcase. "Feel free to borrow a book. Some traveler on the Oregon Trail up yonder dumped the whole caboodle from their wagon. Their loss has been our gain." He appeared to want to say more but deferred to the feast before us.

Spirit Talker nodded. "*Natsuitu piti,*" he observed that it took a strong heart to venture out. "Many Lakota and Cheyenne," he added.

George nodded. "We always pray to God for strength and protection. He hasn't let us down yet."

Running Waters joined us near the fireplace with Topsannah tagging along close behind. The young orphaned girl was already showing signs of recovery from her ordeal. She must have felt something of her mother in Running Waters.

"Have you met the Lakota warrior Otaktay?" I asked.

"Likely been one of the ones I've seen, but he hasn't introduced himself yet," George noted, as he stirred the fire and added a log. "I did meet an interesting young Lakota a couple of weeks back. He sat on his pony maybe fifty yards off. We didn't speak or sign. Just stared at each other. I sensed that he was a smart one, a deep thinker. He smiled at me before moving off into the forest."

"Sounds like Crazy Horse," I suggested.

"Tasunke Witko," added Spirit Talker, nodding agreement as he translated the name into the Lakota tongue.

"We met him and two Lakota warriors, Otaktay and Mato, a few days back. Crazy Horse is young, but clearly had strong influence over his older companions. I think the two warriors wanted our horses, but Crazy Horse wouldn't allow it."

Spirit Talker added, "Next day, Otaktay kill old man called Grandy. Too many Lakota. We could not help."

"Bear Grandy!?" exclaimed George. "Why, he was..." Tears welled up in our black friend's eyes. "He...he helped me lay this place out. Strong Christian, but his own man to God's purposes. He surely rests in heaven." He bowed his head.

I felt just a tad uncomfortable. Sad for George's loss.

He shook off his momentary lament. "So, tell me of your journey," he said, as though to distract from dwelling on Grandy's passing. George produced a hand-carved, beautifully decorated Pawnee pipe, tamped some tobacco in its bowl, and lit it. He took a couple of draws before passing it to me.

"Been about six weeks since we left Spirit Talker's

village. Lost our packhorses to a Cheyenne war party just a couple of weeks ago, so been traveling light." I lost my train of thought as I was still thinking about Bear Grandy. Guess I felt some guilt at not having been able to help, crazy as that might have been. I passed the pipe to Spirit Talker.

Spirit Talker took a long thoughtful pull and puffed out smoke rings.

I wondered where he'd learned to do that.

Spirit Talker smiled and winked at my surprise. "We see many people. They fight each other...try to fight us. Much *aruka, puuka, tasiwoo*," he noted, rattling off some of the plentiful wildlife. He glanced at me. "And *isa*, the wolf." He passed the pipe to George.

"What about the wolf? Another one?" George's curiosity had been piqued as he recalled my mention of the visit by the wolves back in Texas.

I took the pipe and tried my darndest to blow a smoke ring. It was to no avail. George and Spirit Talker repressed the laughs that surely welled up in them. I ignored them. "Yesterday...the Lakota named Otaktay attacked us with a half dozen warriors. Likely figured we'd be easy pickings. I think he coveted Big Red," I paused more for the dramatic effect of what I was about to share.

George's eyes widened at the mention of Otaktay.

"The night was pitch black. Sometime before sunup, I was on watch and surprised by a cold nose nuzzling at me. The clouds parted just enough to reveal the biggest wolf I'd ever seen. Then, I realized it was the same one that I'd met back in Texas. His pack sat off at the edge of our campsite. Once I realized who he was, he loped off into the woods. At daybreak, the Lakota had caught us by surprise. I killed one, but they were determined to kill us and take our horses," I paused and took a pull on the pipe. Admittedly, the pause was for dramatic effect. I passed the pipe to Spirit Talker.

Spirit Talker accepted the pipe. He appreciated my sense of drama and blew no smoke rings this time. "*Isa. Sinupu,*" he said in a slow, very serious tone. "Jack strong medicine. Lakota fear *isa sinupu*. God bring *isa* to Jack. Lakota run away."

As I watched Spirit Talker deliver the message of strong medicine, it struck me how much he had matured. I likely had as well, but I'd never paused long enough to consider it. My Comanche brother's hair hung nearly to his waist, and the scars from the now long-past mountain lion attack had smoothed some, adding character to the frame of his face with its high cheekbones and dark eyes that danced with visions of some future yet to be reached.

George accepted the pipe from Spirit Talker and blew a perfect smoke ring that wafted aloft. "God is all power-ful," he added for emphasis. "What of Topsannah?" he asked, shifting the conversation.

At the mention of her name, the young Comanche girl looked up from her seat behind Running Waters.

I glanced at Spirit Talker and took a pull on the pipe. We hadn't talked about Topsannah's fate. "Perhaps she could stay here?" I suggested. "It's a long dangerous journey back to the Quahadi Comanche."

All eyes fell on Topsannah, and she squirmed uncom-fortably.

Running Waters seized the moment. "What is Topsannah's mind?" she asked.

"No *ap*, no *pia*," lamented Topsannah. She placed her hand on Running Waters's arm. "*Pihi,*" she referred to the heart, that she felt a closeness with Running Waters and her kindness.

George and Running Waters exchanged a long look filled with unspoken words. Unbeknownst to us, she had miscarried just a month back. They dearly wanted children.

Spirit Talker took the pipe and blew three smoke rings in Topsannah's direction. He offered a broad smile as he looked gently upon her. "Topsannah stay here?" he asked. "George and Running Waters *ap* and *pia*."

The young Comanche girl's eyes brightened hopefully, as she nodded.

Running Waters curled an arm around the young girl. "It is good," she added.

With Topsannah's future settled, we men could focus on our next steps. Spirit Talker and I had yearned to visit George and his ranch, but there was more to it. We hoped to supply horses and beeves that George could sell to settlers, the military, and even local tribes.

George snuffed out the pipe. "Tomorrow, we talk of the future. We'll saddle up, and I'll give you a tour," he ordered more than suggested. "Figure y'all already realize that Fort Laramie is a disaster. The Comanche or Cheyenne could wipe them out in a heartbeat."

"Why don't they?" I ventured.

"We'll talk about that tomorrow," George stated. "There's a couple of straw-filled mats over against yonder wall," he said, pointing past us. "Get some shuteye."

I glanced questioningly at Spirit Talker then back to George. "You don't fear attack?"

George laughed. "You haven't met Bear. He's the biggest, loudest watchdog this side of the Missouri."

"Where's he been?" I asked.

"Fear not. He's close by," answered George. With that, he grabbed a bowl of feed and headed out the front door. Upon his return, he laughed again. "Bear says he'll be keeping a good watch." With that, George directed Topsannah to a sleeping mat and disappeared behind a curtain divider with Running Waters tagging along.

———

"*SUNKMANITU TANKA NAGI*," muttered Otaktay, as he sat on the blanket and watched the sun set on the cabin of the dark-skinned one. It was his first acknowledgment that spirit wolves haunted his mind. He'd watched the White teen who called the wolves enter the cabin with the Comanche and the girl. He was at a loss as to how to counter such strong medicine. The Sharps rifle was the least of his worries. His mind twisted around what lay before him and what it might portend for the future of the Oglala Lakota. He felt an irony in his own name, Kills Many. The White teenager's strong medicine had done what arrows and bullets could not.

Mato approached cautiously, ever mindful of Otaktay's flash temper. His chief clearly was frustrated. Worse, he sensed fear. "Tasunke Witko," he said softly so as to not startle Otaktay. He knew he was treading on thin ice with the mention of Crazy Horse given the deep envy of the young warrior that lurked deep within Otaktay's breast.

Otaktay found no comfort in Mato's suggestion. In a passing thought, he wondered why Mato couldn't call up the bear spirit for which he was named. There was far greater medicine at work here. To Otaktay, it overshadowed his abiding concern with the steady onslaught of White settlers into Lakota lands. He glanced at Mato.

Mato returned the glance hopefully. It was clear to him that they needed greater numbers to take on the spirits they faced. They needed stronger medicine to be sure.

"Tasunke Witko," said Otaktay. He arose and began to roll his blanket. He looked up at the canopy of stars and took a deep breath. "It is time," he concluded, mounting his pony and leading his small war party away through the aspens. He would have to face Crazy Horse's likely wrath for attacking the teens and especially for losing a warrior, but honest confrontation seemed the only answer. His succumbing to envy was costing him, but he had no idea as to the ultimate price that he and his people might yet pay.

THIRTEEN
THE TOUR

AFTER A HEARTY BREAKFAST, George, Spirit Talker, and I mounted up for the promised tour of George's ranch. Good feed and well-earned rest topped with an apple treat had Big Red in high spirits and itching for a good ride. Spirit Talker's pinto had caught Big Red's excitement, and it took a few minutes for my Comanche brother to settle him.

George's spread was far greater than had initially met our eyes. While he held a vast area of grassy prairie land, ranch boundaries reached far into the surrounding stands of aspen, cottonwood, and juniper.

Looking back, I occasionally caught sight of Bear. The dog didn't lean toward socializing but was clearly loyal and bent on protecting his people.

We soon found ourselves standing on the southern bank of the North Platte. I looked down at the wagon ruts and at the castoffs of the many travelers journeying westward to whatever opportunity they sought. Discarded chests of drawers, broken wagon wheels, and, sadly, graves littered the trail. It was little wonder that George's cabin enjoyed a full bookcase, a couple of beautiful rocking chairs, and plenty of kitchen furnishings.

"This here is the Oregon Trail," announced George, describing the obvious. "Runs a good ways alongside the North Platte. Marks my northern boundary. If you climb up to the top of yonder Laramie Mountains, you can see the wagon dust kicking up way off to the east. Settlers keep coming." He paused in thought. "Going to push the Indians out. They know it, and while they'll fight it, they know the Whites will keep coming."

I glanced over at Spirit Talker. Clearly, George had given the onslaught of settlers and its impact considerable thought. We'd been riding for better than an hour and seemed to have covered only a small portion of George's ranch. Longhorns were grazing, as were horses. Much to our surprise, there was even a small herd of buffalo. On the far bank of the river stood a large bighorn ram with his herd of ewes. George's ranch was simply teeming with life. "Let's rest our horses, George," I suggested.

We all dismounted and led the horses to the river for a drink. Thirsts satisfied, we moseyed over to a grassy knoll. I hitched Big Red's reins to a broken wagon wheel. Some inner sense told me to keep him near at hand. Perhaps I was still feeling the abundant caution of the past few days of travel.

George was fully relaxed, as though the threat of hostile Cheyenne or Lakota was of no particular concern.

Spirit Talker had been silent during our ride. "George own land?" he asked. He was still coming to grips with the concept of owning land. For the Comanche and other tribes, boundaries were vague if they existed at all. They depended on tribal conquests and the roving of buffalo herds.

George nodded Perhaps, it was his experience as a slave who didn't even own the shirt on his back that drove his next comment. "We set boundaries to protect what we build with our own hands. God gave boundaries to the ancient Iraelites. Judah...Dan...Ephraim all had defined God-given borders. It's a consequence of civilization." George wasn't sure he was getting through to Spirit Talker.

"Buffalo no have boundaries," responded Spirit Talker.

"Buffalo aren't civilized," I responded.

Spirit Talker frowned. "Comanche not civilized?" he queried earnestly.

George recognized that the conversation was turning quite heavy yet its questions needed to be resolved. He sighed thoughtfully. "Comanche are not buffalo," he offered. George scratched his chin as he weighed his next words. "Sad days lie ahead for Lakota, Arapaho, Kiowa, Cheyenne, Comanche...all the Indian nations. They fight each other. Their disunity will destroy them. Like the Fort Laramie Treaty, they will be asked to give up land they do not own. Whites will keep coming and keep taking. The buffalo will disappear, and White man's diseases will kill many. The Indian will be unable to stop them. The Whites will take the land, destroy all who oppose them, build on it, and reap its bounty," he foretold.

Spirit Talker squirmed uncomfortably. "Will God protect Comanche?"

I watched George gaze off as though striving to make the truth as palatable as possible.

He finally looked back at Spirit Talker. "Even those who believe will be tested. Evil lurks among all people. Greed will enslave many, as gold and land beckons. There will surely be cowards and traitors who will betray the Indian people." George grabbed a stick and began to scratch around in the gravel along the riverbank. "The Bible tells us that the truth will set you free. It is God's truth, not man's truth, that frees the soul. We must trust in God's truth to survive. He will place many challenges before us; it is His way. We must rise to those challenges. We must persevere in living a life rooted in His truth." George smiled. "God's challenges will bring opportunities to live a long and fruitful life. He seeks to be known above and beyond mere religious ritual. He asks us to come close to Him, and thus He will come close to us, protect us."

Spirit Talker looked off at the distant mountains to our west. "Is there escape?" he finally asked.

George shook his head. "I escaped my slave master, but still face people who would enslave me. I can never escape that but for the freedom I find in the God who lets me defend it here on the North Platte River. I don't even know who my ancestors were, which one of the many tribes of Africa they were from. But, I am here, and I am an American. My chosen name is George Freeman. There will be many who judge me by my skin rather than by who I am.

"Did you have a name from your ancestors?" I asked.

George smiled. "Nope. Sort of convenient though. Getting to pick my own name, I mean."

"People judge Comanche?" asked Spirit Talker.

George turned to Spirit Talker. "Judgment is not always a fair thing. So it is with the Comanche...with all the Indian nations. Your people are divided, Spirit Talker.

Comanche against Comanche, Comanche against Kiowa. And the Great Father in Washington will further divide your people against each other. Even the White man is divided over the battle over the morality and reality of slavery. Should one man own another? Is slavery God's way? He delivered the enslaved Israelites from their Egyptian masters long ago on the other side of the world. God's grace speaks loudly against subjugating people. Unity seems to be elusive so long as differences are used as wedges to divide us."

"My schooling taught that all men are created equal. Seems unfair to judge by differences," I said, leaning in toward the hearth.

George stroked his chin in deep thought. "That's true, Jack. We are created equal." He pondered another moment. "The founding fathers wrote that in the Declaration of Independence to be free of King George. There are folks who say we are all equal. I don't think so. We are individuals with different strengths and weaknesses by which we can never be equal. But...and this is important...we do have equal opportunity despite all of our inequalities. We can ranch, farm, mine, and more as we so choose. It makes our nation strong. We dare not be defined by race or nation groups. America is like a crucible, a blazing white-hot cauldron casting all who settle here as Americans."

I observed Spirit Talker's face as he struggled with the complexity of George's words. His ever-improving, yet still rudimentary, grasp of the English language made this quite a challenge. "This road not easy," he observed.

"We have already met God's challenges, my brother," I offered. "He has protected us. God is invisible like the air yet with us always."

Spirit Talker nodded. He could hardly deny my truth.

George stood and scanned the stands of aspen and cottonwood on the opposite side of the river. He rightly sensed that we were being watched. It was a given for life out here in the midst of Lakota country. "You are wise beyond your years, Jack."

I looked up at him inquisitively.

"Do you recall how Saint Patrick converted the Celts in Ireland?"

I nodded. I had learned from my pa that Patrick had blended the most-Godly of the Celtic rituals with the tenets of the Catholic faith to bring the heathens to Christ. He was hugely successful, though the Catholics in Europe never fully accepted the Irish Catholics as true believers. To this day, they call the Irish Black Catholics.

George nodded toward Spirit Talker. "Seems to be working," he observed.

I suppose I had unwittingly applied Saint Patrick's methods to my relationship with Spirit Talker and his people.

"Spirit Talker," addressed George, "do you believe in one all-powerful God, the creator of all things, and in his Son the Christ?"

I coughed involuntarily. This was a heavy burden to be placed upon Spirit Talker. "*Tumhyokenu taa narumi*," was my awkward way of trying to translate George's words into simple Comanche. Did Spirit Talker believe in God?

"God sunipu," responded Spirit Talker.

I wondered whether God being strong medicine to Spirit Talker was enough. Was his a soul-felt belief in God and in Christ as his savior?

George caught the uncertainty in my eyes. "It is good," he said in his deepest bass voice. He began to strip off his shirt. His dark skin glistened in the bright mid-morning sun, and the scars on his back from his sufferings under the lash stood out. "You been baptized, Jack?" he asked with his dazzling, ever-sincere smile.

The realization struck me like a bolt of lightning. I was unable to recall ever having been baptized. It rather perplexed me, as I shook my head.

"No time like the present," he bellowed, as he waded waist deep into the frigid North Platte.

I stood and stripped off my own shirt, boots, and trousers. I was about to wade in, when I paused to lay my revolver on top of my clothes. Easy access to your weapons was learned quickly and became routine on the frontier where seconds of response time could spell life or death.

Spirit Talker thought a moment and made his decision. "I believe," he boldly called out.

I went first, following George into the snowmelt-fed waters.

The big rancher gripped my shoulders with those strong black hands, closed his eyes, and plunged me into the frigid river. "I baptize you in the name of the Father, Son, and Holy Ghost," he intoned before letting me come up for air.

I wished in hindsight that I had held my nose and kept my mouth shut tight, as I came up sputtering and coughing. I staggered to the riverbank to get dried out and dressed.

Spirit Talker paused a moment and then waded out to George.

The next moments seemed a blur. As George was about to lay his hands upon Spirit Talker's shoulders and began to close his eyes, the young Comanche suddenly drove his shoulders into the big Black man's midsection with enough force to drive them both under the rushing waters.

A warpaint-bedecked Cheyenne warrior narrowly missed counting coup as he galloped past George and Spirit Talker. He let out a whoop likely born of frustration.

Taken totally unawares by the savage's whooping, I looked up from fumbling with the buttons of my trousers to find the attacker now barreling headlong toward me. In what was a chaotic fury of water, feathers, war whoops, and hooves, I dove with catlike reflexes for my Colt revolver. The savage was nearly on top of me, as I gripped the gun, aimed best I could, and managed to fire off a single round. My bullet went through the poor pony and shattered the leg of the Cheyenne warrior. Lucky shot. He fell in a heap, crippled and writhing in pain. He released a pitiful cry. Striving to collect himself, he gave me an enraged look steeped in evil and grabbed for his knife. Despite what must have been excruciating pain, pure hatred shot from the savage's eyes. He struggled to rise but collapsed.

By now, George's ever-present dog Bear appeared seemingly from nowhere. Snarling, he gripped the Cheyenne's broken leg in his vice-like jaws and pulled with all his might. With a blood-curdling scream, the warrior swiped with his knife at the attacking dog. The luckless savage missed but in rising made himself a target. George and Spirit Talker stood by helplessly in the waters and watched as my well-aimed second shot finished the attacker. Bear released his grip, looked over at me, then at George, and bounded away. He'd apparently figured we were safe.

From across the river at a safe distance came the whoops and yelps of a half dozen Cheyenne hostiles.

They hesitated, seeming to debate whether to follow their fellow warrior into the fray. We'd been so caught up in the baptism that we hadn't seen them arrive on the north bank of the river. How careless of us.

By this time, I had gathered my wits and slipped my Sharps carbine from its scabbard alongside Big Red's saddle. I was pumped with the emotional rush of the attack but took careful aim and squeezed off a shot that splintered the arm of one of the distant Cheyenne warriors.

Now having been made all-too-aware that they were not out of range, they let out a final whoop of feigned bravery and retreated.

I stood there brandishing the Sharps in one hand and holding up my trousers with the other. I began shaking like a leaf, as the stark reality of the moment set in. I took a deep breath to try to calm myself and turned my attention to George and Spirit Talker standing dripping wet in the waist-deep waters of the North Platte. I smiled with false bravado and shrugged, as though it was just a normal day on the frontier.

Without further pause, a seemingly nonplussed George pushed Spirit Talker down into the waters. "I baptize you in the name of the Father, Son, and Holy Ghost," he intoned as calmly as though an attack had never happened. The two of them waded back ashore.

The three of us stood looking down at the dead Cheyenne. His wounded pony lay nearby bleating with pain.

"Foolish courage," said George. He shook his head, then grabbed his gun, walked over to the suffering pony, and mercy-killed the poor beast.

I sensed that an urge to scalp the Cheyenne yet lingered in Spirit Talker's mind, as his eyes lingered on the dead hostile. Cultural instincts were tough to over-come. Of course, any scalping would have been my privilege.

Spirit Talker glanced at me, sighed ever-so-slightly, and looked off at the now-distant band of Cheyenne warriors. "We bury. Take soul," he stated with a finality.

Apparently, the Cheyenne hoped to recover their brother warrior's body to give it a proper departure to whatever other world they worshipped. Our burying the dead warrior underground would frustrate that. Likely anger them, too. For Spirit Talker, disrespecting his enemy was the next best thing to scalping.

———

AFTER BURYING THE DEAD CHEYENNE, we shook off the vestiges of the lingering rush of fending off a Cheyenne war party attack and completed our tour of George's spread.

I was full of questions, but figured to hold them until after dinner. It was already late afternoon when I finished currying Big Red and letting him loose in the fenced portion of the pasture. He sure seemed to love the fresh air here in the North Platte country, but I sensed that he longed for his mares.

Running Waters greeted us at the cabin with another wonderful meal. It was obvious that Topsannah was growing increasingly comfortable in her new home as she puttered about helping her new mother.

As we enjoyed the feast, Running Waters cleared her throat. "Hear much gunfire. Where elk?"

George had apparently decided not to mention the attack on the river, but he was being called out. "I was baptizing Jack and Spirit Talker when some Cheyenne took offense," he hoped that was enough.

"And?" insisted Running Waters.

"Jack dissuaded them," responded George. He was still reluctant to spell it out. Two attacks in two days was concerning.

The expression on Running Waters's face demanded more.

"The boys are baptized."

Still not enough. She folded her arms and cocked her head.

George sighed. "Jack killed one, wounded another. They ran off."

Running Waters smiled. "Truth set you free," she admonished her husband.

What could George do but nod? He drew laughs as he punctuated the moment with a deep belch. "Let's gather by the fire," he said.

———

ONCE AGAIN, George lit the beautifully decorated Pawnee pipe. He jokingly explained that it was a gift from Running Waters's father for taking her off his hands.

Running Waters rolled her eyes, having heard this humor before.

I took the pipe from George and took a pull. "Last night, you mentioned slavery," I ventured. "It doesn't seem right for one person to own another."

My question had grabbed Topsannah's attention given that she had been briefly enslaved to the Arapaho woman back at Fort Laramie.

I passed the pipe to Spirit Talker. He took a long thoughtful pull. "I curious. Comanche have slaves," he stated with nary a single smoke ring. He passed the pipe back to George.

George gestured with the pipe toward the books resting in the bookcase nestled snugly in a corner of the cabin. "Done a bit of reading. Also, I've talked with folks passing through on yonder Oregon Trail. Slavery has been around for a long time. Doesn't mean it's moral or right, mind you, but it has existed since long before history was written down," such was George's opening salvo on the subject. "Mostly, slaves are people that have been conquered. Babylonians, Egyptians, Romans, Spaniards, Comanche, Apache, Cheyenne, and American Whites and even Black folk held slaves. Perhaps blaming conquest is too easy to understand. Slavery gets complicated when it becomes a business like selling livestock or plows or cotton. The supposedly civilized term for slave is chattel, or simply property." He paused and passed the pipe to me.

"By business, do you mean capturing folks and selling them?" I asked almost rhetorically. I knew the answer, but had asked for Spirit Talker's benefit.

Spirit Talker took the pipe from me, said nary a word, pulled on it, and passed it to George.

"When the Spanish first came here three centuries ago, they conquered and enslaved the people who lived here. It didn't take but little more than another century, and the Creek Confederacy of tribes back east began selling captured Indians as slaves to plantation owners in the Carolinas in exchange for blankets and guns. The plantation owners benefited, as they kept expanding their properties westward into Creek territory. Didn't take but another fifty years or so, and those same plantation owners found they could buy Black slaves cheaper from a place called Africa." George took an especially long pull on the pipe. "At some point, my own ancestors were among those enslaved folks."

I looked around our small gathering huddling around the fireplace against the lingering chills of late May. Everyone was hanging on George's words.

Spirit Talker motioned for the pipe. He gazed thoughtfully at each of us. "My people sell slaves." It was more a statement than a question. He recalled how I had reacted to his father Buffalo Hump holding my young brother and sister hostage in exchange for trade goods. I had expressed my indignation at the concept of buying or selling humans. He was beginning to understand. He passed the pipe back to George.

"There's a true moral question," stated the big Black cowboy. "Wasn't long ago that the British outlawed slave trade by its own merchants. Folks across our nation are wrestling with it at this very moment," he said with a deeply concerned expression. "There's emotion, but also some looking at slavery from strictly a business perspective. Neither view gets to the morality of it, to God's love for all humans. Mark my words, it is likely to be settled with much bloodshed." He paused and turned to Spirit Talker. "And that same sort of resorting to violence is sure to be unleashed on your *numunuu*, Spirit Talker."

My mouth gaped.

Spirit Talker looked inquisitively at George.

"The Whites will want more and more of what the Indian cannot give," observed George. "They will pit you against each other. It's called divide and conquer." He looked over at Running Waters's serious expression, then emptied the pipe. She had been a victim of inter-tribal warfare. "That's enough for tonight. Tomorrow, we talk about driving livestock up here from the Rising Cross Ranch," he said with a forced smile aimed at lightening the emotions in the room. "There's plenty of folks up here that'll buy beeves and horses."

I exchanged a glance with Spirit Talker, and we nodded simultaneously. Much opportunity lay ahead that would surely drive out slavery and even the conflicts arising with Indians. Little did we appreciate how naïve we yet were.

FOURTEEN
NEW HORIZONS

"A THOUSAND HEAD," I suggested. In my heart of hearts, I couldn't believe what I'd just proposed. I'd never driven cattle in my young life. I'd have to hire a trail boss, drovers, and a cook, plus outfit the entire enterprise. And it would take some money upfront. It was a lot for my sixteen-year-old brain to wrap around.

Spirit Talker's eyes widened.

George's eyebrows arched as he let out a big breath and scratched his chin. He smiled. "Couple hundred beeves would be a good start. What about horses?"

"Driving a few hundred head of prime Texas longhorns will require a sizable remuda of extra horses. We'd have plenty of horses."

"Too much," observed Spirit Talker.

I'd given the size of the herd plenty of thought as Spirit Talker and I journeyed from Texas. A smaller herd by my reckoning would make us more vulnerable to attacks by Indians and rustlers. "There's greater safety in numbers," I stated.

George leaned forward, resting his elbows on the

table. He took a long sip of coffee. As he put the cup down, a smiling Topsannah happily refilled it. "Thank you, young lady," he responded even as it broke his train of thought. He stared thoughtfully into the steaming coffee. "It's going to take time. Maybe take a couple of trail drives before we build what the money folks call a sustaining business, Jack. I trade horses and beeves with Fort Laramie. The Lakota will take horses before they buy them and prefer buffalo to longhorns. There's plenty of lush meadow to feed livestock, fatten them up. The railroad is on its way, and soon enough we'll be filling cattle cars to ship beeves back east. Yep, it's going to take a few years."

I had to admit that George made perfect sense. "So, you think maybe five hundred head would make sense?" I asked.

"Still a lot, but they won't all make it to the North Platte. Some will be traded to hostile Indians, some will be lost to the trail, some may even be rustled," observed George, gesticulating with his hands.

"Price?" I ventured.

"We're talking next year. No telling what the market might bear," said our Black friend.

Spirit Talker smiled. "Trade for blankets and guns?" He laughed heartily, breaking the slight tension of the moment.

"Likely expect twenty-five dollars a head, Jack," offered George. "Could be more, could be less," he added.

"What about horses?" I asked.

"Indians will likely look to trade for goods. The Army will drive a hard bargain but aren't so fussy about quality. Likely won't fetch more than a hundred dollars a head," postulated George.

Spirit Talker glanced over at me and smiled deviously. "What fifteen ponies worth?" he inquired.

I raised my empty coffee cup toward Topsannah who scurried over and refilled it. That bought me some time to think. "Blue Flower worth more. Fifteen ponies is good." I laughed. We both knew that Buffalo Hump drove a hard bargain.

"You going to marry Blue Flower?" asked George.

I nodded.

"My sister...her heart for Jack," Spirit Talker said with an ever-broadening grin. Even his mountain lion scars seemed to smile.

"Back to driving cattle, men. There will always be uncertainty as to what the market will bear. A year from now, there could be big changes. Up? Down? We simply cannot be certain. Seem to be more and more mouths to be fed out here," said George as he grew serious. "You bring the beeves, and we'll see what happens. I'll do the best I can up here. It's going to take a lot of effort on your part down in Texas. You've grown up, Jack, but a lot of folk will see you as an inexperienced young whippersnapper unworthy of trusting you with their money or their beeves. We'll have to pray on it."

Spirit Talker nodded. "This all good. We strong. Have *sinupu*. We pray." It would indeed take strong medicine, but most of all God's will for our success.

I couldn't have agreed more. Spirit Talker spoke of what the Comanche called *tumhyokenu*, that is, trust or belief. It would take the full strength of our faith coupled with hard work to pull off this cattle venture. Considering all we'd endured since that fateful day the Comanche attacked my folks' homestead and killed nearly all of us, we were feeling reasonably overconfident. I chuckled at that contradiction. Overconfidence and reason are strange bedfellows for sure.

———

WITH THE BUSINESS side of our visit pretty much settled, Spirit Talker and I could enjoy a few days of taking in the majestic spring beauty of the North Platte country with its forests, lush meadows, rushing ice-fed streams, plentiful game, and distant mountains still wearing their snow caps. We helped George with chores around the ranch and thoroughly enjoyed the bounty of Running Waters's cooking. Soon enough, we'd have to be heading south.

One day, I rode out alone to take in the fresh air and awesome grandeur of the landscape. Roughly two miles from George's cabin, I spied an old acquaintance off in the distance. I reined in Big Red. There astride an elaborately decorated pony sat Otaktay. He had no headdress, rather his long black hair simply hung to his waist. His shield was held closely across his chest and lance pointing upward behind it. There was nothing threatening in his manner. He surely saw me, though he made no attempt at connecting. He simply sat proudly with an uplifted chin. After what seemed to be forever, he turned his pony and rode off. There was a certain finality to it, as though I might never see him again. Despite our differences, I did have a yearning to see him again...to talk with him and perhaps his fellow warrior Crazy Horse.

Upon returning to the cabin, I mentioned the encounter to Spirit Talker.

"Otaktay respect Jack *sunipu*," he observed. "He try to understand." With that, Spirit Talker's face turned thoughtful, as though weighing something heavy. "Spirit Talker like talk with Tasunke Witko. Share God."

It was the first time I'd heard Spirit Talker earnestly speak of approaching a fellow Indian about the Christian faith. It warmed me that baptism seemed to have cemented his faith.

Spirit Talker had brought up Blue Flower in jest, but she had been on my mind more than I dared admit. She reached a part of me that I feared I had lost. Whether the way her eyes danced when she looked at me or her saving my life from the Comanche shaman or simply the demure yet coy way she had of posturing when I was near, she reached deep within me. If there was to be a price, fifteen ponies was a bargain.

Spirit Talker and I spent some time teaching George the benefits of the bow and arrow, and he took to it right readily. We managed a bit of target shooting, and George took to it right naturally. He became set on obtaining a bow and quiver of arrows from the Indians at Fort Laramie of whom he was convinced they no longer remembered how to use them.

I couldn't help but appreciate a connection that was flowering between Topsannah and Spirit Talker. The young Comanche seemed to have recovered from her brief travails as an Arapaho slave and had begun to mature physically with Running Waters's and George's love, good nourishment, and plenty of household chores. The looks she gave Spirit Talker began to remind me of Blue Flower's eyes when she was near me. It seemed to me that it would be easy to persuade Spirit Talker to join me for the cattle drive next year...if he could wait that long.

George, bless his heart, made sure we were well-provisioned for our journey home. He convinced us that pack animals would make us far too attractive for hostile Indians and bandits. We already had direct experience, having lost our packhorses to the Cheyenne war party on our travels north. We would travel as efficiently as possible.

Big Red and Spirit Talker's pony were well rested and likely itching to head homeward.

"You might stop briefly at Fort Laramie on your way," advised George. "They're struggling with weak command for now. When you're driving those beeves north next year, they might be in better shape. The folks traveling the Oregon Trail are demanding greater protection, so the Army will be forced to increase the garrison. They will need beeves and horses." George glanced over at Spirit Talker, as he began to impart words of wisdom. "Spirit Talker burn deep in memory the image of those teepees around Fort Laramie. Those people depend on the government for food and blankets. They forgot how to hunt...how to be a *numunuu*, a people. When you sign treaty, you give up freedom; you give up life."

Spirit Talker nodded. He had not missed the desperation in the eyes of the Indians and even the struggling Whites surrounding Fort Laramie. George's words weren't lost on him or me.

I must admit to being quite filled with the prospect of assembling a herd of longhorns and driving them north. I recalled the words in the first chapter of Genesis that my folks drove into me, "subdue the Earth; extract its potential." If I was to be successful in ranching, I would have to raise and deliver livestock. Importantly, this endeavor was to be my calling, to live by God's direction in the fullest sense.

"You might best stay to the east in your travels. There will be more prairies and fewer places vulnerable to ambush," advised George. "Rivers will be a bit easier to cross, too, as they become wider and shallower."

"What of you, George?" I asked. "The Lakotas and Cheyenne don't seem to be your friends."

"God willing, we'll win them over, Jack. If they get smart enough to finally come and talk, they'll learn that we pose no threat. I think that that young warrior Crazy Horse may eventually be a problem. Like Otaktay, he sees the threat to his culture posed by the White settlers. He is smarter than Otaktay. Tasunke Witko is a thinker in the spirit realm sort of like Spirit Talker here, but his warrior blood may exceed his ultimate common sense. It'd be a lot easier if they blended in with the coming cultural forces, but that works two ways. There are far too many who think the only good Indian is a dead Indian. They are often the same ones who disrespect and diminish Black folks. The settlers will come in wave after wave. If sheer numbers and soldiers aren't enough, less game and White man's diseases will surely end the Indian way of life. There will be many treaties, but they will all fail." George had delivered a mouthful of wisdom.

I sat silently digesting George's words. The more time we spent with him, the more impressed I was with his wisdom.

FIFTEEN
HEADING HOME

THE DAY finally arrived for us to begin our trek homeward. We awoke to a cloudless late June sky.

As summer approached, the days have begun to warm considerably. The trees and grasses had become especially lush as fed by the snowmelt waters of the North Platte and its tributaries. We saddled up with decidedly mixed feelings. On the one hand, it would be wonderful to be home, while on the other, we would miss George and Running Waters. Topsannah was thoroughly enjoying her new home and had quite clearly been restored to good health as her radiant smiles attested.

Running Waters had prepared us the last home-cooked breakfast we'd be enjoying for a while, and we relished the opportunity to spend the early morning time with our dear friends before departing.

Topsannah seemed especially happy. She had clearly found a home with George and Running Waters. As she was refilling our coffee cups, she took advantage of a pause in our conversation. She placed her hand on Spirit Talker's shoulder causing him to look up at her. "Topsannah thank Spirit Talker," she said, surprising us with her newfound grasp of English.

"Spirit Talker pleased," my Comanche brother responded.

She smiled and shook her head. With that, Topsannah revealed an exquisitely beaded knife sheath which she placed before Spirit Talker. Boldly placed in the center of the beadwork design was a cross. Topsannah had been truly listening to our discussions of our faith and observing the manner in which we conducted ourselves. It had made a deep, and likely everlasting, impression. She had apparently been secretly working on fashioning the sheath. She turned to return the coffee pot to the wood stove, but Spirit Talker gently grabbed her arm.

"Spirit Talker happy for Topsannah. Grateful for gift." Unsaid was the even greater gift of freedom that Spirit Talker's chance discovery of her captivity at Fort Laramie had bestowed upon her. "May God ever bless you."

It was all I could do to keep from leaping for joy. It had become abundantly clear that my Comanche brother had fully accepted Christ. It gave me pause to wonder what a deep conversation between Spirit Talker and Crazy Horse might have been like. Alas, it was highly unlikely that the two deep thinkers would ever meet again. But one never knows. I turned to George. "Thanks for your hospitality, my friend," I said, as I watched Spirit Talker's eyes follow Topsannah to the stove. I sensed just a tad more than gratitude, though the girl couldn't have been more than twelve years old. There was a tendency on the frontier, especially among the Indians, for the women to mature more rapidly than in the White man's culture.

George stood. "We are grateful for your visit, Jack O'Toole and for the gift you blessed us with," he said, nodding toward Topsannah. He bowed his head and held out his hands with palms up. "Lord, we pray to you, our God and our Savior, that the travels home of Jack and Spirit Talker will be safe. May you ever bless them. Amen." It was a short but heartfelt prayer.

I looked from Spirit Talker to Topsannah.

"We look forward to your return next spring with livestock aplenty," noted George. "Of course you have a home here."

I laughed and glanced over at Spirit Talker. "Oh, I'm sure we will return with or without livestock."

Spirit Talker looked at me with a somewhat disconcerted expression, then joined me in laughter.

George walked over to the bookcase and pulled a single book. He leafed reverently through it before walking back over to the table and handing it to me. "I'd give you more, but you're already packed heavy," he said with a grin.

I looked at the title. It read, *New Testament*. I looked up gratefully.

George smiled. "You must keep His word before you, Jack. You can share with Spirit Talker on your journey home."

———

THE TIME to depart had arrived. The squeak of saddle leather and the taste of the bit excited Big Red. He fully sensed a return to his mares.

Running Waters sidled up to Spirit Talker. We did as she requested.

In each of our extended palms she lay an intricately carved buffalo rib talisman. "Only show to Pawnee. You be safe. Cheyenne or Kiowa will kill," she said, winking.

"She's not joking," added George.

Big Red and Spirit Talker's pinto were fully outfitted for the journey home. We had enough jerky and pemmican to possibly make us never want to eat those necessary culinary surrogates again. Hopefully, our trusty bows and arrows would bring us occasional fresh meat. Owing to their silence, they were often far preferable to the booming report of my Sharps rifle that would echo far and wide.

During our stay, Spirit Talker had continued to work with George concerning the art of the bow and arrow, not only helping him fashion his own weapons but how to hunt with them. Making his own turned out to be a far better experience than trading for a bow and arrows at Fort Laramie. George took up the skills right readily. I expect we would have made an unlikely trio—White boy, Comanche, and Black cowboy—treading the mountains and valleys of this pristine frontier. Any hostile Indian would have surely taken note of the apparent strong medicine.

I must admit that I had begun to think far more frequently about Blue Flower. I hoped and prayed that I'd be able to muster fifteen ponies upon our return home. Much as I didn't want to admit it, given all we'd been through on our journey to the North Platte country, getting home was not a sure thing. It was a given that we'd be praying regularly for our safe passage and being extra vigilant.

Spirit Talker shared a few private words with Topsannah. There was no outward display of affection, but there was some feeling shared between them that required no public display.

It occurred to me that Spirit Talker would not have to put up fifteen ponies.

George and I shared a man-hug. I gave Running Waters and Topsannah hugs before mounting Big Red.

Spirit Talker went through the same hugging ritual.

There was no further point in delay. Rising Cross Ranch awaited, and we had a long journey ahead. We could only pray that the good Lord would deliver us safely. Importantly, we sought a route that would be as easy as possible for driving beeves northward. While that meant staying to the east, well clear of mountains and forests, open prairies meant less cover to shield us from marauding war parties.

We bade our goodbyes and headed eastward along the south bank of the North Platte River. We were wary of hostiles from the very beginning. For the first couple of miles, I saw Bear following us at a distance. Guess he'd taken to us as George's friends. Anyway, I was determined to raise my own loyal dog upon return to Rising Cross Ranch.

OTAKTAY, Mato, Tasunke Witko, and a half dozen warriors watched George's ranch from afar.

"*Tanka* go," observed Otaktay. His comment revealed his obsession with the strong wolf spirit medicine that he'd faced.

"*Kize sapa wikaza,*" the Lakota warrior urged. Kills Many desperately wanted to attack the Black rancher. "*Otaktay katá,*" he added for emphasis. He wanted the honor of killing George Freeman.

Tasunke Witko listened attentively. He had come to understand Otaktay's frustrations and his deep concerns for the future of his people, his *oyate*. As part of the ritual for becoming a warrior, Tasunke Witko had experienced a vision quest in which he went off alone to meditate. He communed with the Great Spirit *Wakan Tanka* and received a vision of his future that fully unsettled him. While he would be a great warrior and leader of his people, Crazy Horse fretted since his dream did not end well. He gazed intently at Otaktay and slowly shook his head. *"No katá sapa wikaza,"* he stated commandingly. This would not be the day for attacking and killing George.

Otaktay grimaced and gave Mato an angry look.

Tasunke Witko pointed skyward at an eagle floating high above on the atmospheric thermals and looking for its breakfast. *"Wanbli,"* he observed. As he began to lower his arm, the eagle dove and swiped a fish from a hapless osprey. What he might not catch himself, the eagle was up for stealing. Crazy Horse smiled. "Lakota like *wanbli*," he stated. He recognized that the Lakota did not have the numbers of warriors or the weapons to wage war on the droves of White settlers heading westward and the accompanying Bluecoats. He also rightly figured that Fort Laramie would soon be re-garrisoned. Like the impoverished Indians and poor Whites surrounding the fort, he feared that the Lakota might all-too-soon fall victim to the largesse of the Great Father in Washington. In exchange for a paltry supply of blankets and food, they would quickly lose their hunting skills and even their ability to wage war. He recognized that killing George Freeman could wreak havoc upon his people. Better to wait for greater opportunity. A long wait it would be, as little could he know that the battle at Greasy Grass, the Little Bighorn, lurked twenty years in the future.

———

WE TRAVELED BLITHELY but guardedly on our way, clueless as to the debates of the hostile Lakota minds we'd left behind. We alternately walked and rode our horses to ensure that they remained strong for the long journey ahead.

The scenery was incredibly beautiful with no shortage of wildlife. Elk, deer, and antelope were abundant. Were we to settle here, we would surely eat well. At night, the heavens opened to a bejeweled sky that at times seemed nearly as bright as daylight. The landscape simply teemed with the sights and sounds of the wild.

SIXTEEN

NEW THREATS

FORT LARAMIE CAME INTO VIEW. From a distance, it didn't appear nearly so decrepit, though the surrounding landscape of ragged teepees and crumbling hovels gave away the truth.

George had suggested that we not linger here. Our aim was to find out when the Army intended to re-garrison and resupply the fort. We hoped there would be someone in authority that might know.

Given the looks of desperation on the folks along the approach to the fort, I feared that we might have to phys-ically defend our supplies. I didn't feature fending off needy folks, but we needed every ounce of food and weapons we had packed. There would be no sharing of our bounty despite the Lord's advice. That wasn't easy to rationalize, but I felt as though we were destined to bring a better future to these people by virtue of our bringing livestock northward. We had to get safely back to Texas to accomplish that goal. Fortunately, no one laid a hand on us, though they came close. It took some glaring eyes on our part to fend them off. That having been said, I did carry the Sharps carbine across my lap as a precaution. Spirit Talker had his hand gripped securely around the hilt of the knife in its beautiful new sheath.

I reined in Big Red at the fort entrance with Spirit Talker alongside. There was no sentry. That gave me a sense of the command structure or lack thereof. Spirit Talker and I exchanged concerned glances. "Is your commanding officer around?" I asked the first soldier we met upon entering the fort.

"Lieutenant be up yonder," he said, pointing to the other side of the parade ground. "Injuns not allowed," he added.

I gave him a cold hard stare and gently put my heels to Big Red's sides.

The soldier shrugged as he took in the buckskins and moccasins that Spirit Talker and I wore along with our rather substantial weaponry.

I reined in before the lieutenant but chose to remain in my saddle. It seemed to me that looking down on someone gave a sense of authority. We were looking to establish terms of discussion from a position of strength.

For his part, the lieutenant didn't appear to be much older than me. He'd shed his tunic as he pitched in to dig a hole for a fence post. A couple of soldiers stood by, seeming to mockingly tolerate the lieutenant's labors. The officer looked up at us and then at the two men beside him. He slowly became aware of his embarrassing predicament. "And that's how it's done," he said, emphatically gathering his wits. He handed the shovel to one of the observers who immediately went to work finishing the post hole. The episode was likely symptomatic of the level of morale at Fort Laramie.

"Just passing through, Lieutenant," I ventured, as he slipped back into his tunic and began to button it.

He fastened the buckle of his saber belt and gave us an appraising look. "I'm

Lieutenant Johnson. Can I help you?" he asked, apparently having sized us up as worthy of engagement.

I didn't figure to waste any time. "My name is Jack O'Toole, and this is my partner Spirit Talker of the Comanche nation. We reckon to be moving some prime Texas beeves and horses up this way next year," I stated.

The officer straightened up and gave Spirit Talker and me a penetrating look as though to ask whether we were serious.

I sized up his reaction before continuing. I wasn't sure how to ask my question without being disrespectful of the condition of the fort and its garrison.

"How many?" he ventured.

Clearly, I had stirred up interest. "At least five hundred head and maybe fifty horses. Would the Army pay market prices?" It was, as they say, an opening gambit.

"You didn't hear it from me, but rumor has it the fort will be strengthened next year," he offered in a low voice with a hand partially covering his mouth. "But, you should talk with the Indian Agent, Thomas Triss."

Unfortunately, Indian Agent Thomas Triss was off visiting with what he deemed friendly tribes, and no one knew how soon he figured to return. I scribbled a note for him to let him know that we planned to be back next year with plenty of longhorns for the government to purchase as part of the annuity to the area tribes. Hopefully, he'd be in a receptive frame of mind.

To my reckoning, the soldiers' morale might have been uplifted by the news, but I figured it couldn't be announced until the decision had been finalized. Driving livestock north was fraught with risk, and the uncertainty of a market served to increase that risk. "We appreciate you being straight with us, Lieutenant Johnson." I handed him the note to pass on to Triss.

"You heading back to Texas?" he asked in an attempt to be friendly. I think he was also beginning to visualize fresh steak dinners and decent horses.

We nodded.

"I'm from San Antonio," he offered.

I chanced a chuckle. "Then you'll appreciate Texas beef, sir," I responded. "I apologize for our short visit, but we have a long journey ahead. See you next year. Do give our best to Mr. Triss."

Johnson looked around him and sighed. I gathered he missed his Texas home. "I reckon I'll still be here." An accent crept into his voice, and he grinned. "Y'all come back, now, y'heah."

Spirit Talker and I turned our cayuses and headed out. There was no point extending our visit. The sooner we returned to Texas, the sooner our cattle venture could be realized.

———

MEMORIES of the poor souls surrounding Fort Laramie and the low morale of the soldiers within the fort were soon behind us. By now, we were three days from Fort Laramie and would soon be leaving the shores of the North Platte River to head due south. Ever more prairie-like landscapes made for faster travel. By my judgment, we would have little trouble driving cattle across this territory. The biggest challenges aside from hostile Indians would be the river crossings. Cattle were pretty decent swimmers, but drovers would need to keep them focused on crossing as opposed to lolling about drinking.

We rested at night but built no fires and took turns as sentry.

On the third night, Spirit Talker broke the silence. "Comanche no believe in Christ," he ventured. This had clearly been something he'd been mulling over during our near-noiseless travels and weighed heavily upon him.

"You are welcome at Rising Cross Ranch," I responded. I caught his appreciative smile as the moon shed its light upon his face.

"That not help Comanche."

I knew he was right. It gave me pause to wonder whether Blue Flower would accept our Christian faith.

It was as though Spirit Talker knew what I was thinking. "She believe," he assured me.

"What of Buffalo Hump?" I asked.

"*Ap* not sure," Spirit Talker responded partially in his Comanche tongue. Referring to his father as *ap* was out of respect.

"Can only plant seeds and see what grows, my brother," I thoughtfully counseled.

That seemed to satisfy Spirit Talker for the moment, and he lay back and fell asleep.

———

WE HAD ARISEN before dawn on the fourth day and rode ever-vigilantly across rolling hills and gentle valleys. Forage for our horses was plentiful and from the tops of the hills we were afforded views at great distances in the crystal-clear atmosphere. I was struck by the large herds of buffalo that we encountered. The beasts were impressive and ornery as could be. I knew there was no way I cared to take one on without my trusty Sharps, though Spirit Talker assured me that a well-placed arrow could bring one down. While he had taught me well, I hadn't the faith in my own bow and arrows to deliver a kill shot. In any case, a buffalo, or *tasiwoo,* could provide a family with meat, sinew, hide, and bone enough for weeks of survival. We were interested in smaller game to meet our meager needs.

We were perhaps a hundred yards from a herd of buffalo when Spirit Talker reined us up short and pointed to something in the distance ahead of us. "Cheyenne," he hissed. His venomous tone actually caught me by surprise.

Sure enough, a party of perhaps a dozen were barely visible a couple of miles to our south. There was no place to hide. If they spotted us, we would be at a great disadvantage. Blessedly, we were upwind so wouldn't be spooking their ponies with smell or sound. A ravine with a creek running through it lay ahead, but my instinct told me to avoid it. Several deer and some antelope were drinking, and a couple of hawks floated above. The Cheyenne very well could be looking for water and the game it attracted.

"Go there," said Spirit Talker, pointing to what appeared to be a forested area a mile or so to the west.

I nodded, and we picked up our pace. Big Red and Spirit Talker's pony seemed to sense our urgency, though they'd likely have loved a long thirst-quenching drink in the stream.

We reined in among a stand of red ash, trying our very best to become one with the trees. We dismounted and hitched our mounts to saplings. Big Red and the pony had been through this sort of drill before and knew to stay quiet. For our part, we sat cross-legged to wait out the Cheyenne threat. The sun was high, likely near midday. We were grateful for the mottled canopy of shade that combined with our tan buckskins tended to offer some camouflage.

I was feeling pretty proud of having avoided discovery. I should have remembered my pa's counsel that pride comes before the fall.

Spirit Talker's face remained deadly serious, as he observed the actions of the Cheyenne. He uncharacteristically squirmed just a tad, the only evidence of any special concern. I was about to say something, when he motioned to be silent. I had never seen him this concerned.

Rather than pursue the wildlife at the stream, the Cheyenne had turned toward our hiding place. So far as Spirit Talker could tell, they had not as yet discovered our presence. We counted eleven warriors. The odds of victory were decidedly in the hostiles favor should they spot us and decide to attack.

Spirit Talker pointed behind us. We had to go deeper into the stand of trees, perhaps all the way through, and then make a run for it when we ran out of cover. He led the way, taking a southeastward course with the sun to our right. We stayed low and moved as swiftly as possible through the low undergrowth. Our moccasins on the soft earth assured silent footfalls.

Blessedly, the Cheyenne were in no hurry to reach the shelter of the trees. Even more blessedly, winds began to kick up, harkening the coming of a sudden summer rain squall. Sure enough, dark clouds rolled in just about the time we emerged from the southern reach of the stand of ash. Being downwind, we could hear the voices of the Cheyenne as they sought shelter from the rain mixed with hail as the storm began its rhythmic cadence against the parched earth.

Much as I didn't feature being drenched, the rain

afforded us a great opportunity to make good our escape from the threat. Drying out our clothes and tack later was far preferable to our scalps drying on Cheyenne lances. We mounted up and rode our cayuses at a fast trot for a couple of miles. The squall soon passed over, and we stopped to rest our mounts and begin to dry out.

"Close," said Spirit Talker with a smile.

I expect we were fast becoming seasoned frontier travelers. I was about to say something to that effect when a motion nearby to my left caught my attention. I grabbed my bow and drew an arrow from my quiver. Rapidly nocking the arrow, I took careful aim, and shot a small doe. Fresh meat for dinner was to be ours this night. I looked over at Spirit Talker. He smiled his approval, upon which I dismounted, field-dressed the deer, and hoisted it over Big Red's rump. We soon found a sheltered spot where we could build a small cooking fire and spend the night.

It turned out to be our last cooking fire for a few days, as we found ourselves traveling through country that seemed to teem with threats.

SEVENTEEN

DANGEROUS ENCOUNTERS

WE WERE three weeks into our journey back to Rising Cross Ranch. I judged that to be roughly halfway home, as we were a day south of what I figured to have been the Arkansas River. We were leaving the lands of the Pawnee and headed into Kiowa country.

We strove to remain ever alert to our surroundings, but the lack of further threats was occasionally challenging our cautiousness. I suppose that better than three weeks on the trail will tend to do that.

I was figuring we wouldn't see a Pawnee, when we crested a hill to find ourselves facing about a dozen Pawnee hunters.

Spirit Talker instantly raised his hand as a gesture of peace, and I followed suit.

The Pawnee hunters were a sad-looking lot, their appearance did not cause us any fear. Coupled with the talismans gifted us by Running Waters, we rightly felt that we had nothing to fear. We had learned from George that in the early 1800s the Pawnee suffered from cholera, measles, and smallpox epidemics as well as devastating raids on villages by Sioux and Cheyenne war parties.

The Pawnee were loosely related to the Caddo and Wichita tribes that lived in Texas. The Pawnee name was an anglicized version of *panis*, the French Canadian term for captured Indians used as slaves. In an 1833 treaty with the United States, the tribe ceded all of their lands south of the Platte River as a common hunting ground for the Pawnee and other supposedly friendly tribes. Importantly, the treaty forbade the Pawnee from going to war with any neighboring tribes and to defer to the United States government to settle any disputes. Unsurprisingly, this severely weakened what had been one of the largest tribes on the Great Plains. To retaliate against Sioux or Cheyenne raiders meant violating the treaty. A recent treaty guaranteed the Pawnee the protection of the US Army, but the fort garrisons in their territory were little better than what we had encountered at Fort Laramie.

The lead Pawnee rode forward cautiously, especially eyeing Spirit Talker. The Comanche were not friends with the Pawnee, and he was apparently trying to determine Spirit Talker's tribal affiliation. He raised his hand in peace and spoke slowly in English. "Me Man Who Steals Horses, chief of Pawnee," he informed us.

I breathed a sigh of relief that we could use English. "I'm Jack O'Toole," I said and motioned toward my Comanche brother. "This is Spirit Talker." I decided to not use his Comanche name.

We had quickly revealed the talismans that Running Waters had given us, but there was really no need for their protection.

Man Who Steals Horses quickly figured out that we were no threat. "We hunt buffalo for Bluecoats," he offered with a smile. Apparently, they were serving as scouts and had been detailed to bring in fresh game. He glanced at our talismans and smiled. "How Running Waters?"

I was fully caught off guard.

Spirit Talker nodded. "Carvings tell story, Jack. Is story of Running Waters," he said with a grin.

"George and Running Waters are well," I shared with Man Who Steals Horses. "They adopted daughter named Topsannah. Have big ranch on North Platte River."

Man Who Steals Horses shook his head. "Many enemies in North Platte. George strong," he said. He smiled. "Running Waters give George many children." It was as much hope as assurance.

We dismounted. Despite our haste to get home, we would pass a pipe and enjoy a bit of conversation. It would be a great opportunity to obtain information about the trail ahead and the dangers we might face.

With much goodwill, we gained an overview of what lay ahead of us over the next several days. Watering holes, Kiowa encampments, best river crossings, and more were shared by our Pawnee friends. The Pawnee offered us a packhorse, but we turned it down with the explanation that we had to travel as light as possible.

We likely could have chatted for hours, but Spirit Talker and I were intent on moving along, and these Pawnee had a hunt to finish. They seemed especially impressed at our intention of driving beeves north to Wyoming.

In the final throes of conversation, we did not hear the rattlesnake. As Spirit Talker went to get up, the serpent struck his high-topped moccasin. The snake's venom-filled fangs barely scratched his skin through the protective buckskin.

A Pawnee quickly dispatched the rattlesnake.

Spirit Talker sat down and pulled off his moccasin to examine the wound. Venom dripped down his ankle. Superficial as it was, there could be enough venom in the wound to make him ill.

Man Who Steals Horses retrieved a bag from his pony and began mixing a poultice. In short order, he applied it to Spirit Talker's wound and wrapped it in place. The Pawnee were proving to be exceptionally efficient. "Heal fast," he assured us.

"No pain," said Spirit Talker. He was concerned but seemed confident in the treatment given him by the Pawnee.

"Tell Comanche brothers that Pawnee help warrior," laughed Man Who Steals Horses. This reminder that the Pawnee and Comanche were mortal enemies made for plenty of irony in his words. He then grew serious. "Spirit Talker wise. Must help his people make peace with Whites."

Spirit Talker nodded. The Pawnee had delivered an accurate counsel, but he knew that the path to accomplishing an enduring peace would yet be littered with death and destruction.

I pulled the mountain lion pelt from behind my saddle and handed it to Spirit Talker.

We exchanged a glance of understanding, and Spirit Talker held the mountain lion skin out as a gift to Man Who Steals Horses.

The Pawnee hunter looked first at Spirit Talker and then at me. "Spirit of mountain lion strong with you. You keep. Next year, you give Pawnee cattle." With that, he motioned his fellow hunters toward their ponies, and they were soon moving off to their hunt.

Spirit Talker slipped his moccasin on. The rattler strike had been a close call.

"God keeps watching over us, my brother," I offered.

"God strong medicine," he responded. "*Sunipu*."

I smiled. Indeed.

———

THE LANDSCAPE HAD BECOME DECIDEDLY FLAT, as vast grasslands extended as far as we could see. We cautiously approached what I reckoned to be the Cimarron River. The crossing the Pawnee had directed us to was at a broad portion of the river and was quite shallow. As we rode out from the north bank, we could see plenty of fish. I was tempted to catch a couple of trout for dinner. As I reined in Big Red to consider a bit of fishing, Spirit Talker pointed animatedly downstream a hundred yards or so.

"*Wasápe!*" Spirit Talker announced.

Indeed, there was a huge grizzly. In between swipes at fish, he looked our way and took a sniff or two. On the south shore was a sow and two cubs feeding on what the giant boar had already caught.

I motioned to Spirit Talker that we ought to move on.

My Comanche brother was already urging his pony on.

The bear had other ideas. Suddenly he arose on his hind legs and let out a bellow. His thick brown fur rippled as he shook his frame.

Big Red reared and nearly dumped me in the Cimarron.

With that, the bear must have decided that we were a threat. He dropped to all fours and came splashing through the water in our direction.

I dug my heels into Big Red's sides and Spirit Talker did likewise with his pony. I'd heard that bears could run right fast, but this grizzly was blazing fast. Our mounts were slowed by the steep slippery bank on the south shore of the river.

Spirit Talker turned with bow and nocked arrow in hand and let fly at the charging bear. The angry beast didn't even pause, as the arrow struck deep into his immense chest.

I drew the Sharps carbine and slipped in a cartridge. The bear was now so close there was no time to aim. The blast from the muzzle echoed across the hills. My 52-caliber bullet brought the bear to an abrupt, skidding halt kicking rocks in all directions. He stood grabbing at the wound in his chest. His bellow brought up blood.

Spirit Talker embedded his second arrow into the grizzly's throat.

Another bellow. The bear pawed helplessly at us. He took another step, made a faltering swipe at Big Red, grunted, and fell in a heap. I put another slug into the hairy monster just to be certain of his demise. Big Red snorted and breathed heavily.

We looked off at the sow and her cubs. She bawled at us before shuttling them away.

"Bear grease good," said Spirit Talker with decided understatement. "Bear meat even better," he added, laughing nervously.

I looked upward and said a few silent words of thanks to my Maker.

Spirit Talker nodded. "Amen," he added.

I scanned the area. "May as well camp here," I suggested. The access to water and shelter of a few trees made for a good site. I did worry that the gunshot from my Sharps carbine might have been heard. In fact, it likely had reached a few Indian ears. We would have to keep a good lookout.

With that, we set up camp and began butchering the bear. We harvested meat and fat. While we had no time to make bear jerky, the fresh meat would sustain us for a couple of days and the fat was a valuable treasure. We made short work of skinning the beast. A bearskin blanket would be welcome come winter.

————

I MUST SAY, the bear meat was excellent. It tasted a tad sweeter than venison, though was just about as gamey. We did our best to render the fat to make bear grease, as I'd heard that it made the very best natural lubricant. Our challenge was what to store it in. Spirit Talker was at his inventive best, as he fashioned a fully adequate container from a red ash branch. It would do until a proper tin could be found.

Full bellies translated to lethargy. I felt as though I could sleep for days. With Kiowa to be on the lookout for, it was an ongoing battle to stay alert.

EIGHTEEN
HOSTILES!

WE WERE DRAWING EVER CLOSER to the Texas border. Sticking with George's advice, we'd traveled farther to the east. In fact, we were about a three-day hard ride due east of Adobe Walls. The country was mostly rolling prairie. Far off to the west and lying in a bluish-gray haze on the horizon stood the granite peaks of the Wichita Mountains. Before us lay the rich bottomlands of the Red River Valley interspersed with forested areas. It was a bountiful landscape by my humble estimation.

My mind increasingly wandered off to thoughts of Blue Flower. By the time I showed up at the Penateka Comanche village with fifteen ponies, would she have waited for me? There were plenty of young warriors who coveted marrying the daughter of a Comanche war chief. I held out assurance that Buffalo Hump was still saving his only daughter for me.

I think Spirit Talker knew what was on my mind, as he occasionally poked fun at me about his sister.

———

THE SUN HANGING EVER CLOSER to the horizon brought me out of my daydreams. We found a naturally defensible spot about a half-day ride north of the Red River. It offered plentiful water from a small stream and a stand of trees on higher ground with a clear view of our surroundings.

We decided it was too risky to build a fire. Our supply of jerky and pemmican was running low, and we had at least two more weeks of travel across rough frontier to reach Rising Cross Ranch. Blessedly, the Pawnee poultice applied to Spirit Talker's rattlesnake bite appeared to be working, as the wound was healing, and there was no swelling or hint of infection.

"Jack feel eyes?" asked Spirit Talker.

I nodded, glad to not be alone in the feeling that we were being watched. If so, it was most likely Kiowa. We'd had good and bad experiences with them. "Why have they not attacked?"

Spirit Talker laughed as he took a final bite of jerky and lay back on his blanket. He looked up at the emerging stars as darkness began to envelop us. A coyote howled far off in the distance. "We *sunipu*," he assured me. "They *kuya akatu*, much fear."

I chuckled and unrolled my own blanket. "Big medicine," I chortled. It seemed always to come to that with the Indians. Their culture of nature-based deities offered no relief from the threats surrounding them. There was no mercy, no forgiveness, no love in their gods. Shamans and prophets found it easy to whip up tribal emotions into frenzies aimed at overcoming fear. Warriors would be assured that enemy weapons would disintegrate or never penetrate their bodies. Little wonder that attacks would often turn into retreats after only one or two warriors were killed. The shaman would cover himself by assuring doubters that something out of his control interfered with the protective *sunipu* he'd placed over the warriors. However, those that encountered Spirit Talker and me were convinced that we possessed truly big medicine, big *sunipu*. It didn't take long for word of our power to spread among the tribes. Pity they weren't aware of the God from whom we received our strength.

All this having been said, we instinctively knew there would be war parties led by warriors intent on proving their strength.

———

WE PRACTICED our usual routine of taking turns keeping watch. The clear starlit sky and half-moon meant that we could see, but any enemy could, too.

The very fact that I knew the hostiles were lurking out there somewhere kept me alert. After months of travel and surviving all manner of threats, I had no intention of falling victim to an attack we didn't know was coming. I figured the Kiowa—I was pretty sure it was those savages—had not yet mustered the medicine to overcome the *sunipu* I represented. They were also naturally quite leery of my Sharps carbine and its accuracy at great distances. I assumed they might have been aware that Spirit Talker was the son of a Comanche war chief, but counting coup on such a prize target would have shown great bravery.

The mournful howl of a coyote broke the stillness.

"No *kutseena*," whispered Spirit Talker from beneath his blanket.

I agreed. I'd been on the frontier long enough to distinguish the Indian's best efforts at mimicking from the real thing. *"Tabu,"* I said. They were cowards, and that was to our benefit.

"Kiowa *kaahaniitu*," Spirit Talker observed.

"Deception? *Kaahaniitu?*" I asked. What might that mean? How might the Kiowa deceive us?

"Sleep. No attack tonight," advised Spirit Talker.

———

THE FIRST RAYS of sunlight had no sooner splashed across my face, than I heard a rustling sound. I glanced at where Spirit Talker had been sleeping, but he had already arisen and was dealing with some disturbance close to our camp.

I sat up and took a quick scan of my surroundings. The hard ground had not been kind to my young body, but I managed to get up. After the sounds of the night and with Spirit Talker off in the nearby brush somewhere, I checked the load in my Colt. I thought to grab the Sharps carbine, but some premonition made me choose my bow and arrows instead. A bit of personal reconnaissance now seemed to be in order.

First off, I made certain that Big Red and the pony were accounted for. It was reassuring to know that they were where they were supposed to be. I loaded our gear on the horses while keeping an ever-watchful eye. I decided it was best to not mount up, so took the leads of both cayuses and headed toward where I'd heard Spirit Talker.

I quickly drew close to where Spirit Talker was hovering over a Kiowa warrior who seemed to be injured. Spirit Talker's words about deception still lingered in my mind.

Spirit Talker looked up at me and rolled his eyes. He

then nodded in the direction of the crest of a hill perhaps fifty yards away. He held up five fingers. It was clear that he was pretending to help the Kiowa while figuring what sort of trap they had in mind.

I ducked low and took a path toward the hill but well clear of Spirit Talker and the Kiowa decoy. By my calculations, their strategy was to weaken our *sunipu* by splitting us up. Well, we could be equally deceptive. My not joining Spirit Talker with the supposedly injured warrior would encourage them to think they had succeeded. I was well hidden among the brush that was over my head. They likely had no idea that I was moving toward them. I nocked an arrow, so as to be at the ready. My moccasins enabled me to move stealthily.

Unbeknownst to me, Spirit Talker had eliminated the Kiowa decoy with a deft stroke of his knife. He'd noted where I was headed, so moved in the opposite direction such that we would catch the Kiowa in their own trap with a pincer movement.

I heard a rustling in the brush not ten yards ahead of me. I brought up my bow with an arrow ready and waited for the Kiowa to appear. They didn't disappoint.

The wide-eyed expression on the first warrior's face gave testament to his total surprise. The last thing he heard was the twang of my bow and whoosh of the arrow I put deep into his chest. The Kiowa plan had gone totally awry. A second warrior stepped past his fallen brother and was about to level his lance at me when an arrow from Spirit Talker ended his threat. Another Kiowa shot an arrow toward me, but I was already on the move, and he missed. By now, the fight was at closer quarters, and I brought my Colt into play. A bullet dispatched another warrior and still another fell to Spirit Talker's arrows. An eerie silence followed.

"*Kwakuru*," said Spirit Talker, emerging from the brush. "All *kooitu*."

The Kiowa band had been defeated. Indeed, all the warriors were dead. I actually felt saddened. Squaws would never see their husbands again and children would never again play with their fathers. God had used us to punish evil, but was it that clear? As often happened, the Kiowa's gods had let them down. The false incantations of their shamans had failed them. I so wished I had an opportunity to tell them of the one God of love and redemption.

Spirit Talker and I mounted up. With nary a backward glance, we would leave the dead Kiowa warriors for the buzzards and as a warning to others with ill intentions. How many more would die before they accepted the coming waves of settlers? Settlers moving west were hungry for a new life, new opportunity. Pity that it was at the expense of the Indians.

As we resumed our journey southward with Spirit Talker riding beside me, he turned toward me. "Kiowa no listen to God," he said flatly.

"How's that?" I asked.

Spirit Talker shook his head. "Kiowa *kaahaniitu*. Spirit Talker offer God to save Kiowa. No listen."

It hit me that Spirit Talker had offered a chance at redemption to the Kiowa warrior. When he refused, he had no choice but to kill him for fear he might warn the others. "Not all understand God's way," I said.

Spirit Talker shook his head. He looked off into the distance ahead. "Blue Flower knows God."

The observation after having fought off Kiowa mere moments before blindsided me. Comparing Blue Flower's faith to the refusal by a Kiowa warrior was a tad extreme. I found myself having to quickly recover my wits. "Do you think so?" I responded with a hopeful expression writ large across my face.

Spirit Talker nodded. "Home soon. You see." Then he laughed. "Fifteen ponies," he chided.

I must have turned a deep crimson as I felt the blood surge to my face and neck.

Home was tantalizingly close. We'd soon cross the Brazos River and be swimming across the Guadalupe.

NINETEEN
HOME

WE'D CROSSED the broad and shallow Brazos River days back. Crossing the Colorado River was our sign that we were nearly home. Another couple of days, and the Guadalupe would bring us home.

We made camp about a day's ride north of the Guadalupe in the northern reaches of the hill country. Ever more stands of juniper and live oak fed our anticipation of arriving home. We felt secure enough to make a cooking fire. Spirit Talker had shot a rabbit, so we'd enjoy fresh roasted meat.

The sun danced tantalizingly on the horizon, and we were enjoying a tasty bit of that rabbit when a deep gravelly voice came to us from the shadows.

"*Salud* the camp!" announced the voice with a decidedly Spanish accent.

Spirit Talker and I looked at each other. A mutual sense of trepidation enveloped us.

I stood with Colt in my holster and hand gripping the Sharps carbine. "Who are you and what's your business?"

Silence, then the click of the hammer of a gun being drawn back.

I motioned Spirit Talker to move off to a stand of junipers with his bow and a nocked arrow at the ready. I lifted the Sharps carbine, cocked it, and pointed the muzzle in the direction of the voice.

"Move a muscle, and Carlos will blow your head off," came the voice.

Despite the morning chill, I felt beads of nervous perspiration on my brow.

"*Carlos, toma su arma,*" ordered the voice.

I sensed movement to my left and saw a short man with beady little eyes, drooping mustache, and big hat approaching hesitantly to disarm me. He held a gun but foolishly aimed it downward. He wasn't about to blow anyone's head off. I sensed that there was no way we'd be talking our way out of this situation. I took a chance that there were only two of these apparent bandits. I swung the Sharps and fired point blank at Carlos.

Carlos's eyes bulged as he looked down at the hole in the center of his chest. His mouth opened, but no sound came forth.

I heard the dreaded click of a hammer on a frizzen, heard a blast, and went over backward as something plowed into my chest.

Almost simultaneous with the blast from my rifle and subsequent gunfire from the shadows came a thud and a grunt as Spirit Talker's arrow found a home with the source of the gunshot.

"*Madre de Dios,*" came a near-muffled sound. Then, in a near whisper, "*me muero.*" Silence followed. It was a chilling reminder of the finality of death.

Spirit Talker emerged from the trees and kneeled beside me near the fire.

I was lying on my back with the air pretty much knocked from me.

"*Sunipu!*" declared Spirit Talker as he pulled the New Testament from my pocket. A musket ball was embedded in its pages. "*Sunipu,*" he said again in near disbelief.

I stared at the book as he held it in front of me. "God is good," I managed to gasp.

Spirit Talker simply nodded.

I caught my breath and worked my way into a sitting position.

"Is Good Book," observed Spirit Talker, not realizing he was describing what many folks called the Bible.

By now, I'd pretty much gathered my wits. It had been a close call, and I said a silent prayer to God for sparing me once again. "Guess it'd be right to bury them, whoever they are," I urged. Burial was actually a must obligation, as the bodies could attract unwelcome guests. The howl of a distant coyote was an all-too-real reminder.

We found the body of the man who had spoken from the shadows.

I found a pouch beside him and opened it, as I sought a name to go with the body. A card in the pouch read "Theodore Alfonso Waters" but gave no further information other than Brownsville, Texas. "At least we know his name," I said, assuming the pouch was indeed his. For all we knew, it could have been stolen.

We had one small shovel between us, but our fortune was that the sandy soil was reasonably soft. We made short work of the burial, before taking any time to think on all that had just happened within spitting distance of Rising Cross Ranch. We returned to our fire and sat silently.

"What was that about?" I asked absentmindedly.

"Bad men," said Spirit Talker with a tone of finality.

"What did they want from us?" I retorted, though my real question was what made them bad.

"Horses," responded Spirit Talker. "Maybe food?" He didn't know either.

Why had they not simply approached our camp? What made them so desperate? What drove folks to evil deeds? I gazed thoughtfully into the flickering flames of our fire. Answers were not coming to me. Afore long, I found myself staring at embers while Spirit Talker had fallen asleep.

———

WE PASSED my favorite fishing spot on the Guadalupe River. It brought back memories of the day my pa had sent me off to fish, and while I was hooking bass, the Comanche killed my parents and a brother and a sister. Could I ever shake the scene from my mind? Did I want to? From it had come a strengthening of my faith. Anger, guilt, and vengeance were replaced by forgiveness and mercy. And God delivered my surviving brother and sister from the clutches of the Comanche, forged my friendship with Spirit Talker, and sent me a mentor in George.

I was determined not to get emotional as Rising Cross Ranch came into view. The elation for both me and Spirit Talker felt akin to a spiny cactus or a porcupine pricking at our senses. The first hint of having reached the ranch came from our horses. Big Red's ears went on full alert as he surely sensed the mares awaiting his return.

"There it is, my brother," I announced to Spirit Talker

as the cabin came into view. It felt great to be home again.

"Big," responded Spirit Talker.

I did a double-take and realized that Isaac had not only built a place for he, Sarah, and baby Jack, but had added to my own cabin. They had entered my life as squatters on Rising Cross Ranch and had become a true blessing to me and my kin.

"Plenty *puuka*," he said with a sweep of his hand across the rolling prairie, having observed a couple of dozen horses.

I had a feeling he was already beginning to pick out horses that Buffalo Hump would accept. But there were a few beeves grazing in the far pasture. They sported impressive horn spreads worthy of their longhorn moniker. I looked forward to inspecting them up close, but that would have to wait.

I persuaded Spirit Talker to spend a few days at my ranch before we headed off to his people. It would also give me time to gather fifteen horses. Despite Spirit Talker's observation, I suspected that we'd have to supplement the existing herd. There were plenty of horses running wild, so I was optimistic.

As I was about to respond to his comment about there being plenty of horses, my eyes fell on my brother Buck and sister Kate running toward me as fast as their legs could muster. I fairly leaped from my saddle to sweep them into my arms.

"Jack...Jack...you're home," were Kate's words muffled in the folds of my buckskin shirt.

Buck simply hung on to me with all the strength his six-year-old arms could deliver.

Spirit Talker simply sat silently waiting to be noticed.

After what seemed forever, Kate broke free and looked up at the Comanche who'd been instrumental in freeing her and Buck from captivity. "Wild Horse!" she cried.

Spirit Talker slid from the pinto's back and stretched his arms out in greeting. "Is Mukwooru now; means Spirit Talker to you, young one," he chided as she slipped into his arms.

Buck finally tore himself away from me to take in our arrival. "Though you might never get back," he said in wonderment while gazing at the two buckskin-clad, travel-toughened men standing before him.

I found myself taken with the realization that Spirit Talker and I had matured quite a bit while on our journey. Encounters with wild people and wildlife along with the rigors of the landscape will tend to do that. We had a seemingly endless supply of tales to share around the hearth after dinners. Guess I liked George's tradition of such family gatherings.

"Let's head home," I finally said, lifting Kate and Buck up into my saddle. Spirit Talker and I led the horses toward the cabin. Of course, Buck was happy as a bee in clover riding Big Red.

Soon enough, Isaac and Sarah looked up from their chores and saw us approaching. Isaac dropped his saw, dusted himself off, and headed to greet us. Sarah stopped her butter churning, wiped buttery hands on her apron, and followed close behind her husband. Smiles were a mix of joy and relief at our safe return.

After a round of hugs, we all settled into an easy walk to the cabin.

"My oh my, Isaac. Look at what you've done," I said while looking admiringly at the large room he'd added to our cabin.

Isaac uncharacteristically blushed. "It was Sarah's idea," he confessed.

"I figured you might be needing it," added Sarah. Unsaid was her thinking that I might be wanting a private space with Blue Flower.

I might never figure out how women think, and Sarah was surely a step ahead of me.

"How's baby Jack?" I asked.

"Wait until you see him. He's growing faster than Texas catclaw," she responded with a broad smile.

I was taken with her use of colloquialisms. She was fast becoming so typical of frontier settlers who were so very fond of the folksy use of metaphors whether to describe conditions or offer advice. My ma once described a passing salesman by saying, "Why he's so tight, his boots squeak." She was put off by a local preacher, saying, "His halo fits too tight." My momentary reminiscing ended quickly with Buck calling out for help in getting dismounted from Big Red. I helped him down, then turned to Isaac. "Thanks so much for looking after Rising Cross while we were gone. Was there any trouble?"

Isaac's face went serious for a moment. "Nothing we couldn't handle. Texas Rangers came by a few times to check on us."

Spirit Talker and I stole a quick glance at each other. Having the Texas Rangers around was reassuring but left us to wonder what might be brewing that caused them to be active in the region.

I looked over at the barn and corral. They had been kept in great shape. It reinforced how impressed and blessed I was with Isaac having taken responsibility for looking after the ranch.

Kate pulled at my arm. "Can I take the horses to the barn?" she pleaded.

"Me too," chimed in Buck.

"How about we go with you?" I responded. "We have to unpack our gear." I earnestly wanted to peek inside the cabin first but had little choice but to yield to my young siblings. Kate even brought some lumps of sugar for the horses. They sure had earned it.

We unloaded our travel gear, curried the horses, and set them loose in the corral. Big Red already had his eyes on a couple of mares as he pranced around. Spirit Talker's pinto simply watched.

After settling our cayuses, we all shared in hauling our outfits to the cabin. The first step through the door just about took my breath away. It was downright spotless and done up about as comfy as could ever be imagined.

Kate and Sarah had fixed the place up right fine. The original floor plan had been a single great room roughly twenty by twelve feet and divided by hung tarpaulins into a kitchen and eating area and a sort of bedroom. The tarpaulins had been replaced by a wooden divider. With a theatrical sweeping gesture, Kate waved me to a new door at the rear of the cabin that led to the new bedroom. It was right spacious by frontier standards and even had its own entry door. The windows, such as they were, were mere vertical gunports. Sadly, we still had to be prepared to defend our home. Not more than a dozen feet from the door was a convenience contraption folks called an outhouse. Well, I was speechless.

Spirit Talker stood behind me mouth agape.

The room featured an ample bed, a beautiful rocking chair that Isaac had apparently fashioned, and even a chest of drawers.

Spirit Talker finally caught my eye and gave me a look that said Blue Flower would be a happy wife.

———

THE NEXT FEW evenings featured Spirit Talker and I gathering everyone together at the hearth after dinner and sharing tales of our adventures. Buck was totally taken with all we had encountered, and I sensed a bit of wanderlust developing in his young bones. Kate and Sarah were duly horrified at some of what we had to deal with but, like strong frontier women, strove not to show their distress. Isaac spent the time whittling toy figurines while taking in our stories.

I must admit that I did not sleep in the new bed. Maybe it was God bending my ear, but I was figuring to wait and christen it with my future bride.

It had become evident that Isaac was quite a craftsman. He seemed to work magic with wood. That he had managed the ranch while building out my cabin and caring for the livestock fully impressed me. Isaac was fascinated with my bow and arrow and determined to fashion his own. He listened intently to Spirit Talker and me as to the best materials and the processes for making the bow and arrows.

Sarah, meanwhile, was like a mother to Kate, as she taught my sister all sorts of household skills in addition to tending the family garden.

If there was a definition of civilization, Rising Cross Ranch seemed to be that very definition. I chuckled to myself at the thought of Rising Cross being a town that had a schoolhouse, church, and post office.

———

BLUE FLOWER LISTENED INTENTLY. She only picked up tidbits of the conversation between the scout and her father. She so wished she could draw closer.

"Spirit Talker...*tosa*," one scout whispered to Buffalo Hump with one hand covering his mouth so as not to be easily overheard.

The scout went into greater detail, but Blue Flower was unable to hear.

Buffalo Hump nodded. The report of the scout offered no surprises. His son was still with the White man. It both gratified and concerned him, as he sensed that Spirit Talker's falling into the *tosa* religion with its single all-powerful deity was another sign toward the eventual loss of traditional Comanche culture.

Blue Flower heard enough to feel an involuntary tingle course its way up her spine, as though all her nerve endings were afire. Her heart raced. Jack was not far off.

Buffalo Hump and the scout exchanged more information and then parted with the chief directing him to continue to watch his son but not intervene.

"*Ap?*" asked Blue Flower, trying to contain her excitement.

The chief's facial expression belied any concerns. "Spirit Talker come," he shared. Then, he couldn't help but smile, "Jack...and *puukas!*"

Blue Flower had been dreaming of Jack's arrival with the fifteen horses. Her father's assurance brought unbounded joy to her heart. She gave her father a hug, then backed away upon realizing she was showing affection in a public place.

Buffalo Hump nodded. It was okay. He might never fully understand the thinking of his son and daughter, but he understood the power of love. This warrior chief who had exacted his share of dealing frontier death, torturing captives, burning entire towns, and lifting scalps still had a heart beating under his breast. The family unit was essential to the future of his Penateka Comanche. He nevertheless had not fully accommodated his son taking up with a *tosa* and daughter wishing to marry that same one. What he saw as the *tosa* God seemed all powerful; more powerful even than the Comanche deities. Jack O'Toole's *sunipu* was impressive, as Spirit Talker had borne witness. Still, he was unable to fully grasp this religion that his children were taking into their very souls. "Prepare yourself, Blue Flower," were his parting words, as he lifted the entry flap of the teepee and ducked inside.

TWENTY
SERIOUS BUSINESS

A MERE WEEK had passed since our arrival from the journey to the North Platte country, and we began to pull together sufficient supplies for the ride to Spirit Talker's village.

Spirit Talker was anxious to be heading back to his village but waited patiently for me to be ready. He helped cut fifteen of the best horses from the growing herd. "Have horses. We go?" he asked as much as pleaded.

I had already discussed with everyone at Rising Cross Ranch the preparation for next year's venture to Fort Laramie. We would need to find a trail boss and hire drovers. Most importantly, I would need to gather beeves —better than five hundred head. And more horses would be a must. A single drover might use as many as three horses in a day. With half a dozen drovers, that meant at least twenty cayuses in the cattle drive remuda. Needless to say but I will, the cattle business was already a tad distracting from family.

"We go soon?" Spirit Talker asked his question.

I ashamedly realized I hadn't been paying attention. "Got serious business to talk about. We go soon," I assured Spirit Talker. As much as anything, his reminder brought me back to dealing with the here and now. Spirit Talker had family to return to, and I needed to be sensitive to that.

I did manage to learn where I was likely to find a trail boss. Seemed that Bandera, roughly a one day ride south of Kerrville, was becoming a gathering place for what folks had begun to call cowboys. Having been advised by George to seek out the Mexican cowboys, or *vaqueros*, I reckoned my needs would be met.

There were just enough ranches springing up that, while gathering a sizable herd might not be easy, it was a realistic possibility. I hadn't figured on competition from other cattle outfits, so I would have to deal with that upon my return from Spirit Talker's village. George had also counseled establishment of a banking relationship. Doggone, but driving cattle was going to be complicated, a major undertaking. I also hadn't counted on the challenge of folks placing their trust in a teen. I'd cross that bridge when I came to it. Reckoned I'd have some proving to do.

———

TIME WAS WASTING. We really had to get Spirit Talker home and, most importantly...well, there was Blue Flower.

The evening before our departure, Spirit Talker and I found ourselves alone in the barn pulling together supplies. I held up a beautiful coat that Sarah had fashioned as a gift to Buffalo Hump. Isaac had carved a beautiful pipe and a flute for gifts. I looked out at Big Red prancing around the corral. The big stallion had a sense of upcoming adventures.

"What should I expect?" I asked, referring to marrying Blue Flower. I was aware that weddings in the Anglo culture could be quite elaborate events. What of the Comanche? Plus, it had occurred to me that a Christian wedding might be necessary to legitimize the marriage.

Spirit Talker laughed. "You give fifteen *puuka* to Buffalo Hump," explained my Comanche brother trying hard to be serious. He laughed again. "Buffalo Hump give Blue Flower. Jack *kuhmabai*."

"That's all?" I asked. "*Kuhmabai*," rolled off my tongue, the Comanche word for married.

"Blue Flower wear pretty dress," Spirit Talker added with a shrug and another laugh. He was quite taken with my distress over the lack of ceremony.

It seemed to me more like the purchase one might encounter at a general store or a livestock auction.

"Jack spend three or four days in village," Spirit Talker advised. He was advising that this must not be a quick visit, even though there was much to do toward planning next year's cattle drive. He looked at me and sensed my anxiety. Spirit Talker finally smiled knowingly. "Spirit Talker bless marriage as under God."

I exhaled, finally satisfied that Spirit Talker's blessing would make the union acceptable to God.

Satisfied that we need only load packs on our pack-horse and saddle up, we strolled from the barn. The corral was filled near overflowing with the horses we would be taking to Buffalo Hump. We had also decided to make a gift of the bearskin to the chief. Kate and Buck had been especially fascinated with our tale of the bear attack, and I could tell they'd have liked to have made a carpet of the bearskin. I had to convince them that it was better to give than receive, and God intended that we give the bearskin as a gift.

The air was fresh as a gentle breeze floated over the prairie. The sound of hoofbeats broke the surrounding peacefulness.

Texas Ranger Captain Benton and his company came galloping into our barnyard, reining in with a cloud of dust. "Welcome home, Mr. O'Toole!" he shouted over the din of neighing horses and Rangers barking commands.

I gave him a welcoming nod. "Pull up a spell," I invited him.

He didn't dismount. "Sorry, O'Toole. Can't be dallying. Looking for some Kiowa hostiles north of here." He scanned the ranch. "Seems all is at peace," he said, then glanced at Spirit Talker.

I didn't like the squinty judgmental look in his eyes. "Yes it is, Captain."

He couldn't hold himself back. "See you're still hanging with that redskin," he blurted.

Spirit Talker looked at me questioningly.

I seethed inside but was determined to not let the captain's prejudice get to me. "He's my brother, Captain," I said, then had second thoughts. "Thanks for stopping by to check on Rising Cross Ranch, but I suggest you get to chasing those Kiowa before I let Spirit Talker here take your scalp." I added a bit of a chuckle to take the edge off my comment.

Benton's eyes grew large for a moment. He got the message. "Y'all have a good day," he finally said as he turned his horse and motioned for his company of Texas Rangers to follow him.

As the dust cleared, I turned to Spirit Talker. "I think

he got the message, my brother," I said with a big grin. "His sort of people take extra time to understand."

Spirit Talker shook his head. "Is sad. They say all equal under God, but they not show by action. Tongues forked like snake, like *wutsutsuki*."

My Comanche brother's response was all-too well put. All I could do was nod.

———

"YOU THINK JUST the two of you can handle all those horses?" asked Isaac as he scanned the small herd.

It seemed clear to me that he was concerned that we'd be attractive targets for thieving Indians or bandits. With a nearly three-day travel time through rough country, we would surely be vulnerable. I looked over at Spirit Talker. "They'll follow Big Red anywhere." I laughed.

Spirit Talker shrugged. "No worry. *Sunipu*."

By my estimation, he was relying a bit too much on *sunipu*. I fully believed that God would see us through, but sensed there was more to Spirit Talker's assurance than he was letting on.

As we tightened the cinches on our saddles, Kate appeared at my side. She handed me a warm package of something wrapped in cloth. "Hurry home safe, brother," she said.

I sniffed at the cloth-wrapped bundle. "Cornbread!" I whispered as though it was our secret.

"Share with Spirit Talker," she laughingly admonished and kissed me lightly on the cheek.

I held her hand as she slowly took a step back. As I looked upon her, I felt so grateful, so blessed, that we'd saved her from the ravages of the heathen Comanche.

God willing, we'd all have a wonderful life ahead of us. My brief idyll was interrupted by Buck tapping my leg.

"Can I come?" asked Buck. He'd already pestered me endlessly about the trip.

"Like I've told you, Buck. We need men here at Rising Cross. You must help Isaac."

"But..." he persisted.

"Buck!" I said firmly. "I promise we'll go on an adventure."

My little brother had far too much of me in him. Loving as home was, he'd bust out as soon as he was old enough...maybe before. He'd even snuck out and practiced with my bow and arrows, enough so that I asked Isaac to make him a bow to suit his height.

Spirit Talker was mounted and ready to go. "Come, Jack," he urged.

I thanked Isaac and Sarah again and swung into the saddle. I felt Big Red shudder with excitement under me. I must admit, a sensation of anticipated adventure coursed through me. I turned the big stallion and headed our herd out toward the Guadalupe River.

The cabin and waving hands soon faded from sight, and we focused on the trail ahead. Our immediate goal was to reach the Pinta Trail before sundown.

TWENTY-ONE
TRAIL TO THE FUTURE

SPIRIT TALKER and I held to the emotions wrapped around anticipation of our arrival at the Penateka Comanche village. We had traveled no more than a dozen miles, mostly in silent reflection, when I reined in. A cold wash of reality had set in. We were out here on the Comanchería with a valuable herd of prime horseflesh. Why didn't we simply shout out an invitation to be attacked? "Watch for Kiowa and Apache," I cautioned Spirit Talker.

Spirit Talker gave me a broad grin and pointed to a bluff overlooking the river.

At least a half dozen Comanche warriors mounted on their ponies were watching us. Upon being spotted, they waved and turned away. Apparently, they were a guard sent by Buffalo Hump to ensure our safe passage.

The trail to our future lay ahead, and it would apparently be a safe one to travel–for now.

———

THE PINTA TRAIL from the Guadalupe to the Pedernales River was as rough as we'd remembered it. Most folks that used the trail traveled alone. They'd rarely have more than a single horse if any. Here we were pushing along with a string of fifteen ponies plus our packhorse.

Now that Spirit Talker had made me aware of them, I caught sight of our escorts now and then. They especially impressed me, as they kept up with us despite traveling in far rougher terrain. Occasionally along narrow segments of the trail, I would realize that they'd passed ahead of us. It seemed as though we were being guarded by ghostly spirits.

We camped the first night roughly five miles up the Pinta Trail.

I wasn't surprised when Spirit Talker disappeared after we'd finished the dinner that Sarah had sent us off with. Naturally, I shared the cornbread. I was stirring the embers of our cooking fire, looked up, and Spirit Talker was gone. Poof! Just disappeared with nary a sound.

I sat back against my saddle and gazed up at the stars. The quiet might have been unnerving were it not for the security of Buffalo Hump's warriors. Still it was so silent I swear I could hear the stars twinkle. Now and then, an owl would hoot—I was certain it was an owl—or a coyote howl. One of the horses would occasionally nicker or snort. These noises were far preferable to the unearthly scream of a mountain lion or *pia wa'óo*, as the Comanche called the beasts.

I had just closed my eyes and felt myself being transported to dreamland, when I heard Spirit Talker return.

"Wake up, Jack," he said.

"Where you been?" I asked, although I felt sure he'd gone off to chat with our escorts.

"Must go," Spirit Talker insisted. "Kiowa near."

Well, he didn't have to ask me twice. I reckoned that the Kiowa war party must have outnumbered us, or it wouldn't be such a great concern. While we had to protect ourselves, our Comanche escort apparently was concerned with protecting the fifteen ponies as well.

We didn't waste any time packing up. While I was grateful for a nearly full moon that gave sufficient light to enable us to follow the trail, it meant any enemy could see us, too. I noted that our escort party had split up. Two warriors scouted ahead while two more trailed to be sure we were not being followed.

"Kiowa *hoikwa*," observed Spirit Talker. Indeed, we had become hunted prey to the Kiowa war party.

I spotted a couple of our Comanche escorts. Both now wore war paint. This was very serious business. They were committed to doing whatever was necessary to protect Spirit Talker and me.

I saw the trail ahead narrow through a ravine and turned to Spirit Talker. I pointed ahead. "I don't like this," I said. I knew that two of our Comanche escorts had gone through ahead but had a strange feeling that an ambush lay ahead. *Kaahaniitu* or deceptive Kiowa could have permitted the Comanche to pass while we rode into their trap.

Spirit Talker pulled up alongside.

I drew the Sharps carbine from its scabbard and shoved a cartridge into the breech.

The Comanche on either side of us pulled up just as we had. Spirit Talker signaled to them to be ready to fight. The two Comanche behind us took charge of our herd of horses.

I urged Big Red along slowly toward the ravine. I pulled back the hammer and aimed the Sharps ahead of me.

Our stopping must have tipped off the Kiowa that we were on to them. One stepped onto the trail ahead with an arrow nocked on his bowstring. He didn't have time to aim, as my bullet quickly ended his foolish bravery. A second Kiowa appeared from high above the ravine trail but fell to a couple of Comanche arrows. There was a flurry of muffled sounds from unshod ponies galloping away.

"*Sunipu*," observed Spirit Talker.

Was it strong medicine that caused me to suspect trouble ahead? Apparently, God was delivering strong medicine to keep us alive on this rough and tumble frontier called the Comanchería. "*Sunipu*," I agreed. "God is good."

Spirit Talker stroked the carved cross hanging between the mountain lion claws on his necklace. "God is good," he repeated.

I looked ahead to our escorts and received a wave that all was well on the trail. Apparently, the Kiowa had more than enough of our *sunipu*. I smiled reassuringly at Spirit Talker and urged Big Red to move forward.

———

THE PEDERNALES RIVER was just about dry as a bone. Tepid pools of water were all that remained of any spring and early summer runoff. Didn't matter. The Pedernales signaled that we were close to Spirit Talker's *numunuu*.

With less than a day's ride ahead of us, we gave serious consideration to riding through the night. "We camp here," said Spirit Talker decisively. He signaled to our escorts to gather. After a brief conversation, he sent two ahead to his Penateka Comanche home village. The remaining warriors would continue their protective role.

"Figure we should arrive by mid-morning," I ventured.

Spirit Talker smiled. "Too soon," he said with a laugh. "Jack *kuhmabai* soon," he assured me.

Marriage. Kuhmabai now hung huge on my mind. I was going to be a sixteen-year-old husband to a fifteen-year-old Comanche woman. It struck me like a deer haunch struck up the side of my head that I'd grown up awfully fast. The frontier tended to mature young folks, but the loss of my family, my adventures with Spirit Talker, and now the making of a new family seemed to be a destiny determined by God to mature me. God was indeed mapping a trail to the future. I needed only follow Him. I smiled at Spirit Talker. "No hurry," I said in a vain attempt to sound calm and collected.

I looked off in the distance at gathering storm clouds. They were far enough away to be of no special concern other than to enjoy an eventual display of lightning and a few claps of thunder. I hoped the distant storm portended no future troubles. Up to now, our travels had been blessed with mostly clear skies.

It did get me to thinking about the work ahead to hire a trail boss and drovers, gather a herd, and move the beeves to Wyoming. I shook that off, as I brought myself back to the here and now.

"Jack distracted," observed Spirit Talker. "Not worry. Blue Flower take mind off cattle," he added with an understanding smile.

How did he know what I was thinking? I nodded. "*Ana o'a hi'it*," I said, suggesting that we eat. Food would go a long way to allaying any nerves I might have concerning tomorrow's delivery of the fifteen ponies to Buffalo Hump.

———

THE ENTIRE PENATEKA Comanche village had turned out for our arrival. Blue Flower was radiant in a white buckskin dress. Of course, I had donned my own buckskin shirt and trousers along with the moccasins she had made for me. What could possibly go wrong?

Spirit Talker nudged me as we rode in side by side.

I followed his eyes to a somber figure standing off behind Buffalo Hump. I dare say, this Comanche's appearance was more than somber; it reeked of sheer evil. Even from a distance, I could see the blackness within his eyes. He wore a buffalo horn headdress and white shirt and leggings. His lance was decorated with many eagle feathers and more scalps than I could count. A shiver went through me.

We reined in before Buffalo Hump and dismounted. His smile seemed a good sign despite the dour-faced warrior behind him. There was no hint of any trouble.

Spirit Talker wasted no time. He hugged his father and nodded to Blue Flower and to his father's wife. He gave a derisive glance at the all-too-serious-looking stranger. "*Ana o'a hi'it, ap.*" We must eat.

I shook Buffalo Hump's extended hand, smiled at Blue Flower, and followed everyone into the teepee. As I was about to enter, I caught sight of a new teepee standing a few yards away. I shrugged and thought little of it. Curious though.

Following behind me into the teepee and a bit too close for comfort was the evil-looking Comanche whom I'd never seen before in the encampment.

We sat around the fire burning in the center of the teepee, and Buffalo Hump produced a pipe.

Spirit Talker caught his father's eye and nodded

toward the stranger. "*Unha haksi nahniaka?*" he asked, inquiring as to his name.

Buffalo Hump gave an apologetic expression and motioned his hand toward the warrior. "Hakan," he said grimly and with an air of reluctance.

Hakan nodded and gave me a piercing glare. He then unexpectedly did the same to Spirit Talker.

I gathered that this Hakan, whose name translated to Fire, appeared soon after Spirit Talker and I departed on our Wyoming quest. He apparently was having some sort of deep spiritual influence on the tribe.

Buffalo Hump ignored Hakan's rudeness and lit the pipe. He took an especially long draw and slowly exhaled. "Buffalo Hump pleased at Spirit Talker return to *numunuu*." He handed the pipe to Spirit Talker.

"*Sunipu* strong. Fight Kiowa, Arapaho, Lakota, and Cheyenne. Kill bear and mountain lion. Jack God strong. Bring *isa*," he added seemingly for the direct benefit of Hakan.

By now, it didn't take much thinking to figure that Hakan was claiming great power and ability to prophesize. Spirit Talker had told me how tribal shamans would convince warriors that they were impervious to enemy lances and arrows before being sent into battle. When the assurances of divine protection failed, the shaman would simply claim that a warrior must have done something wrong and broken his spirit power of invulnerability. Before I could think much further on Hakan, Spirit Talker handed me the pipe.

As I drew on the pipe, I could see Blue Flower, her incredible winsome smile aglow, standing a few feet behind her father. "Spirit Talker speak truth. *Peeka wasápe.*" With that, I pulled a bag from behind me, stood, and drew out the bearskin gift. I handed it to Buffalo Hump.

The chief's eyes went wide. This was impressive. Strong *sunipu* for certain. He was quite clearly pleased with the gift. That he was speechless only served to add to the obvious pleasure. Buffalo Hump wrapped the bearskin over his shoulders.

Hakan appeared to be growing increasingly uncomfortable as an evermore-powerful *sunipu* was being revealed before him.

I took another draw on the pipe. Normally, after such a dramatic gift offering, the pipe would be passed. I was ignoring protocol. Hakan sneered. "Prayed to God. Brought *isa sunipu* to defeat the Oglala Lakota. Lakota run, Lakota *tabu*," I stated.

Relating our story of the appearance of the wolves to run off the attacking Lakota and calling the warriors cowards was bordering on being too much for Hakan, as he contained a seething anger.

I ignored Hakan and looked directly at Buffalo Hump. I took another pull on the pipe.

As if to defuse any growing ill feelings with Hakan, food and drink was distributed.

I didn't take my eyes from Buffalo Hump. "Bring fifteen *puuka*." I handed the pipe across to the chief, ignoring Hakan. The sleight was intentional. In my peripheral vision, I saw Spirit Talker smile approval. He didn't like the interloper either. I glanced up at Blue Flower. There was a glow about her.

Buffalo Hump smiled at my announcement of the gift of fifteen ponies in exchange for his daughter. He hesitated. "Eat first," he meekly directed. Clearly, something was on his mind, something was distracting him.

Spirit Talker frowned. This was unlike his father. He

glared at Hakan as though asking what influence the shaman had on the chief.

Hakan ignored the pipe. "*Taa Narumi sunipu.* Blue Flower follow *Taa Narumi.*"

My mouth dropped. I understood enough of the Comanche tongue to recognize that he was saying that Blue Flower must serve the Comanche gods, not the one God.

Spirit Talker gave Hakan a look that could have melted steel.

Hakan met his gaze. His deep black eyes seemed on fire with hatred. His very person exuded evil.

I looked over at Blue Flower. Tears were beginning to well in her eyes.

Buffalo Hump shifted uncomfortably. He looked at Hakan and then at Spirit Talker. He loved his son, but Hakan had stoked fear in the hearts of the Penateka Comanche. Did Spirit Talker hold the superior *sunipu*? Dare he doubt his son?

What happened next totally surprised me.

Spirit Talker drew his knife from the beautiful scabbard that Topsannah had fashioned for him and waved it toward the shaman. "Hakan *kaahaniitu.*" He called Hakan a cheat and deceiver.

Buffalo Hump's jaw dropped.

Hakan stood and grabbed his lance.

"Stop!" I said loudly. I also stood up, and my hand gravitated to the grip of my Colt revolver. I wrapped my hand around it just in case to send a strong message to Hakan. "Man cannot serve two masters. God stronger than *Taa Narumi*. Defeat *Taa Narumi* many times," I said with authority.

Spirit Talker translated my words to ensure that

Hakan fully understood. "God *sunipu!*" he concluded emphatically.

Blue Flower held back with arms raised toward her father in a silent cry for help.

By now, Buffalo Hump had decided to take charge before any blood was shed. He had seen enough, having realized that Hakan had been deceiving him, had been a *kaahaniitu.* "Hakan *wutsutsuki.* Leave Penateka Comanche or *kooitu.*" Calling the shaman a rattlesnake and ordering him to leave or die was pretty heavy. He waved his hand from Hakan to the teepee entrance.

Hakan's dark eyes flitted between Spirit Talker's knife and my Colt revolver. He gave Buffalo Hump an evil glare and stalked from the teepee.

Buffalo Hump breathed a sigh of relief. He slowly turned to Blue Flower, gently took her hand, and drew her forward toward me. "Buffalo Hump like *puuka.* Blue Flower yours. *Kuhmabai,*" he intoned in a mix of English and Comanche. Seemed as though the horses pleased him.

That was it. I was now married to Blue Flower in the eyes of the Comanche. A new life with God's guidance lay ahead.

Spirit Talker slid his knife back into the scabbard. He nodded to me.

I took Blue Flower's hands and looked into eyes filled with love.

Spirit Talker arose, nodded to his father, and turned to me and Blue Flower. "Spirit Talker bless Jack and Blue Flower forever in name of Father, Son, and Holy Spirit," he intoned about as well as any church preacher.

That was as close to a Christian wedding as we'd enjoy.

Buffalo Hump looked perplexed but shrugged and

smiled. He hadn't quite figured out what was going on with this God business but was not hostile to it. Maybe he'd figure it out.

My eyes melted into those of Blue Flower. Before I could react to Spirit Talker's blessing, she pressed herself against me. It was more than any sane male could endure.

Spirit Talker nodded his head toward the teepee entrance and winked.

Blue Flower took my hand and led me out.

I learned what the new teepee was for.

———

AFTER FOUR DAYS with the Comanche, I grew restless. Despite my deep love for Blue Flower and joys of the teepee, thoughts of the tasks ahead began creeping into my mind. Even Blue Flower's cooking skills couldn't dissuade me from dealing with the future.

I was grateful that Blue Flower remembered the limited English she'd learned, as communication was important. She would be a key contributor to our cattle venture. In fact, all the folks at Rising Cross Ranch would have to be involved.

Blue Flower smiled lovingly as she placed venison sausage and eggs before me.

"Coffee good," I said as I sat cross-legged before the fire. I wasn't joking. She brewed excellent coffee. I wasn't sure that it was pure coffee, but I wasn't going to try rooting out whatever secret ingredients contributed to its flavor.

"Eggs good?" she asked.

I nodded.

"Quail," she added. She paused. "Blue Flower

kamakuna kahni," she cooed. She placed her warm hands on my broad shoulders as she assured me in the Comanche language that she would love me all her life. With gentle fingers, she turned my head upward toward her and kissed me ever-so-lightly. She pulled back with a soft smile, then a deep soulfulness caressed her face. "When go Rising Cross, Jack?" she murmured in my ear.

I had been dreading facing up to the inevitability of returning to the ranch owing to the combination of the idyllic time spent in the teepee as juxtaposed with the business of the future cattle venture. "Two days," I said with as gentle a smile as I could muster while her fragrance wafted across my soul.

"Spirit Talker come?" she wondered.

I knew that Spirit Talker was conflicted. He dearly wanted to join in the cattle drive but feared that Hakan might return and impart more of his evil prophecies on the Penateka Comanche. His heartfelt desire was to further plant the seeds of his faith within his tribe. He recognized that his *numunuu* could not, must not, serve two masters. "Is his choice," I said. As I forked the last piece of sausage into my mouth, Blue Flower pulled me toward the blankets.

"Two days," she murmured and kissed me lightly on my ear.

I laughed…it tickled.

———

THE DAY for our return to Rising Cross Ranch arrived. I arose bright and early. A ray of sunlight peeked through the edges of the teepee entrance flap. Sitting reflectively for a few moments watching Blue Flower sleep with the sun's rays dancing across her face, peace lay upon me. I decided to take a stroll and enjoy the crisp morning air before our journey got underway. We had packed up most of what we needed the night before, so I felt comfortable taking a little extra time to reflect. Returning to Rising Cross with a wife created a new perspective on life. A great sense of responsibility came with marriage and eventually family.

A sense of purpose had come upon me. Jack O'Toole would not become a person who wondered what life was about. I had arrived at the opinion that unsuccessful folks tended to not look past their noses toward the future and that prevented them having a greater vision. I did not want to be thrown into that mucky mire of life with its bleak future. God's desire in Genesis to subdue the earth and extract its potential lingered large within me. Driving a herd of beeves to Wyoming would be a beginning. I harkened back to my pa's words from Psalm 37 to take delight in the Lord, and He will give you your heart's desires…trust in Him, and He will act. Indeed, I would trust in my faith. In the end, I prayed to hear those heavenly words, "Well done, good and faithful servant."

Taking in the early morning air with my senses filled with dreams of the future, I walked with an easy stride toward the horses. Big Red perked up his ears and gave a soft nicker at my approach. An apple brought an affectionate nuzzle. As I stroked his back and looked beyond into a stand of live oak, a chill ran up my spine. I shuddered involuntarily. There, perhaps a hundred yards off among the trees, was none other than Hakan. His face was painted as black as his eyes, and his hair fell in a single long braid down his back. He wore his mystical white buckskins and buffalo horn headdress.

Hakan knew I'd seen him as he vigorously shook

some sort of medicine stick in my direction. His upper lip curled into a sneer of derision.

Cowing to his diabolical antics was out of the question. I expect I was high on what might be called Godfidence. I raised my hand up toward the evil savage, pointed a finger at him like it was a gun, and pretended to shoot.

His dark eyes grew so wide I thought they'd explode. His painted face grew blacker as he glared angrily at me, shook his medicine stick at me one more time, and disappeared.

In the next instant, Spirit Talker appeared behind me. "What you do, Jack?" he asked.

"Nothing, my brother. Nothing," I assured him. What was the point of sharing a threat until it became a true threat?

He nodded. "Spirit Talker stay with *numunuu* until spring," he advised me.

"I thought you might." So far as I could tell, he seemed worried about Hakan's impact on his village.

"Want go on cattle drive," he said. "Be cowboy," he added with a broad grin. He quickly grew serious. "Comanche go with Jack to ranch. Much danger on trail." He couldn't hold back a sheepish grin. "See Topsannah," he said, as his reddish-brown face took on a decided blush.

I wasn't certain as to whether he was concerned more for me or for his sister. No matter. The escort would be wise. "You worry for your people?" I asked.

Spirit Talker nodded. "Texas Rangers...crazy shaman...Spirit Talker worry," he said with a sadness. "*Ap* get old," he added. Indeed, his father was getting on in years, and my Comanche brother feared at what might follow for his people.

"There are bad people," I counseled the obvious. I looked off thoughtfully and harkened back best I could to the Bible teachings my ma and pa shared not so many years ago in advising me about the dangerous ways of the world. "Bible says in Romans that there are many who don't know God, don't fear God; they vomit *kaahaniitu* from their tongues, bloodshed is in their paths, and they don't know the path of peace." I knew that wasn't exactly what the Bible said, but it was close enough and made my point.

Spirit Talker gave me a disconcerted look as though seeking reassurance on what Christ would do about evil.

"Forgive but punish," I said. Was it that simple? Just then, I saw Blue Flower appear back at the teepee entrance. "We must leave soon, my brother. God will give you *sunipu* to defeat evil." I almost felt as though I was sharing my own apparent strong medicine, a *sunipu* grounded in my faith in God. Spirit Talker had it. He needed only believe, to have *tumhyokenu*.

TWENTY-TWO

HEADED HOME

"YOU EVER GOING to name that pony?" I teased Spirit Talker upon my climbing into Big Red's saddle for the journey back to Rising Cross Ranch. It had been months since I had gifted him with the cayuse. The pinto was beautifully marked and had easily kept pace with Big Red on our travel to the North Platte River country, yet he steadfastly refrained from giving a name.

Spirit Talker smiled. "Give *nahniaka* soon," he responded. It was as though he was waiting for the right moment or right deed, much as his *numunuu* waited to give warriors their adult names.

What could I say? I laughed. "Six moons," I reminded him when he was to be at Rising Cross Ranch.

Blue Flower had mounted a white mare that Buffalo Hump had given her. She sat resplendent in her traveling buckskin dress upon a colorful blanket that served as padding for the Comanche saddle. I found the Indian saddles uncomfortable but could hardly argue with how they contributed to Comanche warriors being among the best horsemen on the frontier. My wife pulled up along-side with our packhorse in tow.

We had already said our goodbyes. Buffalo Hump struck a majestic farewell pose as he stood wrapped in the bearskin I had gifted to him. Spirit Talker's silent farewell offered a mix of joy for our future but sadness at our leaving.

Our escort of Comanche warriors left little doubt that we would be protected. Spirit Talker had assured me that the six were the bravest and most battle-worthy in the village. Looking at them, I couldn't argue. They were dressed more for battle than travel, as they virtually bristled with their lances, war clubs, and bows and arrows. Any enemy war party or bandit would surely think twice before challenging us. Of course, I had my own bow and arrows along with my trusty Colt revolver, knife, and Sharps carbine. I even had the New Testament George had gifted me, though it was of limited use for reading owing to the hole from the lead musket ball. It was simply an ever-present reminder of God's presence.

———

THE FIRST FEW hours riding along the southern bank of the Pedernales River was uneventful. I took joy in describing Rising Cross Ranch to Blue Flower. She seemed ever curious about Kate and Buck and my Amish friends Isaac and Sarah.

Our Comanche warrior escort was ever-vigilant early on but seemed to be lulling into a false sense of security as we encountered no threats.

We could feel the warm rays of the sun behind us as it dropped toward the horizon. There's something to be said for travel with the sun at your back, as it's easier on the eyes and illuminates the trail ahead. We figured to reach the northern end of the Pinta Trail before sunset and pitch camp there.

We heard noises as we approached the trailhead. I motioned to the lead warriors of our escort to scout further ahead. They quickly came galloping back from their scouting. Kobe, the lead warrior, rode up beside me. "Texas Rangers," he shared in a near whisper.

The last thing I wanted was an encounter with Captain Benton and his prejudice against Indians. I dreaded even the threat of any sort of fight.

"What is it?" asked Blue Flower.

I shook my head. "Texas Rangers," I responded. "No *kuya akatu*." I tried to assure her not to be afraid. With that, I motioned the two warriors to follow behind me and placed the remaining Comanche roughly twenty-five yards away on either side with arrows nocked in their bows. I would take the lead but was taking no chances with Captain Benton.

I pulled the Sharps carbine from its scabbard and nudged Big Red ahead with Blue Flower and the pack-horse close behind. If Benton was going to engage us, he'd have to deal with me first.

We'd traveled perhaps a half mile when we came upon Captain Benton and about twenty Rangers blocking our trail. Benton had a quirky smile on his lips as his still-mounted company spread behind him with rifles across their saddle horns.

"Where you heading with them savages, Mr. O'Toole?" he asked.

Dang, but his question was almost rhetorical. He knew where we were headed. "Taking my wife home to Rising Cross Ranch, Captain. We appreciate your concern for our safe passage, and I pray you'll be kind enough to let us pass."

"Holy smoke, O'Toole! You got yourself a squaw!" Benton retorted.

I gave him a look that would melt steel, a look that said to watch his language. "My wife understands English, Captain, so please watch your tongue. Now, if you will, please stand aside."

"My men might enjoy playing with your squaw," he replied with a sneer.

My fuse was growing ever shorter, and Blue Flower shifted uncomfortably on her pony. Benton was being unusually obnoxious. "We reckon to remain peaceful, Captain. But if you or one of your men comes close enough to breathe on my wife, it will be the final breath he takes."

"You threatening me, O'Toole?"

"You seem to have become a Ranger who threatens innocent folks, Captain Benton. I figure we're outnumbered three to one, but I can guarantee you will be first to meet God. And I suspect God won't be welcoming you to the Promised Land this day."

Benton sat silently astride his horse. A fly buzzed around, and he refrained from making any motion to shoo it away. The silence was deafening.

Big Red nickered as though to break the trancelike quiet.

Benton thoughtfully looked off to his right at the two Comanche with nocked arrows and then to his left for a similar sight.

The click of my pulling back the hammer of the Sharps broke the quiet tension. It was my way of telling Benton to make his play or stand aside.

Who knows what thoughts were running through

the Texas Ranger captain's mind. Perhaps he was calculating how many men it would likely cost him to engage with me and my Comanche escort. It would surely be a high price, and his Texas Ranger career would be over.

I swung the barrel of the Sharps just slightly toward Benton without actually aiming at him.

Finally, he leveled his steely gray eyes at me with a cold hard look and backed his horse off the trail. "You breathe a word of this to anybody, and I'll get you, O'Toole," he cautioned as he waved us through. "Folks like you making nice with the savages gets the Redskins thinking Whites are weak. They attack innocent settlers. Then they call me to clean up the mess. Mark my words, but the days of the Redskins are numbered O'Toole. You're just delaying the end."

I didn't respond at first. There seemed little point. Benton had his mind made up. Was he a Godly man? Should I judge? He was right in his own mind. Unfortunately, many folks thought as he did. "Bless you, Captain. Do stop by Rising Cross and enjoy our hospitality." I pressed my heels into Big Red's sides, and we slowly and silently moved forward through a corridor of Texas Rangers. There were ugly murmurs but nothing intelligible as we passed through. I kept my eyes focused ahead.

As we cleared free of the Rangers, Blue Flower rode up beside me. "Jack brave, strong *sunipu*," she cooed.

Every now and then I was confronted with my own vulnerability. Was I over-reliant on my faith in Christ? A sixteen-year-old boy-man and a fifteen-year-old Comanche bride had just faced down a company of frontier-hardened Texas Rangers. Strong *sunipu* indeed! I smiled just a tad bashfully.

———

FOLLOWING the encounter with the Texas Rangers, we rode an extra hour past sunset before making camp. We were actually a couple of miles down the Pinta Trail and felt we could finally breathe easy.

"Bad men?" asked Blue Flower as we unpacked.

"It's called prejudice, my love," I replied. "There are good men with a dark spot in their *pihi*." The dark spot was more than in Benton's heart; he needed a salve for the dark spot in his soul.

"Comanche, too," she added, recalling the shaman Tosahwi whom she killed and more recently the shaman prophet Hakan. "Jack good man. Strong *sunipu*."

If standing up to a wayward Texas Ranger was *sunipu*, then I certainly had *sunipu*. I'd say it was akin to having more guts than common sense. What if I'd gotten us all killed? Thank goodness Captain Benton made the right decision. He might have gotten away with killing a bunch of Comanche, but not a sixteen-year-old White rancher.

Our warrior escorts shared a meal of fresh venison with us before moving off a distance to graciously afford some privacy for Blue Flower and me. I must say that I had long since dismissed any notion of savagery from my Comanche friends...except in battle.

As the fire died to a pile of embers, Blue Flower and I curled up together under a blanket. I took a long look up at the vast starlit sky and then down at Blue Flower. I kissed her lightly and fell asleep having admired God's majestic creation and the beautiful spirited young woman I'd taken for my wife.

———

I AWAKENED to the sounds of our warrior escort preparing for our journey. There would be no breakfast, as something had spooked them into figuring that smoke from a fire wouldn't be a good move.

Blue Flower had gone off to tend to personal needs. As I stood rolling the blanket, Kobe came over to me.

"See Kiowa sign," he confided. He seemed intent on moving quickly down the trail and avoiding any engagement.

"Where Blue Flower?" I asked.

Just then, she appeared.

"We must go," I said with a serious expression.

She smiled, then read my face and realized my concern.

We were soon mounted and headed south on the Pinta Trail. I was evermore appreciative of our Comanche warrior escorts.

With the sun high above us, I reckoned we had traveled about a half-day when Kobe rode up to me.

"Must leave trail," he cautioned. He promptly headed us eastward through a stand of live oak and on through tall grass. We could barely see above the grass, and the scrubby trees had offered a screen from whatever danger Kobe had spotted. After roughly a quarter mile, he pulled us up and had us dismount. "We wait," he whispered. "Stay quiet."

We were downwind from whomever was passing on the trail. The voices were in Spanish, but I couldn't quite make out what was being said. There was a boastful tenor to their chatter. They had apparently been celebrating something and had likely consumed just a bit too much booze. I think the Comanche called it firewater.

Looking over at Kobe, I had a feeling that he would have liked to have attacked the unsuspecting travelers, counted coup, and taken scalps. Blessedly, he stuck to his duty of protecting us.

Kobe caught me watching him. "Bad *tosa*," he explained. "Steal cattle, sell skins," he added.

The passersby were what were called hiders. They rustled cattle and took only the hides to sell. Disgustingly, they left the carcasses to rot on the prairie. These were truly nasty men. I wished Captain Benton and his Texas Ranger company were close at hand. I nodded to Kobe. "Bad *tosa*," I repeated. I wasn't going to argue that we considered the Mexicans brown-skinned rather than White, but a bad human was a bad human, and skin color didn't really matter.

Once we were certain that the hiders had passed, we made our way back to the Pinta Trail. The putrid aroma of the hiders lingered in the air; a mix of booze, sweat, leather, and mule droppings. We were right pleased to leave the scene behind and resume our journey home.

TWENTY-THREE
RISING CROSS BRAND

AT LAST, Rising Cross Ranch came into view. As I scanned the ranchland, I noticed a few cattle and horses had been added in the two short weeks that we'd been away. I turned to Blue Flower and pointed to the cabin in the distance ahead of us. A broad smile creased her face, and her eyes lit up with anticipation.

I turned to Kobe. *"Ana o'a hi'it,"* I said inviting him and our escorts to enjoy the hospitality of a home-cooked meal.

Kobe smiled friendly-like but apparently considered his obligation ended. "Kobe find hiders. Jack visit *numunuu,*" he invited. Then he smiled and added, "Bring Blue Flower and little ones." He winked.

"Kobe brave. English plenty good. Travel safe. Watch for Texas Rangers." I worried that they'd run afoul of Captain Benton's company. "Tell Spirit Talker six moons," I said, smiling.

Kobe gave me a quizzical look.

"Topsannah," I responded with a grin.

The Comanche warrior offered up an aha smile as he

nodded his understanding. He thumped his hand against his heart before turning and leading his band away.

Our escorts had barely departed, and a plaintive cry reached our ears. "Jack! Jack!" called out Buck.

Blue Flower saw him, put heels to her pony, and galloped to meet him.

Caught off guard watching Kobe depart, I followed a few lengths behind.

Pulling up in a cloud of dust, Blue Flower dismounted and ran to greet my little brother.

She swept him up in a hug.

For his part, Buck looked startled. Barely able to breathe in her grasp, he looked quizzically past her shoulder at me.

"Blue Flower is my wife now, Buck. She'll be living here with us."

He wrestled himself free and sucked in air. He held her at arm's length, looked her over, and shrugged. "Er, welcome," he managed to blurt.

If Blue Flower was disappointed in the six-year-old's greeting, it didn't show. Youngsters could react strangely at times, especially at surprises.

"Come mount up, Buck," I invited, extending my hand.

Buck didn't hesitate to climb aboard, and we rode toward the cabin with him sitting in front of me on Big Red. His curious eyes never left Blue Flower.

———

BUCK'S SHOUTS had alerted everyone.

Upon seeing Blue Flower, Kate's face was filled with joy. She ran over and nearly pulled my new wife from the pony in the effort to hug her. Blue Flower remained in the saddle, and Kate wound up hugging her leg.

Nonplussed at the affection, Blue Flower lovingly tousled Kate's hair. "Pretty hair," she said.

Kate hugged her leg even tighter at the compliment.

Isaac and Sarah stood by quietly, as they patiently awaited introduction. Sarah lovingly held their baby son Jack, who was as yet so young as to not know what sort of event was occurring.

Finally, I let Buck slide down from Big Red and dismounted. I eased over to Blue Flower and helped her from her pony. I stood with one arm around her waist. "Blue Flower O'Toole, these are my good friends Isaac and Sarah Fisher and their son, Jack." It occurred to me that it was the first time I'd appended the name O'Toole to Blue Flower. It seemed to hold a spirit apropos to the uniting of White man and Red man.

Introduction completed, Isaac nodded a reserved but warm welcome while Sarah moved forward and delivered a hug.

"Are y'all hungry?" asked Kate.

I was caught a tad off guard. "Something I must do first, sister," I said with a wink. With that, I swept a surprised Blue Flower off her feet, kicked open the cabin door, and carried her over the threshold. The others were frozen in place at my unexpected action. Alone for the moment, Blue Flower and I indulged in what was intended to be a long kiss. It all felt so right.

Too soon, three faces peered in through the doorway. "Can we come in and eat?" asked Buck. Isaac hung back, rolling his eyes at Sarah and the kids with their lack of appreciation for my very brief romantic interlude.

Blue Flower and I broke free of our embrace. "You know we must take care of the horses first, Buck."

"We can do that," said Buck and Kate in unison. The sooner the cayuses were tended to, the sooner we'd eat.

Isaac was already busy unfastening the load from the packhorse.

We laughed at Buck's and Kate's anxiousness to complete chores and get to eating. Horses were a high priority, far too important to not be properly tended to. We were soon finishing up currying and feeding the horses. We set Blue Flower's horse and the packhorse free in the corral. I gave Big Red his head toward the pasture and the herd of mares awaiting him. He whinnied with joy as he galloped off.

Horses cared for, we headed for the cabin to enjoy Kate's and Sarah's culinary skills. Blue Flower stayed close to me, not clingy mind you, but close. She was usually on the feisty side of spirit, but the new surroundings would take some getting used to. In any case, we were all home at last.

———

IT DIDN'T TAKE LONG for Blue Flower to begin putting her cultural and womanly touches on our living spaces. After nearly two years on my own, it took a bit of getting used to. She hung beautiful blankets with unique designs on the walls and laid out her combs, necklaces, and the like on a small table. Somehow, Isaac had acquired a mirror. It fascinated Blue Flower, and she propped it as a centerpiece on the table. But for seeing her reflection in rippling pools of water, she had never before experienced full appreciation of her own beauty. There had been no other such affirmation other than me telling her how pretty she was.

I padded silently into our bedroom the morning of

our second day at Rising Cross and quietly eased up behind her.

She was combing out her waist-length dark hair and smiled as she caught my image in the mirror.

I stood transfixed, fully appreciating her gemlike brown eyes, long lashes, and high cheekbones set off by a straight nose and full lips.

She ceased her combing and looked up at me. "Jack *kamakuna*," she cooed.

Oh yes, we were in love.

I lifted her from her chair and let our passions take over.

———

IN LESS THAN SIX MONTHS, or six moons to Spirit Talker, we reckoned to be driving a herd of longhorns northward to Fort Laramie. While it was easy to become fully immersed in my new wife, there was much to do.

Blue Flower quickly fell into the routines of keeping up a ranch on the frontier. We remained ever-vigilant lest we be surprised by Indians or bandits. Out here on the Comanchería, there was no shortage of danger. I helped with the myriad chores around the spread, stuff like repairing fencing, mucking stalls, and helping mares and cows birth their young'uns. Other than the livestock, none of this would contribute to putting together a cattle drive. I decided that I needed to become familiar with the goings on down in Bandera. Ranches were springing up around the region, but they were still few and far between. Still, word got around that Bandera was destined to become a key hub for cattle and cattlemen.

One morning I stood with one leg on the bottom

fence rail of the corral and observed a newcomer to Rising Cross.

"Big, isn't he?" observed Isaac.

"Never seen a spread like that before," I responded.

"Better than eight feet tip to tip. Unless you object, I figured we'd call him Atlas in keeping with his size."

At the sound of his name the massive longhorn nonchalantly laid a pair of big brown eyes on Isaac and snorted as if approving. He turned his attention back to a half dozen cows in the adjoining corral.

I was impressed at how Isaac had configured the corrals around the barn to accommodate various live-stock. "Seems Atlas is ready to make us a herd," I said with a laugh.

"Got some advice from the fellow with the ranch east of here, Jack. Been very helpful."

"Where'd you find Atlas?"

"There are an amazing number of beeves roaming free. I've been rounding them up one by one and driving them here to Rising Cross."

I noted that Atlas had no brand. "I expect that we'd best create and register our Rising Cross brand," I said.

"Mind a suggestion?"

"You have something in mind?" I asked.

Isaac shuffled his feet in the dust a moment as though engaged in deep thought. "Well, I was thinking that we needed to come up with a design that would likely foil rustlers trying to alter it with a running iron. I think a simple cross with an upward pointing arrow and a wing on each side might be good."

"Dang, but that sounds perfect, Isaac. Can you sketch it up? I'll take it to Bandera and register it."

Isaac beamed with delight at my having readily accepted his design. Importantly, we now had the Rising

Cross Ranch brand. He looked over at Atlas. "Hear that, Atlas. You'll be getting branded."

Atlas snorted.

"One other thing, Jack," said Isaac with a concerned look.

"What's that?"

"With all this livestock, I'm thinking we need some help. Buck's too small, the ladies have their work, and I'm only one man. When you're not here...well, it's a lot to handle." He paused for effect. "And there's the matter of hiders and Indians lurking about."

That caught my attention. "You have anyone in mind?" I figured that in his local travels he might have found a man or two with the right skills.

"There was a fellow at the Running N spread, but he feared for his hair and lit out after a Comanche attack. Maybe you'll find someone in Bandera."

I nodded. "I'll do what I can," I responded. This cattle business wasn't going to be easy. I looked over at Atlas. He was busy eyeing the cows. Me? I was growing up right fast.

———

I WAS all set to head to Bandera, when I was reminded that it wasn't all about me and what I wanted. Blue Flower had talked with Kate and Sarah. They had planted a desire in her for some female fashion accoutrements. I can't say as I was excited about this newfound need, as I fully appreciated the naturalness of her buckskin dresses and unadorned braided hair. I considered myself a simple man with simple desires. This having been said, the ladies wanted to go with me to Bandera.

Lurking in the back of my mind was the very likely

prospect of having to deal with folks prejudiced against Indians. These were often the very same folks who professed to be church-going Christians but held deeply rooted hatred, hostility, and scorn of Indians, Blacks, and Mexicans. While they often expressed these feelings with disgusting language, they dealt in violence as well. I didn't find subjecting Blue Flower to these prejudices an especially attractive eventuality. But...what was I to do? I prayed that meeting the ladies' needs wouldn't interfere over much with my getting acquainted with folks I'd need to be doing cattle-related business with.

Isaac, Buck, and Kate stayed home to tend the ranch. We figured that my having to shepherd three ladies to Bandera would be just a tad too much of a burden from a security point of view. While Bandera was an easy day's ride by horseback, pulling a wagon was going to push the limits of accomplishing the roughly twenty-five-mile trip in a day through rough and surely dangerous frontier territory. We would necessarily be staying overnight in Bandera. Again, the very idea of camping overnight with the ladies seemed daunting.

I did take some comfort in the Army having established nearby Camp Verde, though I understood that it housed the military's experiment with camels. There were apparently nearly three dozen of the nasty unruly beasts, and soldiers dealt with horses and other necessary livestock not getting along with the humped critters.

WE PLANNED to depart Rising Cross Ranch at daybreak. The wagon was mostly empty save for the ladies' overnight necessities and a few camping supplies.

"Pretty dress," Blue Flower observed, dancing before

the mirror in our bedroom before we departed. She was especially excited to experience a White settlement town but didn't quite understand why I persuaded her to wear one of Sarah's dresses and an oversized sunbonnet with a wide brim that hid her beautiful face. It was complicated.

How was I to get her to fully comprehend the prejudices that lurked in the White man's world? The closest I could compare it to was the degrading ways the Comanche treated their captives, yet it wasn't the same. Men and women had the God-given freedom to think as they would. It didn't make the thinking right. By any measure, the frontier was a savage place despite the advances of civilization. And yet, the west presented the freedom to seize opportunities, much as I was reckoning to do with my cattle-driving enterprise. Not everyone saw it that way, as many were wholly in the frontier adventure for themselves as driven by greed, violence, lust, and other evils constituting God's abominations. As I said, it was complicated.

Isaac urged me to seek out August Klappenbach, a German immigrant who owned the building housing the general store and post office. He held a possibility of helping finance our venture. There were increasing numbers of German settlers in the region, and I had found them to be solid business folks. There were some Mormons that settled near Bandera, but they mostly stayed to themselves. The cypress shingle business was still flourishing so far as I knew. I figured that would continue so long as there were plenty of cypress trees to harvest along the Medina River.

I had made only a couple of trips to Bandera to purchase supplies in the interval since the Comanche attack on my home. I figured the residents would not be thinking of me as part of their community. At least, not yet.

I featured myself as a reasonably fast learner. It struck me that reciprocity went a long way among folks out west. Do someone a good turn, and they will tend to reciprocate. The key was to find what would spark the reciprocal response. Would the prospect of making money selling beeves in Wyoming be that spark? Would they trust a sixteen-year-old? Throw in prejudices against Indians, Mexicans, and Negroes, and it appeared that I had my work cut out for me.

We had acquired a couple of mules, and they were more than up to the task of pulling our wagon to Bandera. I tied Big Red to the back of the wagon, while Blue Flower sat with me and Sarah enjoyed a bouncy ride in the wagon bed with little baby Jack. Buck had protested, but we convinced him to stay behind with Kate and help Isaac protect Rising Cross Ranch.

We had to cross the Medina River twice on our journey, but it was actually a refreshing experience given the still hot late summer weather. I was grateful that the waters ran a tad shallow this time of year. Afore long, we reached the outskirts of Bandera.

———

I TOOK A DEEP BREATH. We were about to find out what sort of hospitality would present itself in Bandera. The river and cypress trees made for an idyllic introduction to the town. There was plenty of grass about the area for our mules and Big Red to graze along with stands of cedar, oak, pecan, and the aforementioned cypress trees There wasn't much to the town just yet save for the shingle manufacturing adjoining the sawmill and the general store with its post office. There were a couple of nondescript homes, no church, no saloon, and no jail. There was what passed for a blacksmith shop of sorts with an adjoining corral. As I understood it, most of the residents were Polish immigrants.

We were losing daylight, so there was no time to waste. I gave a chuck to the mules, and we headed into the town. I pulled us up in front of what I figured to be August Klappenbach's store and climbed down.

"Wait here," I said to Blue Flower and Sarah.

As I reached for the door latch, the doors swung open, and I found myself facing a large square-jawed man. He gave a look at Blue Flower and Sarah before connecting with me. "Welcome to Bandera," he offered with another sideways glance at the ladies.

"Howdy, my name is Jack O'Toole. Our spread is about a day's ride north, and we've come for supplies and other business," I said, delivering a mouthful of information. I waited patiently for the man to turn his eyes from Blue Flower and Sarah. I was beginning to get the impression that women might be a rarity in Bandera.

"Er, sorry. I'm August Klappenbach," he finally blurted out. "If you plan to spend the night, you can set your rig out back."

"Thanks kindly," I responded. He seemed right friendly enough after all.

"Go set your camp, then come on in for a bite to eat," he said with another even more intense look at Blue Flower and Sarah.

It occurred to me that introducing the ladies might be awkward depending upon Klappenbach's disposition toward Indians. As soon as I might utter Blue Flower's name, it would be a dead giveaway despite her flimsy disguise. Upon consideration, it seemed to make sense to just be honest about my wife's name and heritage and to trust in my Lord to ensure a proper outcome.

It didn't take long to set camp and care for Big Red and the mules, so it didn't take long for us to enter Klappenbach's fine establishment. There was actually a small bell at the front door that jingled upon entering.

"Come on back here," called Klappenbach from the rear of the store.

We walked past stacks of merchandise to a couple of tables with chairs that qualified as a small but serviceable dining room. We sat at the chairs our host motioned us to. Aromas of sausage and some vegetable concoction wafted into the room. I'd learn soon enough that the vegetable concoction was called sauerkraut. I saw a woman, likely Klappenbach's wife, preparing food in the adjoining room from which those aromas originated.

"Who might these beautiful ladies be?" asked Klappenbach.

I motioned first to Sarah. "This is Sarah Fisher with her young son Jack. And this," I said with a sweeping motion, "is Blue Flower."

"Nice that Sarah here has some Injun help," retorted Klappenbach quickly.

I shook my head. "Sarah's husband is back at our spread. Blue Flower is my wife."

Klappenbach's eyebrows arched. "Oh," he said.

Blessedly, Mrs. Klappenbach entered the room and plunked plates brimming with delectables before us just as her husband was about to say something. "About time we accepted the Indian folk into our lives," she offered. "What is your wife's tribe, Mr. O'Toole?"

I wasn't sure whether to breathe a sigh of relief just yet, as Klappenbach looked disconcerted. I turned to his wife. "Blue Flower is a…"

"Penateka Comanche," chimed in Blue Flower. "I love your town," she added in perfect English.

"Well, you're welcome to shop your little heart out, dear," responded Mrs. Klappenbach.

I was about to stuff a mouthful of potatoes into my gaping mouth when I felt a nudge from Blue Flower. I nodded. "I expect we should bless this fine meal," I offered.

There were nods, and everyone bowed heads as I delivered a brief thanks to God.

August Klappenbach appeared to yet be just a bit uncomfortable about my mixed marriage but decided to ignore it for now. While it had been common practice for mountain men and early settlers on the frontier to take Indian wives, it was clear that mixed-race marriages hadn't taken hold in this part of Texas. "Did you say you had some other business, Mr. O'Toole?"

"You may call me Jack, Mr. Klappenbach," I offered with a friendly smile. "Yes, I need to register my brand. Also, I'm fixing to drive cattle north to Wyoming, and I'm looking for help in pulling the venture together."

"You're young, Jack. You ever driven a herd of cattle over open range before?" he asked.

"No, but I handle livestock right well. I returned a few weeks back from Fort Laramie in the North Platte River country, and there are ready buyers for good beeves."

"You expect to find help here in Bandera?"

"I hoped. I need a trail boss, some hands, a cook, and a bit of upfront financing in addition to other ranchers contributing cattle to the drive," I said, feeling as though I was likely scatter-gunning the information.

"You have cattle of your own?" Klappenbach inquired.

"Have a few head, but we'll need closer to five hundred plus extra horses for the drovers." I wasn't quite ready to admit to barely having a half dozen beeves at Rising Cross.

Klappenbach whistled. "Tall order you have here, Jack."

"Can you help?" I figured nothing ventured, nothing gained.

Mrs. Klappenbach strode from the kitchen and placed a hot-from-the-oven apple pie in the middle of the table. "Of course he can help, young man."

Her husband gave her a don't-get-ahead-of-me look. "You traveled all the way to Fort Laramie and kept your scalp?" he said with a chuckle. "That's quite an accomplishment."

I tried to appear humble and delivered my best can-you-help look. "Guess I was lucky." Why did I say that? I needed to give credit where credit was due. "I think God was looking out for me...and my Comanche warrior companion." I didn't mention the wolf.

Klappenbach took a deep breath. "Actually, there haven't been too many cattle drives out of Texas, Jack. Fellow named Piper put one together back in '46. Drove about a thousand head to Ohio, as I recall. There's been some success since driving beeves to the gold miners in California. Getting near a hundred dollars a head, but it's a rugged trail, and prices are dropping," he said while laying a seriously intense gaze on me. "Hear tell there are difficulties in Missouri and Kansas with what they call Texas fever. They blame ticks carried by longhorns for infecting their herds. So, you driving beeves north to Wyoming makes good sense to me."

I breathed a sigh of relief as I felt as though I had grabbed Klappenbach's interest.

He continued. "Bandera is beginning to attract cattle folks. The Army has those stupid camels over at Camp Verde. Some of the troops are frustrated and looking to muster out. Might be some possible hands in the bunch. As to a cook, you cannot have my wife," he said with a laugh. Then, he grew serious again. "It's going to take time to get the word out, Jack. Let me see what I can do. Oh, and you can call me August. My wife here is Stella."

"I'd be most obliged for your help, August," I said, reaching over and shaking hands. "Oh, and I have that brand to register. Where might I…"

"We can handle that here, Jack. Bandera is the county seat."

Klappenbach had definitely warmed up to me and what may initially have come across as a hair-brained venture. He didn't seem put off by my youth or my Comanche wife. Somehow, I think Stella exerted some influence over that. "I'd be much obliged for any help, August."

We spent another hour chattering around our hosts' table, especially enjoying second helpings of that awesome apple pie. Klappenbach was genuinely interested in how I had overcome the loss of my parents and a brother and sister but then trusted God in saving Sarah and Buck and then journeying to the North Platte River country toward seizing the bold opportunity to start a cattle venture. That I had made peace with a band of Comanche and even married one especially seemed to intrigue him, as Comanche, Kiowa, and Apache were feared in the Bandera region despite the presence of Texas Rangers and the troops at Camp Verde. Bandera sat on the southern periphery of the Comanchería and all the danger that portended. I agreed that we needed more of the likes of Texas Ranger Captain Benton.

I realized that Blue Flower's and Sarah's eyes were growing heavy and baby Jack was getting cranky. It was a signal to call it a night. We thanked the Klappenbachs and retired to the wagon.

———

STELLA PREPARED A WONDERFUL BREAKFAST, and Blue Flower and Sarah enjoyed an early morning perusal of the stacks of merchandise the Klappenbach's displayed. Apparently, there were few women around Bandera, so Stella truly treasured their frivolous dancing through the plentiful selection of mentionables and unmentionables that caught Blue Flower's and Sarah's fancy. I loved watching Blue Flower playfully prance in a pale-blue sundress before a full-length mirror.

Stella was assuring the ladies that she only stocked the latest fashions. She likely stretched the truth a tad, but it was really no matter here on the Texas frontier. I was confident that the store was not exactly overflowing day-to-day with female shoppers.

Klappenbach finally emerged and stood beside me as I ordered supplies for Rising Cross and watched the ladies having fun. "You are a lucky man, Jack," he said.

I nodded.

"I'm talking about more than the ladies. I've given it some thought, and I believe I can help you pull this cattle drive together."

"Much obliged, August. Much obliged indeed."

"We will need a business arrangement, Jack. Perhaps, a percentage of the profits?"

Klappenbach's proposal didn't surprise me. I hardly expected him to help me simply out of the goodness of his heart. He was a businessman first and foremost. "You have my attention, August."

Klappenbach cut to the chase right quickly. "I'll finance your venture and help recruit drovers and a cook," he said, looking me in the eye. "The cookie will need a wagon and oxen to pull the contraption. I figure my efforts should be worth at least half."

"Drovers?" I asked.

Klappenbach chuckled and rolled his eyes in a friendly sort of way. "Better get up on the lingo, Jack. Drovers drive the cattle; drover in the rear rides drag, one in front is point, along sides are swing riders and flank riders. The best drovers these days are of Mexican *vaquero* heritage. In Texas, we call them cowboys or cowpokes, cattlemen, cowpunchers, punchers, waddies, or whatever they'll answer to. Understanding cattle behaviors is critically important. Good drovers know cattle inside and out; they even get inside the heads of the beeves," he said by way of educating me. "While I'm thinking on it, you'll be needing a lead bull too." He paused and extended his hand. "We have a deal?" he asked.

I thought on Atlas. He'd likely make a great lead bull for any herd. Then again, he was my breeder bull. Seems that I had a decision ahead.

Clearly, I was about to be doing business with a man who knew a bit about cattle. I got to thinking on the possible profit. I was ever mindful of my biblical teaching as to the evils of the worship of money, but we did need to make a profit. I had calculated this venture's take more than once on a 500-head drive. Assuming most of the beeves made it to Fort Laramie, and we experienced minimal hindrances along the way, profits could be handsome. On the upside, kicking off a cattle drive from

Bandera could also begin to establish the little town as a hub for the cattle trade. That could bring a huge business upside to Klappenbach, as well as build the influence of Rising Cross Ranch in the region. "Fair enough, August," I responded and shook his hand. "We figure to leave come start of April. I'll work on gathering the herd."

"We'll be ready, Jack."

"One more thing," I said.

"What's that?" responded Klappenbach.

"I'm going to need a hand to help my foreman at the Rising Cross while we're on the trail drive. I'd appreciate it if you could keep your eyes out for a good man." I realized it was the first time that I had thought of Isaac as my ranch foreman, but he was doing all associated with that role.

———

IT WAS mid-morning by the time we began heading home with a full wagon. Sarah now lay with baby Jack across sacks of flour, sugar, feed, some new tack, and a few farming implements. Laying aside it all was our brand-spanking-new Rising Cross Ranch branding iron that I'd troubled the local smithy to fashion. Alongside Sarah were a couple of packages specially wrapped to protect from the trail dust the dresses inside as well as a couple of right-pretty ladies' hats. Blue Flower had even found one for Kate. We were all in good spirits. I let Blue Flower drive the wagon while I rode alongside on Big Red. The weather was unseasonably dry and right pleasant.

Shortly after making our second crossing of the Medina River in the early afternoon, the sounds of shod horses reached my ears. Reflexively, I slipped the Sharps carbine from its scabbard and laid it across my saddle pommel.

Blue Flower heard the sounds too. She smiled nervously at me and glanced furtively at the Colt revolver lying beside her on the wagon seat. She hadn't fired a gun since saving me from the evil-intentioned Comanche shaman many months back.

Sure enough, a few minutes later, three riders appeared. They were heavily armed, rode well-lathered cayuses coated with trail dust, and looked to be about as swarthy a set of characters as could be imagined. That lather on their horses gave ample evidence that they'd been riding hard. They reined in about twenty yards in front of us, looking about as surprised as we were.

The apparent leader looked back over his shoulder as though they were being followed. He glared at me, then shifted his gaze to Blue Flower and Sarah. "Y'all betta turn this rig 'round an' git!" he blurted. "Be Comanche behind us!"

Given that each of the men carried plenty of guns and weren't standing and fighting, I quickly figured there must be a large war party pursuing them. I saw an arrow sticking out from the cantle of one of the saddles.

Blue Flower and I locked eyes and smiled. We realized from the design that it was a Comanche arrow.

"Get behind us and lay low," I directed the three riders.

Just about this time, a half dozen Comanche warriors in full warpaint emerged on the trail ahead and pulled up their ponies in a cloud of dust. Arrows were nocked on bowstrings and expressions were about as fierce as could be mustered.

"*Unha haksi nahniaka,*" I shouted, raising my hand as a peace sign. "No *peeka numunuu.*"

Challenging them in the Comanche tongue for their name and telling them not to kill their people caught them totally unawares. Their expressions turned from serious to perplexed.

"*Ana o'a hi'it,*" I added, causing more consternation by dismounting and inviting them to join us for a meal.

By now, Blue Flower had shed her bonnet and displayed her long dark braided hair and decidedly Indian facial features. She nodded to the apparent leader. "Me Blue Flower, Penateka Comanche, daughter of Buffalo Hump."

A reverence seemed to sweep through the war party at the reference to the much-revered Buffalo Hump.

Behind us, the three riders could be heard breathing sighs of relief.

The war party leader inched toward us with a hand raised in peace. He gave Blue Flower an almost imperceptible bow of respect. "Tasiwoo Tenahpu," he said pointing to himself.

"Buffalo Man," translated Blue Flower.

"*Tosa peeka tasiwoo,*" added Buffalo Man. He was accusing the fleeing riders of killing buffalo. Worse, it was apparently his buffalo.

I nodded. "*Aitu,*" I said to emphasize that I understood that it wasn't good.

Apparently, Comanche tempers were cooling in the face of a Comanche princess and a White man who spoke some Comanche.

Buffalo Man turned his attention to the three riders. He made a slicing motion across his forehead. He wanted their scalps.

I turned to the lead rider. "Is what he is saying true?"

"We was huntin' just like them. Rifle worked faster than bow an' arrow."

I shook my head. "Where's the dead buffalo?"

"Couple of miles up the trail."

I turned back to Buffalo Man. "*Ana o'a hi'it tasiwoo*," I said, inviting them to feast on buffalo.

Buffalo Man scanned the faces of his band. The fire seemed to have gone from their spirits. "*Ana o'a hi'it tasiwoo*," he repeated and nodded toward the three riders. He turned his pony around and began to lead his band back toward the kill site. He glanced back over his shoulder and nodded his head up the trail as an invitation to follow him.

"It's your lucky day," I said to the lead rider.

I nodded to Blue Flower to follow the Comanche.

"Looks like we'll enjoy a nice peaceful dinner," I added with a chuckle. "My name's Jack O'Toole. I own the Rising Cross spread north of here."

"Sam Collins," the lead rider responded. "I run the Circle C east of here."

"We eatin' with them Injuns, Sam?" interjected one of the riders. "They be takin' our hair."

Collins winced and shook his head. "Mr. O'Toole heah has jus' saved our skins. We be makin' nice an' eatin' buffalo steak with them Injuns like it or not."

"Not me. I quit," said the rider emphatically, promptly turning his horse and riding off.

Collins shook his head. "Dang, lost another one. Where the hell is Captain Benton when ya need him?" With that, he began to follow me and our wagon.

The remaining rider with Collins shrugged and urged his horse along behind us.

———

WE ENJOYED a buffalo feast with the Comanche, even reaching an agreement with Buffalo Man to divide the buffalo between the two hunting parties. An unexpected benefit was my getting Collins interested in adding some of his beeves to our trail drive.

By the time our dinner was over and all our guests had departed, the sun was hanging close to the horizon, and we decided to camp for the night. Better to be traveling in the daylight. Having stopped a violent encounter between Comanche and White cowboys, we reckoned that the rest of our travel home would be right easy. It was nevertheless another reminder of how the frontier was ever a meeting point between savagery and civilization. I praised God that the encounter had ended well. We needed civilization to win out more frequently, and the church contributed to that eventuality.

———

A COUPLE of hours out from Rising Cross, a strange feeling settled over me. "Blue Flower, stay here." Something or someone was ahead of us, and I had long ago learned to listen to my intuition about such things.

She pulled the wagon to a halt.

"I'll be back," I said, urging Big Red ahead at a cautious walk. My eyes and ears were intently focused on the rough trail ahead. I was downwind of whatever was drawing me through the scrub and tall grass. At last, the faint sound of voices came to me. Mexicans! Could they be the dreaded hiders?

This close to Rising Cross, it concerned me that they

might come after our small herd of longhorns. Worse yet, they might already have been there!

I pulled my Sharps carbine from the saddle scabbard and quietly dismounted. I ground-hitched Big Red and snuck forward in a low crouch. At the top of a slight rise, I was able to see five swarthy-looking Mexicans with a wagon heaped with cattle skins. They'd been hard at work at their unlawful craft and the going was tough for their heavy load of stolen hides. Outnumbered and with the ladies' safety paramount, I wasn't about to confront them. I decided that my best course of action was to get our rig off the trail and hidden with the hope that the hiders would be too busy to notice any sign of us. Discretion was certainly the better part of valor.

I slipped on back to Blue Flower, Sarah, and our wagon. "We must hide," I said, directing Blue Flower to drive the wagon behind a thick stand of low-hanging live oak and tall grasses about a hundred yards off the trail. Once the rig was situated, I snuck back to the trail with a tree branch and did my best to wipe away any trace of wagon wheels and hoofprints. I could only hope that the hiders wouldn't notice any of our tracks farther south.

We watched from our hiding place as the hiders went past us laughing and carrying on about how much money they'd make from selling the hides from the *gringo* ranches. Big Red seemed to sense the danger but remained calm. I worried about the mules. Sarah and Blue Flower stood stroking the mules' muzzles in an effort to keep them still.

The hiders were nearly safely past our position when one of the mules was bitten by a fly and let out a fearsome bray.

The laughing and boastful talk among the hiders ceased. "*Qué es?*" queried the leader.

I readied the Sharps. Blue Flower released the mule and grabbed the Colt revolver from the wagon seat. Where were my *isa*? We needed big *sunipu*. We needed God's grace and mercy desperately!

EPILOGUE

THE AMERICAN WESTERN frontier was mostly unforgiving, a meeting of savagery and civilization. Imagine the perils of the trail from Texas to Wyoming (see the map on page X). Then envision the hazards encountered in traveling north through that uncharted wild country. Some folks said it was the very roughest part of our western frontier. What made it so? It was Lakota, Crow, Cheyenne, Pawnee, Kiowa, Shoshone, and Comanche territory for one thing. Stretching hundreds of miles northward from Texas all the way to the upper reaches of the North Platte River, the region was a virtual no-man's-land for White settlers. *Wyoming Calls: Jack's Risky Quest* offers insights into the courage, faith, endurance, and pure grit entailed in the conquest of the West. It presages the decades it would take to reap the bounty the region would eventually deliver.

Life expectancy on the frontier was nothing like today. A male Indian did well to live beyond age thirty and women could expect to live a tad less. Little wonder that older tribesmen were highly respected. Life expectancy for Whites wasn't much better. A White man on the frontier tended not to live beyond his late thirties. Notably, the brevity of life generally meant that folks had to mature sooner. By the time a man or woman reached age fifteen or sixteen, he or she was pretty much an adult in terms of others expecting him or her to carry an adult set of responsibilities.

Oh, I do refer to bison as buffalo. Just for the record, bison and buffalo are quite different. Visualize the water buffalo and then the shaggy awkward bulk of the American bison. Seems that "buffalo" came into common usage in America to refer to the bison, so I've chosen to use it in my writings. Also, note that what is today's Colorado was referred to as part of the Kansas Territory and for a brief time after 1859 as the Jefferson Territory.

Dangers? Anthropology-minded folks claim there were as many as thirteen tribes of Comanche from the Quahadi, or "antelope eaters," in the north to the Penateka, or "honey eaters," in the south. Mix in Kiowa, Apache, and Tonkawa, and settlers had their hands full. The very name Comanche loosely translates in the Ute tribal language as "enemy." Capture by the Comanche invariably led to terrible outcomes. A fearsome lot these tribes were. Notably, Penateka Comanche Chief Buffalo Hump led more than 600 warriors on a raid through the heart of Texas in August 1840, murdering Texans, looting the city of Victoria, and looting and burning Linnville on their march to the Gulf of Mexico. It was not until 1858 that Texas Ranger John Salmon "Rip" Ford led a force of 102 heavily armed Texas Rangers into the Comanchería and brought the Comanche to their knees at the Battle of Little Robe Creek on the Canadian River.

The northwest plains were peopled by the Sioux, comprised of three groups: Dakota, Nakota, and Lakota.

Wyoming Calls: Jack's Risky Quest focuses on the Lakota, in turn made up of seven subgroups: Oglalas (famed for Red Cloud and Crazy Horse), Hunkpapas (famed for Sitting Bull), Miniconjous, Oohenunpas (Two Kettles), Itazipacolas (Sans Arcs), Brulés (Burnt Thighs), and Sihasapas (Blackfeet). The Lakota history was no less combative than Comanche or Cheyenne. For example, there was the Grattan Massacre, or Cow Incident of August 19, 1854, in which the Army erroneously accused the Lakota of stealing a Mormon settler's cow and resulted in a confrontation in which the entire 30-man company was killed, including 2nd Lieutenant John Grattan. Troops under Brigadier General William Harney avenged that massacre a year later at the Battle of Ash Hollow. Most folks have heard of the Little Bighorn (called Greasy Grass by the Lakota) where troops under General George Armstrong Custer on June 25, 1876, were massacred by Sioux and their allies.

Far fewer are aware of the Fetterman Massacre on December 21, 1866, also known as the Battle of the Hundred-in-the-Hands, or the Battle of a Hundred Slain, during Red Cloud's War. It involved a confederation of the Lakota, Cheyenne, and Arapaho tribes and a detachment of the United States Army based at Fort Phil Kearny, Wyoming. Oglala Lakota chief Crazy Horse lured an entire 81-man detachment of troops into a trap where they were all killed. Massacres cut both ways. There was the Sand Creek Massacre of November 29, 1864, in which members of the Colorado Militia attacked a peaceful Cheyenne village, killing up to 600 men, women, and children at Sand Creek in Kiowa County. Despite the violence of the frontier, it's worthy of note that the Lakota held to a worthy set of virtues: generosity, courage, fortitude, and wisdom.

In *Wyoming Calls: Jack's Risky Quest* young Jack O'Toole ventures north with his friend Spirit Talker while facing an unforgiving land featuring savage Indians, unpredictable weather, predatory beasts, and vegetation that could literally tear flesh from bone. It is said the United States' western frontier offered new opportunities for hearty folks willing to endure its rigors. It might also be said that folks that settled certain parts of the frontier like the Yellowstone region with its Lakota tribe and the Comanchería with its Comanche tribes were not playing with a full deck. They had to be crazy.

Jack had no modern creature comforts. Invention of cell phones and social media was a century and a half into the future. Transportation? Horses and mules were the vehicles of choice. Jack had no refrigerator to preserve sweet treats. There were no flush toilets or showers. Folks mostly ate what grazed upon or grew from the land. Learning was squeezed from the few books that might be found, especially the Holy Bible. By way of example, my own great great-great-grandfather brought his collection of books from Ireland in 1851. As a serious and religious-minded pioneer, he had gathered quite an impressive library for his time. It included *The Holy Bible;* three volumes of *Lives of the Saints, Lives of Irish Saints and Martyrs*; Geoffrey Keating's *History of Ireland*; Edward Clarendon's *History of Ireland*; a *History of the Christian Church*; lectures and sermons by Father Burke titled *Instructions for Youth*; Hume's *History of England, Trials of a Mind*; Moore's *Life of Lord Edward Fitzgerald*; *Washington and His Generals*; a *Bible History*; and Cobbet's *History of the Reformation*. Sort of makes a head swim, doesn't it?

Can't say as the living of the era was luxurious unless you counted the sheer grandeur of majestic landscapes and of nights so quiet you could hear the stars twinkling. To fully appreciate the place, you simply had to love the beauty of the outdoors. Fishing the meandering Guadalupe River in Texas or the chill waters of Wyoming's North Platte River, hunting deer and antelope, raising cattle and horses, and reaping the bounteous yield of the rich soil was sheer joy for a courageous visionary few. For a teen on the frontier, life could be pretty good...mostly. Otherwise, it was downright dangerous.

Thus far, Jack O'Toole has grown to manhood, conquered fears and prejudices, fought Indians and bandits, taken on prairie fires and storms, defended against wild beasts, traveled the wild country, driven cattle, and found the love of his life. As you have seen, he especially draws upon his faith and what he was taught by his parents. He has to learn to trust in instincts forged from his biblical lessons. Yes, Jack is on a frontier adventure and more.

A LOOK AT BOOK THREE:
LONGHORNS NORTH: JACK'S GREAT TRAIL DRIVE

Climb into your saddle with *Longhorns North: Jack's Great Trail Drive*, the third spellbinding installment of The Frontier Chronicles YA series.

Now seventeen-years-old, Jack O'Toole and his Comanche friend Spirit Talker must find the courage and endurance to take on the tough challenges faced in driving a herd of longhorn cattle northward through a hostile frontier to Wyoming. Storm-driven stampedes, wildfires, raging rivers, and attacks by Cheyenne and dreaded Blackfeet warriors test their resolve.

Along the trail to the fledgling ranch of their Black cowboy friend George Freeman, Jack and Spirit Talker must also deal with vulnerable caravans of prairie schooners headed west on the Oregon Trail, defend themselves against a huge angry grizzly, and find a way to free an enslaved Comanche girl.

Does Jack's faith and friendship with Spirit Talker result in the success of their cattle venture despite the rigors of the trail? Will Jack make it home to Rising Cross Ranch in time for the birth of his first children? And what of the mystery surrounding Zeb, the ever-present wolf?

AVAILABLE OCTOBER 2024

ACKNOWLEDGMENTS

Authoring books doesn't simply happen in a vacuum. The author provides the creative talent and crafts the stories, but there's so much more that demands acknowledgment. There are lots of folks and places that contribute to my authoring endeavors. So it is with *Wyoming Calls: Jack's Risky Quest*. The tale is set in 1856 and shares the trials and tribulations of a teen forced to meet the challenges inherent in the dangerous vastness of the western frontier; but this novel stands apart. At its core, it is also about the taming of the frontier. Step in two teen boys becoming men. The protagonist epitomizes the freedom of America's western frontier and represents a final bastion of honor in America. The tale follows Jack O'Toole's adventures in *Perilous Trails: Jack's Adventure Begins*. Hopefully, readers will find *Wyoming Calls: Jack's Risky Quest* worthy of their time and emotional involvement.

I've been blessed with many friends and family who have supported my writings. My wife Carolyn's reviews and encouragement were a huge help along with very important tech support from our sons Mike and Matt. Thanks to my nephew Shawn for his faith insights. Many more friends and family have contributed support at some level to the creation and publication of *Wyoming Calls: Jack's Risky Quest* be it encouragement or advice.

Naturally, I am majorly grateful to the great folks at Wise Wolf Books. The team they bring to publishing is first-rate in editing, cover design, narration, and the myriad tasks that lead to successful book sales.

It's only right to acknowledge my ancestors who were actual settlers of the south Texas frontier. In addition to inspiring me, they provided a quite helpful true-to-life framework as to the life and times on the Texas Nueces Strip. It has been appropriate to weave them into the tapestry of my western novels. Matthew Dunn (1815-1855) immigrated to Corpus Christi from County Kildare in 1845, established a homestead on Upriver Road, and served as a sutler to General Zachary Taylor's Army in the Mexican-American War. Peter Dunn (1807-1890) immigrated from Ireland in 1850 and established a blacksmith shop in Corpus Christi; John Dunn (1803-1889), my great-great-great-grandfather, raised cattle and grew thousands of acres of cotton; Lawrence Dunn (1837-1864) fought and died with Captain Ware's Confederate cavalry; and my great-great-grandfather Nicholas Dunn (1835-1912) was a rancher, drover, live-stock speculator, and Comanche fighter of some repute. My cousin John Beamond "Red John" Dunn (1851-1940) served as a Texas Ranger in the 1870s under Captain Bland Chamberlain (Company H), subsequently joined a "vigilance committee," became a farmer and merchant, and curated a museum of military weapons displayed to this day in the Corpus Christi Museum of Science & History. Red John Dunn's brother Matthew Dunn also served as a Texas Ranger, and another cousin Rut Evans served as a Texas Ranger in the 1890s (Company E, Frontier Battalion, Alice, TX). My cousin Patrick Dunn was quite successful at raising longhorns on North Padre Island just east of Corpus Christi from 1883 to 1937. John Hillard Dunn (1883-1958) whose personal narra-tive about his family and his own adventures drove my pursuit of my Texas family legacy, inspired my own writings, and led me to write his yet-to-be-published biography *Tough Hombre–Recollections of a True Texan*. Finally, my grandfather, Horace Charles Greathouse served as a Texas Ranger in 1920 (Company C, Austin, TX). Such real-life characters coupled with actual events have served to reinforce the historical settings for my writings.

Most of my authoring has occurred in my office as decorated to channel my inner Texan, but my creative juices have often been inspired and imagination stoked in cafés and coffee houses across America. My favorites were Hester's Café & Coffee Bar in Corpus Christi, TX; Nueces Café in Robstown, TX; Java Ranch Espresso Bar & Café in Fredericksburg, TX; PAX Coffee & Goods in Kerrville, TX; Ragged Edge Coffee House and Bantam Coffee Roasters in Gettysburg, PA; 1889 Coffee House in Helena, MT; Dunn Brothers Coffee in Rapid City, SD; Postmasters Coffee & Bakery and Brio Coffeehouse in Waynesboro, PA; Birdie's Café and American Ice Co Café in Westminster, MD; Deja Brew Coffee House, New Oxford and Deja Brew at Miney Branch, Carroll Valley, PA; and Baltimore Coffee & Tea Co., Frederick Coffee Company & Café, and Dublin Roasters in Frederick, MD. I must admit to also frequenting a few Dunkin Donuts and Starbucks around our fine nation. The décors and easy-listening music in these fine establishments combined with savory cups of coffee and mostly friendly folks tended to set me in the right creative frame of mind.

Last but not least, I'm especially thankful for the many folks who have read and enjoyed my books.

I do believe it's important to acknowledge how the Old West represents the brave pioneering spirit of settlers that met the challenges and transcended mere survival to enable America to achieve exceptional growth. The settling of the American frontier west is replete with tales of leveraging freedom for individual achievement. I hope you'll agree that reliving our past– even through history-based fiction–often has the effect of pointing the way to an ever-brighter future. Might we be up to it? I hope that the inspiration I've drawn from my having walked the very earth my characters have trodden coupled with my extensive historical research will enable readers to fully experience the grit, adventure, and passion of my characters while sensing aromas of gunsmoke, trail dust, leather, and bluebonnets.

Thanks kindly to all of you and I hope you enjoyed *Wyoming Calls: Jack's Risky Quest*.

ABOUT THE AUTHOR

Award-winning author Mark Greathouse's love for the western genre draws upon his deep family roots and love of the outdoors honed from teen years hiking the Appalachian Trail and family travels across America's frontier. He began writing full time after a successful career as a business executive and later as an entrepreneurial investor and advisor. His service as president of several business and community nonprofits led to their extraordinary growth. He holds a BA in English and MBA in marketing. Greathouse donates time and books annually to support wounded military warriors.

A member of Western Writers of America and the Wild West History Association, he also contributes articles on the history of America's west to western-themed magazines. Greathouse was recognized as a 2024 Finalist in western genre by the American Literary Book Awards for his sixth Tumbleweed Saga, *Nueces Truth: Texans Face War's Realities*.

His *Frontier Chronicles,* a series of western novels aimed at adventure-minded teens and young adults while weaving a Christian message within their fabric, are aimed at lighting fires of truth, faith, hope, and life purpose in the bellies of today's teen boys and girls. Just as seeds must be sown to reap the harvest, so the seeds of faith must be planted to raise tomorrow's men and women.

GLOSSARY

DEFINITIONS

Big Father—All-powerful Comanche deity.

Bota bag—A canteen fashioned from leather and popular among Indians, mountain men, and many travelers of the western frontier.

Life debt—A cultural phenomenon in which someone whose life is saved or spared by another becomes indebted or in some way connected to their savior.

Pemmican—Lean dried strips of meat pounded into a paste, mixed with fat and berries, and then pressed into small cakes.

Possibles bag—A leather or canvas sack carried by cowboys and containing essentials like soap, matches, bandages, extra spur, smoke makings, and playing cards

Remuda—A herd of horses frequently used on trail drives and by Plains Indians.

Shaman—Comanche medicine man.

Teepee—An enclosed conical transportable shelter constructed of long poles and buffalo hides with a vent at the top to permit smoke to escape.

COMANCHE TRANSLATIONS

Aitu—Not good

Ana o'a hi'it—Phrase for *desire to eat*

Ap—Father

Aruka—Deer

Eetu—Bow

Ekakwitsụbaitụ—Lightning

Ekapitu—Red

Eekạsahpana paraiboo—Army officer (soldier chief)

Hawokatu—Hollow, loose

Hoikwa—Hunt, look for prey

Isa—Wolf

Isa wasu—Poison

Kaahaniitu—deceive, cheat

Kahni—Life

Kamakuna—Loved one

Kee—No

Kobe—Wild Horse

Kohto—Build a fire

Kooitu—Die

Kutseena—Coyote

Kwakuru—Defeat someone

Nahuu—Knife

Natsuitu—Strong

Numu—Teepee

Numunuu—Referring to the members of the Comanche tribes. Literally: people.

Ohapitu—Yellow

Paa—Water

Paaka—Arrow

Peeka—Kill

Pia—Mother

Pia huutsuu—Bald eagle

Pia wa'óo—Comanche words for mountain lion, puma, or cougar.

Pihi—Heart

Puuka—Horse

Sunipu—Medicine (as in strong medicine)

Suumaru—Ten

Taa Narumi—Master/God

Tabu—Coward

Tamu—Rabbit

Tasiwoo—Buffalo

Tenahpu—Man

Tomoobi—Sky

Tosa—White man or woman

Tosaabitu—White

Tumah tuyai—After life

Tuhibitu—Black

Tumhyokenu—Believe, trust

Tu Taiboo—Black man

Umaru—Rain

Unha haksi nahniaka—Phrase for *what's your name?*

Wa'ipu—Woman

Wasápe—Bear

Wutsutsuki—Rattlesnake